VOICES EAST and WEST

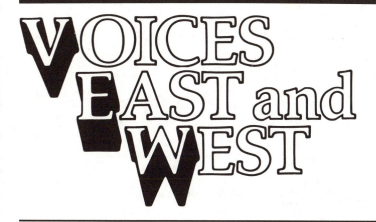

VOICES EAST and WEST

German Short Stories since 1945

Translations and introduction by
ROGER C. NORTON

FREDERICK UNGAR PUBLISHING CO. /
New York

Copyright © 1984 by **Frederick Ungar Publishing Co., Inc.**
Printed in the United States of America

Designed by David Lunn

Library of Congress Cataloging in Publication Data
Main entry under title:

Voices East and West.

1. Short stories, German—Germany (West)—Translations into English. 2. Short stories, German—Germany (East)—Translations into English. 3. German fiction—20th century—Translations into English. 4. Short stories, English—Translations from German. 5. English fiction—Translations from German. I. Norton, Roger C. (Roger Cecil), 1921—
PT1327.V65   1984   833'.01'08   84-8899
ISBN 0-8044-2660-0
ISBN 0-8044-6608-4 (pbk.)

Acknowledgments

For the right to publish the stories in this volume, I am indebted to the following authors, agents, and publishers:

Becher, Ulrich. "A Very Baltic Story" ("Eine sehr baltische Geschichte"). From *Deutsche Erzähler der Gegenwart* (Stuttgart: Reclam, 1964). Published by permission of the author.

Bender, Hans. "La Paloma, or the Food of Love" ("La Paloma oder Der Liebe Nahrung"). From Hans Bender, *Worte, Bilder, Menschen* (München: Carl Hanser Verlag, copyright 1969, Sonderausgabe). Published by permission of Carl Hanser Verlag.

Böll, Heinrich. "My Sad Face" ("Mein trauriges Gesicht"). From Heinrich Böll, *Wo warst du, Adam? und Erzählungen* (Köln: Friedrich Middelhauve Verlag, 1967). Published by permission of Middelhauve Verlag.

Borchert, Wolfgang. "Stories from a First Reader" ("Lesebuchgeschichten") and "The Three Dark Kings" ("Die drei dunklen Könige"). From the German text in *The Man Outside.* Copyright 1949 by Rowohlt Verlag GMBH. All rights reserved. Published by permission of New Directions Publishing Corporation.

Brězan, Jurij. "How Krabat Lost Smjala" ("Wie Krabat die Smjala verlor"). From *Auskunft: Neue Prosa aus der DDR*, ed. Stefan Heym (München, Gütersloh, Wien: C. Bertelsmann Verlag, 1974). Excerpted from a subsequently published novel. Published by permission of the author.

Claudius, Eduard. "How the Jungle Soldiers Became Sons of Heaven" ("Wie die Dschungelsoldaten zu Söhnen des Himmels wurden"). From *Fünfzig Erzähler der DDR* (Berlin & Weimar: Aufbau-Verlag, 1974). Originally published in Eduard Claudius, *Aus den nahen und fernen Städten* (Berlin: Verlag Volk und Welt, 1964). Published by permission of the author.

De Bruyn, Günter. "Someday He Really Will Come Home" ("Eines Tages ist er wirklich da"). From Günter de Bruyn, *Ein schwarzer abgrundtiefer See* (Halle/S: Mitteldeutscher Verlag, copyright 1966). Published by permission of Mitteldeutscher Verlag.

Görlich, Günter. "The Decision" ("Der Entschluss"). From *Berliner Schriftsteller erzählen* (Berlin & Weimar: Aufbau-Verlag, 1976). Published by permission of the author.

ACKNOWLEDGMENTS

Grass, Günter. "The Left-Handers" ("Die Linkshänder"). From *Deutschland erzählt*, ed. Benno v. Wiese (Frankfurt a.M.: Fischer, 1973). Published by permission of the author.

Heym, Stefan. "My Richard" ("Mein Richard"). From *Geschichten aus der DDR* (Hamburg: Hoffmann & Campe, 1979). Published by permission of Betty Marks and Hoffmann & Campe.

Kant, Uwe. "A Letter to Comrade Ernst L." ("Brief an den Genossen Ernst L."). From *Berliner Schriftsteller erzählen* (Berlin & Weimar: Aufbau-Verlag, 1976). Published by permission of the author.

Kaschnitz, Marie Luise. "The Fat Child" ("Das dicke Kind"). From *Deutschland erzählt*, ed. Benno v. Wiese (Frankfurt a.M.: Fischer, 1973). Published by permission of Scherpe Verlag, Krefeld.

Kohlhaase, Wolfgang. "Invention of a Language" ("Erfindung einer Sprache"). In *Neue Erzähler der DDR* (Frankfurt a.M.: Fischer, 1977). Published by permission of the author.

Körner, Wolfgang. "Bleep, crash, zap, wow!: Accidents in the Ruhr": ("Blimpp, crash, zack, wow!: Unfälle im Ruhrgebiet"). From *Ausserdem: Deutsche Literatur minus Gruppe 47-Wieviel?* (München & Bern: Scherz Verlag, 1967). Published by permission of the author.

Kusenberg, Kurt. "Who Am I?" ("Wer ist man?"). From Kurt Kusenberg, *Sonnenblumen* (Hamburg: Rowohlt, 1951). Also in *Gesammelte Erzählungen*. Published by permission of Sanford J. Greenburger Associates and Rowohlt Verlag.

Lenz, Siegfried. "The Amusement-Doctor" ("Der Amüsierdoktor"). From Siegfried Lenz, *Das Feuerschiff: Zehr Erzählungen* (München: Taschenbuch Verlag, 1978). Copyright 1960 Hoffmann & Campe Verlag.

Mundstock, Karl. "A Judgment Worthy of Solomon" ("Salomonisches Urteil"). From *Nachrichten aus Deutschland*, ed. Hildegard Brenner (Hamburg: Rowohlt, 1967). Published by permission of Sanford J. Greenburger Associates and Rowohlt Verlag.

Nowotny, Joachim. "Hic sunt leones." From Joachim Nowotny, *Sonntag unter Leuten* (Halle/S: Mitteldeutscher Verlag, copyright 1971). Published by permission of Mitteldeutscher Verlag.

Rinser, Luise. "A Handful of White Daffodils" ("Ein Bündel weisser Narzissen"). From Luise Rinser, *Ein Bündel weißer Narzissen: Erzählungen* (Frankfurt a.M.: Fischer, 1964). Published by permission of Fisher Verlag.

ACKNOWLEDGMENTS

Risse, Heinz. "Traffic Accident" ("Verkehrsunfall"). From Heinz Risse, *Der Buchhalter Gottes* (München: Langen-Müller Verlag, 1958). Published by permission of Langen-Müller Verlag.

Schneider, Rolf. "Border Crossers" ("Grenzgänger"). From *Auskunft: Neue Prosa aus der DDR,* ed. Stefan Heym (München, Gütersloh, Wien: C. Bertelsmann Verlag, 1974). Published by permission of the author.

Schnurre, Wolfdietrich. "Diary of a Dayfly" ("Tagebuch einer Eintagsfliege"). From Wolfdietrich Schnurre, *Ohne Einsatz kein Spiel* (Olten & Freiburg i.Br.: Walter-Verlag, 1964). Published by permission of the author.

Schulze, Axel. "Eighteen Minutes" ("Achtzehn Minuten"). From *Fünfzig Erzähler der DDR* (Berlin & Weimar: Aufbau-Verlag, 1973). Also in *Das Gastmahl Balthasars,* 1973. Published by permission of Aufbau-Verlag.

Seghers, Anna. "The Reed" ("Das Schilfrohr"). From Anna Seghers, *Die Kraft der Schwachen* (Darmstadt und Neuwied: Hermann Luchterhand Verlag, 1966). Published by permission of the author and Luchterhand Verlag.

Stephan, Martin. "The Tub" ("Der Bottich"). From *Auskunft: Neue Prosa aus der DDR,* ed. Stefan Heym (München, Gütersloh, Wien: C. Bertelsmann Verlag, 1974). Published by permission of the author.

Wohmann, Gabriele. "The Swan" ("Der Schwan"). From *Das Atelier: Zeitgenössische Prosa* (Frankfurt, a.M.: Fischer, 1970). Published by permission of the author and Eremiten-Presse.

Wolf, Christa. "A Certain Date" ("Zu einem Datum"). From *Erzähler aus der DDR,* ed. Franke & Langenbucher (Tübingen & Basel: Horst Erdmann Verlag, 1973). Published by permission of Aufbau-Verlag.

Contents

Introduction / xiii

Part One: *WEST GERMAN AUTHORS*

Wolfgang Borchert /   **Stories from a First Reader** /   3
                        The Three Dark Kings /   7
Heinrich Böll /   **My Sad Face** /   10
Ulrich Becher /   **A Very Baltic Story** /   16
Hans Bender /   **La Paloma, or the Food of Love** /   20
Kurt Kusenberg /   **Who Am I?** /   25
Marie Luise Kaschnitz /   **The Fat Child** /   30
Heinz Risse /   **Traffic Accident** /   37
Günter Grass /   **The Left-Handers** /   42
Gabriele Wohmann /   **The Swan** /   49
Luise Rinser /   **A Handful of White Daffodils** /   53
Wolfdietrich Schnurre /   **Diary of a Dayfly** /   60
Wolfgang Körner /   **Bleep, crash, zap, wow:**
                      Accidents in the Ruhr /   65
Siegfried Lenz /   **The Amusement-Doctor** /   68

Part Two: *EAST GERMAN AUTHORS*

Anna Seghers /   **The Reed** /   77
Wolfgang Kohlhaase /   **Invention of a Language** /   88
Christa Wolf /   **A Certain Date** /   99
Günter de Bruyn /   **Someday He Really Will Come**
                      Home /   105
Uwe Kant /   **A Letter to Comrade Ernst L.** /   109
Rolf Schneider /   **Border Crossers** /   114
Stefan Heym /   **My Richard** /   123
Eduard Claudius /   **How the Jungle Soldiers**
                      Became Sons of Heaven /   138
Karl Mundstock /   **A Judgment Worthy of Solomon** /   142
Joachim Nowotny /   **Hic sunt leones** /   148
Günter Görlich /   **The Decision** /   155

Axel Schulze / **Eighteen Minutes** / 162
Martin Stephan / **The Tub** / 166
Jurij Brězan / **How Krabat Lost Smjala** / 170
Biographical Sketches / 174

Translator's Note

I have adhered as closely as possible to the particular linguistic flavor of the original, while trying to avoid unnatural English. My hope is that my work will inspire and justify the reader's confidence that in those passages where my English may sound unusual, be it old-fashioned and cliché-ridden or, on the other hand, daring or slangy, the original German was faithfully rendered.

In introducing quotations I have followed the style of the original and rarely changed the authors' usage, which varies frequently, sometimes within the same work—regular punctuation, dashes, a combination of the two, or even no punctuation at all.

I am grateful to my colleagues Gerard Schmidt and Elfriede Heyer for their help in interpreting unusual German expressions.

R.N.

Introduction

At the beginning of the twentieth century, the German short story had little status as a separate literary form. It was considered more or less as a catchall for short prose pieces of indeterminate character. But by the 1950s it had grown into a popular and proudly independent genre; it established the reputation of many of the country's best authors. The main reason for the story's phenomenal growth was — in addition to its brevity and thus its greater accessibility to the reader — its flexibility of structure, style, and outlook, which made it the ideal vehicle to portray the volatile postwar situation in both East and West Germany. But its approach has not been parochial. Whereas Irving, Poe, and Hawthorne had once been inspired by the German Romantics, the Germans now learned mainly from Americans such as Bret Harte, O. Henry, Ring Lardner, Ernest Hemingway, and Eudora Welty, and were able to develop their own original styles. Lesser influences came from other countries, notably England, France, and Russia. The particular character of the twentieth century—its political traumas, its destruction of the comfortable and narrower bourgeois realities of the nineteenth century—demanded new and more open approaches in order to express the new conditions of their time.

Despite the great divergence of theme and style, one can say that in general the unifying factor in the twentieth-century stories is their authors' attempt to reconcile themselves to the rapidly changing values, man's alienation, fragmentation, and the revolutions of a period in which a belief in new social systems and technological panaceas clashes with still powerful humanistic traditions. This search for new ways was especially pronounced in Germany among the ruins of World War II. The younger generation of authors demanded liberation from the institutions and attitudes that had produced these ruins. Their cultivation of strong but simple language to illuminate realistically basic human relations, and, at the same time, their frequent use of satire, whimsy, and also of poetical language, give their works international significance and appeal. Kay Boyle, for example, wrote in 1971, in her foreword to *The Man Outside* (a collection of Wolfgang Borchert's stories and one drama)[1] that this book had been a unique and constant companion, to which she turned again and again as a model and inspiration for her own work.

INTRODUCTION

As far as form is concerned, the German short story is paradoxical in the sense that, despite its apparent openness and freedom of narration, it has a rather demanding set of formal constraints. These are based, however, less on style or subject matter than on subtleties of structure and on the particular type of relationship it establishes between author and reader. Like avant-garde drama, which has abandoned the closed stage and thrust out into the audience, the short story has learned to reach out to its reader with lyric conciseness and intensity, not to lead or coerce him but rather to let life itself speak to him directly through and between the lines of the story. It correspondingly tends not to focus on a finished episode but rather on the ongoing moment, and its most prominent single trait is its openness, not only at the start and finish but throughout its narration. It often juxtaposes seemingly unrelated events, thoughts, or even syntactical elements, all of which invite the reader to make the connections, in other words, to construct his own story in collaboration with the author. Wolfdietrich Schnurre, in one of his essays, discusses the short story's more particular characteristics of form and expression: "What is a short story? . . . Roughly speaking, it is a piece torn out of life. Beginnings and endings are a matter of indifference to it: what it has to say, it says with every line. It prefers unity of time; its language is simple but never banal. Its characters never speak like this in reality, yet one always has the feeling they *could* do so. Its strength lies in what it omits; its special knack is understatement."[2] Schnurre very appropriately does not depict this "piece torn out of life" as a miniature of life, but as a vital segment, a particular moment. And this "piece" will be a part of every word, sentence and paragraph, each of which, however, is a facet of something universal that encompasses the story. When it has been read, the reader will not know much more about a particular character's life but he will have learned a good deal about life in general, having explored one segment of it inventively and creatively, hand in hand with the author, who has suggested things to the reader but has never been so presumptuous as to try to lead him toward a precise goal.

In addition to the short story, this collection offers various examples of related short prose forms, to serve as a contrast and to illustrate some of the potentialities of, for example, the parable, short-short story, and "text." Nearly all of these are one to two pages in length, whereas the short stories themselves vary from about three to fourteen manuscript pages, with an average of five and a half, which is within the range of length that Ludwig Rohner, for example, considers the most representative of the genre, namely four to eight printed pages. The influence of the forerunner of the short story, the *Novelle*, which dominated short prose in the nineteenth century, may be seen in a few of the stories. The *Novelle* followed a rather closely defined set of requirements which primarily stipulated a clear and simple focus on a certain historical event and/or a psychological perception and was given a rounded-off structure, i.e., a linear plot narration with a well-defined beginning and ending. In recent decades the *Novelle* has been largely eclipsed either by the short story or by the tale (*Erzählung*).

As the title of this anthology suggests, an important purpose is to introduce representative authors of East and West Germany. Within these groupings the stories are arranged in a sequence that represents a compromise between chronology of publication and, on the other hand, thematic and/or stylistic similarity. A considerable difference of approach will be evident both between and within the two main groupings, but the reader may also note certain overall traits which transcend political boundaries. In general, the stories of the first years after the war furnished a vital intellectual stimulus for new social and political approaches to life in Germany. Their authors were to a large degree successful in doing what many of their predecessors had not done after World War I, that is, divorcing themselves from narrow nationalistic goals and resentment against their wartime enemies, and freeing themselves from conventional literary approaches. These were the authors who, in their first years of writing, had seen around them nearly total spiritual and physical devastation, a life among ruins, where people had to forage like animals. Something as basic as a piece of bread could have enormous value for them both as a physical necessity and as a symbol of a spiritual sustenance that could no longer be found except in the most fundamental things and relationships. As one reads many of these stories, one is amazed at the lightness of touch, the ability to smile at human idiosyncracies, the almost complete lack of recrimination and spite. The style is simple, strong, lyrical; the satire is often gentle but incisive.

A majority of the stories in the Western group were produced by the so-called Gruppe 47 (founded in 1947), which consisted of writers of similar sympathies who met yearly for the next 25 years as a forum to present and criticize each other's works. Among its better known representatives here are Böll, Grass, Schnurre, and Bender. Through its informality, spontaneity, and bluntness of criticism, Gruppe 47 encouraged independence of thought and discouraged literary lionization and retreat to the ivory tower. One main point of contention, which was intensified within the literary world in general in the following years, pitted activistic writers against those of mere aesthetic or fanciful tendencies. It was essentially a quarrel between those who insisted on overt, direct commitment on the part of the writer to a political or social cause, and those who were not less concerned with human values and conventionally conceived reality but directed their writing at those values which underlie all things of the spirit and of creation of any kind. Another important and related element in several stories of both groups is the conflict between Eastern and Western political ideologies. The majority of West German writers tend to treat the theme more lightly and whimsically, more in terms of human emotions and personal problems, while those of East Germany tend to strike a more ideological, somewhat didactic tone, although here too one can find very sensitive personal touches. In general, the East German stories adhere to the principles of social realism enunciated by the Communist government and its one-party system, which fosters a literature that is written to further the socialistic ideals and goals of the state. Yet here too, satire and criticism appear, although more subtly expressed, and also poetical language and whimsical treatment of themes. I have found it advisable to insert explanatory notes to clarify the rather frequent allusions to East German organizations and procedures with which many Western readers may not be familiar.

In both groups I have included stories that illustrate certain recent developments and trends. Some of these are experimental variations of existing directions, while others make a clean break with the past. They give evidence of a desire to create new forms of expression, to establish a different relationship between words and subject matter. Wolfgang Körner imitates the sounds and sights of a society exploited and corrupted by communication overkill. Schnurre presents the diary of a dayfly-turned-author, who changes his style moment by moment during his frenetically short life, and seems to parody the dizzying tempo of change in modern life. Some of the East German authors are also stylistically innovative within a framework conditioned by Marxist dialectic. In Christa Wolf's story, the heroine makes individualistic judgments expressed in a very original way. Nowotny, in a narrative

INTRODUCTION

that seems to take its departure from Ring Lardner's slangy style, describes a taxi-driver's yearning to break away from his daily routine into uncharted territories of emotion and dreams. Schulze effectively mingles poetry and social realism. Brězan leads us into a fairy-tale world whose spiritual essence, however, is intensely real.

This anthology is, as far as we know, the first to include a substantial number of stories from both East and West Germany in the same volume. Despite the differences of approach in the two groups, the short story as a genre proves its adaptability to the most varied styles and contents. The conflict of ideologies proves to be less of a dividing factor than one might have expected. We believe that the reader will be able to gain both a greater awareness of the relevance of literature in general for our time and a better understanding of the particular societies and individuals depicted.

Notes

[1]New York: New Directions, 1971.

[2]"Kritik und Waffe," *Deutsche Rundschau,* Jg. 87 (1961), 61. I am indebted to Ludwig Rohner (*Theorie der Kurzgeschichte,* Frankfurt a.M.: Athenäum, 1973) for drawing my attention to Schnurre's essay and for miscellaneous information on the structure and character of the short story.

Part One

WEST GERMAN AUTHORS

Stories from a First Reader

Wolfgang Borchert

All the people have a sewing machine, a radio, a refrigerator, and a telephone. What shall we make now? asked the factory owner.

Bombs, said the inventor.

War, said the general.

If we absolutely have to, said the factory owner.

The man in the white smock wrote figures on the paper.

He added very small, delicate letters.

Then he took off his white smock and for an hour tended the flowers on his window sill. When he noticed that a flower had faded he became very sad and wept.

The figures were on the paper. According to them a thousand people could be killed within two hours with half a gram.

The sun was shining on the flowers.

And on the paper.

Two men were talking to each other.

Cost estimate?

With tiles?

With green tiles, naturally.

Ten thousand.

Ten thousand? Good. You know, my friend, if I hadn't gone from chocolates to gun powder at the right time I couldn't give you that ten thousand now.
And I couldn't give you a shower stall.
With green tiles.
With green tiles.
The two men walked away.
It was a factory owner and a building contractor.
It was war.

Bowling alley. Two men were talking to each other.
Well, Professor, you're wearing a dark suit. Death in the family?
Not at all, not at all. Had a celebration. Boys going to the front. Gave a little talk. Mentioned Sparta. Quoted Clausewitz. Gave them a few ideas to take along: Honor, Country. Told them to read Hölderlin.
Thought of Verdun. A touching send-off. Very touching. The boys sang:
God, who made the Weapons Bloom. Eyes were shining. Touching. Very touching.
For God's sake, Professor, stop it. That's horrible.

The Professor stared at the others indignantly. While he'd been talking he had drawn nothing but little crosses on the score sheet. Nothing but little crosses. He stood up and laughed. Took another ball and rolled it down the alley. There was a gentle thunder. Then the pins back there fell. They looked like little men.

Two men were talking together.
Well, how are things going?
Not so good.
How many do you still have?
If I'm lucky, four thousand.
How many can you give me?
Eight hundred at the most.
They won't last long.
All right, a thousand.
Thanks.

The two men walked away.

Wolfgang Borchert

They were talking about human beings.
They were generals.
It was war.

Two men were talking to each other.
Volunteer?
Sure.
How old?
Eighteen. You?
Me too.
The two men walked away.
Both of them were soldiers.
Then one of them fell over. He was dead.
It was war.

When the war was over the soldier came home. But he had
no bread.
Then he saw a man who had some bread. He killed him.
You shouldn't kill people, said the judge.
Why not, asked the soldier.

When the peace conference was over, the government officials made a tour of the city. They passed a shooting gallery.
Sir, want to try a few shots? the girls with the red lips called
out. Then the officials all took a gun and shot at little men
made out of cardboard.
In the midst of the shooting an old woman came by and took
the guns out of their hands. When one of the officials wanted
it back, she boxed their ears.
It was a mother.

Once there were two children. When they were two years old
they hit each other with their fists.
When they were twelve they hit each other with sticks and
threw stones.
When they were twenty-two they shot at each other with
guns.
When they were forty-two they dropped bombs.
When they were sixty-two they used bacteria.
When they were eighty-two they died. They were buried
next to each other.
A hundred years later, when a worm ate its way into their

two graves, it had no idea that two different men were buried there. It was the same earth. All the same earth.

In the year 5000, when a mole peeked out of the earth he calmly took note:
The trees are still trees.
The crows still caw.
The dogs still lift their legs.
The sturgeon and the stars,
The moss and the ocean main
And the mites:
All have remained the same
And every now and then—
Every now and then you meet a human being.

The Three Dark Kings

Wolfgang Borchert

He groped through the dark suburb. The buildings stood broken against the sky. There was no moon and the pavement was startled by the late footsteps. Then he found an old plank fence. He kicked it with his foot until one of the boards gave a crumbly sigh and broke loose. The wood had a mellow, sweet smell. Then he groped home through the dark suburb. There were no stars.

As he opened the door (it whimpered when he opened it) the pale blue eyes of his wife watched him. They watched from a weary face. Her breath hung whitish in the room, it was so cold. He bent his bony knee and broke the wood. The wood sighed. Then there was a mellow and sweet smell around them. He held a piece of the wood under his nose. Smells almost like cake, he laughed softly. Don't, said his wife's eyes, don't laugh. He's asleep.

The man put the sweet mellow wood into the little iron stove. Then it flamed and cast a handful of warm light across the room. The light fell brightly upon a tiny round face and stayed a moment. The face was only an hour old, but it already had everything it was supposed to have: ears, nose, mouth, and eyes. The eyes must be big, you could see that although they were shut. But the mouth was open and made soft breathing sounds. The nose and ears were red. He's alive, thought the mother. And the little face was asleep.

We still have oatmeal, said the man. Yes, answered the woman, that's good. It's cold. The man took more of the sweet soft wood. Now she's had her baby and has to freeze. But he had nobody to hit in the face and blame for that. When he opened the door of the stove, another handful of light fell upon the sleeping face. The woman said softly: Look, it's like a halo, do you see? Halo! he thought and he had nobody he could hit in the face with his fist.

Then there were people at the door. We saw the light, they said, through the window. We want to sit down for a few minutes.

But we have a baby, the man said to them. Then they said nothing more but came into the room anyway, puffing mist from their nostrils, stepping softly. We're very quiet, they whispered, and stepped softly. Then the light fell upon them. There were three. In three old uniforms. One had a cardboard carton, one a bag. And the third had no hands. Frozen, he said, and held up the stumps. Then he emptied his coatpocket for the man. There was tobacco in it and thin paper. They rolled cigarettes. But the woman said: No, the child.

Then the four went outside and their cigarettes were four dots in the night. One of them had heavily wrapped feet. He took a piece of wood out of his bag. A donkey, he said, I carved on it for seven months. For the baby. He said that and gave it to the man. What's wrong with your feet? asked the man. Swollen, said the donkey-carver, from hunger. And the other, the third? asked the man and in the dark ran his fingers over the donkey. The third man trembled in his uniform. Oh, nothing, he whispered, it's only nerves. There was just too much to be afraid of. Then they put out their cigarettes and went back in.

They stepped softly and looked at the little sleeping face. The trembling man took two yellow candies out of his cardboard carton and said: They're for your wife. The woman opened her pale blue eyes wide when she saw the three dark men bending over the baby. She was afraid. And then the baby braced his legs against her breast and screeched so hard that the three dark men went on tiptoe to the door. Here they nodded once more then stepped into the night.

The man watched them go. Three funny wise men, he said to his wife. Then he closed the door. Fine wise men, he grumbled and went to look for the oatmeal.

And there was no face for his fist.

Wolfgang Borchert

But the child was screaming, whispered his wife. He was screaming very loud. Then they left. Look how lively he is, she said proudly. The little face opened its mouth and screamed.

Is he crying? asked the man.

No, I think he is laughing, the woman answered.

It's almost like cake, said the man, and sniffed the piece of wood—like cake. Very sweet.

Today is Christmas too, the woman said.

Yes, Christmas, he grumbled, and from the stove a handful of light fell bright upon the little sleeping face.

My Sad Face

Heinrich Böll

As I stood by the harbor, looking at the gulls, my sad face caught the attention of a policeman patrolling the area. I was completely engrossed watching the birds swoop and plunge in vain searching for something to eat. The harbor was desolate, the water greenish, thick with dirty oil, and on its crusted surface all sorts of discarded trash was floating; there were no ships to be seen, the cranes were rusty and the storehouses dilapidated; the black hulks along the docks seemed devoid even of rats; everything was still. For many years all connection with the outside world had been cut off.

I had my eye on a certain gull whose flight I was studying. As anxiously as a swallow sensing a storm, it usually hovered close to the surface of the water, but now and then it screechingly risked an upward swoop to rejoin its companions. If I could have had my wish, it would have been for bread to feed the gulls, to break crumbs for them and give their aimless flying a white point as a goal, to tauten this screeching web of confused paths by casting a piece of bread, which would draw them together like a bundle of strings within my grasp. But I was as hungry as they, and tired too, although happy despite my sadness because it was good to stand there with my hands in my pockets watching the gulls and drinking in the sadness.

But suddenly an authoritative hand was laid on my shoulder and a voice said: "Come along!" Then the hand tried to pull my shoulder and twist me around. I stayed where I was, shook it off and said quietly: "You're crazy."

"Comrade," the still invisible person said to me, "I warn you."

"But sir . . ." I answered.

"There are no 'sirs'," he shouted angrily. "We are all comrades." And now he came closer, looked at me from the side, and I was forced to bring my happily wandering glance back and focus it on his earnest eyes: he was as serious as a buffalo which has eaten nothing but duty for years and years.

"On what grounds . . ." I started to ask . . .

"Grounds enough," he said. "Your sad face."

I laughed.

"Don't laugh!" His anger was genuine. At first I thought he had gotten bored because there was nobody to arrest: no unregistered prostitutes, no drunken sailors, no thieves or runaways, but now I could see that he was serious, he wanted to arrest me.

"Come along . . . !"

"Why?" I asked calmly.

Before I realized what was happening my left wrist was locked in a handcuff, and at this moment I knew that I was again lost. For a last time I turned toward the soaring gulls, looked at the beautiful gray sky and then tried, with a sudden twist of my body, to jump into the water, because it seemed better to drown by myself in this filthy brew than to be choked to death in some alley by their lackeys or to be locked up again. But the policeman, with a sudden jerk, had pulled me so close to him that there was no chance to escape.

"Why?" I asked once more.

"There's a law that says you have to be happy."

"I *am* happy!" I cried.

"Your sad face . . . ," he shook his head.

"But that's a new law," I said.

"It is thirty-six hours old, and you know very well that every law goes into effect twenty-four hours after it is proclaimed."

"But I know nothing about it."

"That does not excuse you from punishment. It was proclaimed day before yesterday by every loudspeaker, every newspaper, and, for those persons," he looked at me scornfully, "for those persons who do not share in the blessings of either press or radio, it was announced by means of leaflets that were scattered over every street and road in the whole country. So now we'll find out where you have spent the last thirty-six hours, comrade."

He dragged me away. Only now did I notice that it was cold and that I didn't have a coat on, and my hunger was making my stomach growl in earnest. I realized for the first time, too, that I was dirty, unshaven, shabby, although there were laws which said that every comrade had to be clean, neatly shaven, happy, and well-fed. He pulled me along like a scarecrow which has been accused of robbery and forced to leave its place of reverie at the edge of the field. The streets were empty and it wasn't far to the station, and although I had known that they would soon find another reason to arrest me, my heart grew heavy, because he led me through an area I had known in my childhood and had wanted to visit after looking at the harbor: gardens that used to be full of bushes growing in beautiful disorder, overgrown paths—all this was leveled out now and arranged in neat and orderly rectangles for the patriotic clubs which had their parades here on Monday, Wednesday, and Saturday. Only the sky was the way it used to be and the air just as it was in those days when my mind was full of dreams.

Here and there as we passed, I noticed the official sign posted in front of certain of the love barracks, reminding those whose turn came on Wednesdays that they might participate in hygienic pleasure. Also some of the bars were apparently authorized to hang out drinking signs, which had the shape of a beer glass stamped in tin and exhibiting the striped colors of the nation: light brown — dark brown — light brown. Joy undoubtedly filled the hearts of those who were on the list of Wednesday drinkers and thus could partake of the Wednesday beer.

All the people we saw bore an unmistakable stamp of eagerness; an aura of busyness enveloped them, and, indeed, the more so after they noticed the policeman; they all started walking faster, assumed an air of complete dedication to duty, and the women who came out of the stores tried to make their faces express the joy expected of them since the order had been given to show joy and cheerful contentment with their role as housewives whose duty in the evening was to strengthen the employees of the state with a good meal.

But all these people moved so skillfully out of our way that no one was forced to confront us directly. All signs of activity on the street disappeared when we came within twenty yards. Everyone managed to step into a store or turn a corner, and some may even have entered a stranger's house and waited anxiously behind the door until our footsteps faded.

But once, at a street corner, we came upon an elderly man whom I quickly identified as a schoolteacher type. He couldn't avoid us and so, after he had saluted the policeman in the prescribed way—that is, by slapping his own head three times and assuming a look of absolute humility—he attempted to fulfill the additional duty required of him by spitting in my face three times and shouting at me the prescribed words: "Traitorous pig!" His aim was good but it was a hot day and his throat was probably dry, because only a few thin and quite insignificant droplets struck me. I tried involuntarily—and against regulations—to wipe them off, upon which the policeman kicked me in the rear and hit the small of my back with his fist, adding in a low voice "Stage One," which means something like: "First and mildest form of punishment applied by all policemen."

The schoolteacher had quickly hurried off. Everyone else successfully avoided us except one woman. She was standing in front of a love barracks, taking her prescribed allotment of fresh air before the evening's pleasures began; she was a pale, puffy blond. She threw me a fleeting kiss and I smiled gratefully, while the policeman tried to act as if he hadn't seen it. They have instructions to allow these women freedoms that would bring certain and severe punishment for any other comrade; and since they make a very essential contribution toward increasing the laborers' general level of joy, they are allowed to remain outside the law—a concession whose implications the governmental philosopher Bleigoeth, possessor of three doctor's degrees, has condemned (in the officially sanctioned *Journal of Governmental Philosophy*) as a sign of incipient liberalization. I had read it the day before on my way to the capital city when I happened to be sitting in a farmer's privy and found a few pages of the Journal, which a student—perhaps the farmer's son—had provided with very witty marginal notations.

Fortunately we reached the station just before the sirens sounded, which meant that the streets would be overflowing with people whose faces would express mild pleasure (since it had been decreed that only a limited degree of pleasure should be shown at the end of the workday, otherwise it might look as if their jobs were a burden; on the other hand, at the beginning of the workday great joy was supposed to prevail—joy and singing) and all these thousands of people would have to spit on me. Of course, the siren meant that there were still ten minutes before quitting time, because everyone was required to wash thoroughly for ten minutes in accordance with the words of the present chief of state: "Happiness and Soapsuds."

The door of the district police station, a building made of cement blocks, was guarded by two sentries who administered to me the customary "physical measures" as I passed, that is, they gave me a sharp blow on my temple with their sidearms and smacked my collarbone with the barrels of their pistols in conformance with the preamble of Governmental Ordinance No. 1: "Every policeman must forcibly demonstrate his authority to every person held in legal restraint (they mean "arrest"); the only exception is the person who restrains him, since this person will have the pleasure of applying the necessary physical measures during the interrogation. Governmental Ordinance No. 1 further asserts: Any policeman *can* punish anybody and *must* punish anybody who is guilty of an infringement. No comrade possesses immunity as a prerogative—only as a possibility."

We now walked through a long, bare corridor with many large windows, then a door opened automatically before us, because in the meantime the guards had relayed the news of our arrival, and in these days when everybody was happy, well-behaved, neat, and took pains to use up the prescribed pound of soap per day to keep himself clean, the arrival of a person under legal restraint (arrest) was an event.

We entered an almost empty room that contained only a desk with a telephone and two chairs. I was told to stand in the middle of the room. The policeman took off his helmet and sat down.

At first everything was quiet and nothing happened; that's the way they always do it, and it's the worst part. I felt my composure slipping away. I was tired and hungry, and the last trace of my pleasant sadness had now disappeared because I knew I was lost.

After a few seconds a tall, pale man walked in silently, wearing the brownish uniform of the Preliminary Interrogator. He sat down and looked at me.

"Profession?"

"Simple comrade."

"Born?"

"First day, first month, first year," I said.

"Most recent occupation?"

"Convict."

The two men looked at each other.

"When and where released?"

"Yesterday, Building 12, cell 13."

"For what destination?"

"The capital."

"Papers."

I took my release papers out of my pocket and handed them to him. He clipped them to the green card that he had begun to write my answers on.

"Previous offense?"

"Happy face."

The two men looked at each other.

"Explain," the Preliminary Interrogator said.

"My happy face attracted the attention of a policeman on a day when general mourning was prescribed. It was the day the Leader died."

"Length of incarceration?"

"Five."

"Conduct?"

"Bad."

"Reason?"

"Insufficient attention to assigned tasks."

"That's all."

Then the Preliminary Interrogator stood up, walked over to me, and with precision knocked out my three middle front teeth—as a sign that I was being branded as a repeater—a more severe procedure than I had anticipated. Then the Preliminary Interrogator left the room and a fat fellow in a dark-brown uniform walked in—the Interrogator.

They all beat me—the Interrogator, the Chief Interrogator, the Supervisory Interrogator, the Judge of First Instance, and the Judge of Last Instance, while, at the same time, the policeman administered all the "physical measures" prescribed by law; and they gave me a ten-year sentence for my sad face the same way they had given me five years for my happy face.

But I will have to try to be completely faceless from now on if I hope to survive the next years of happiness and soapsuds.

A Very Baltic Story

Ulrich Becher

The Baroness Lena von Kockspur was born on the family estate Tiflisana in the Baltic province of Livonia, a part of the Russian Empire. Her grandfather on the maternal side, General Vladimir Fedorovich Fermin, had been the Czar's Governor of Trans-caucasian Georgia in Tiflis, where he had married a local girl. Georgian women are famous for their beauty; Lena's grandmother was still pretty as a picture in her old age and, in addition, very eccentric. When the retired general died at an advanced age, she concealed his death and burial with refined circumspection; she moved into the city residence of the Fermins in Tartu without telling a soul about her widowhood. She stuffed her husband, that is to say, his stiffly epauletted general's coat, with an eiderdown quilt, and she perched his officer's cap on the tip of the quilt that protruded from the collar of the uniform. She then ensconced this effigy in a wing chair which she had placed in front of a window, facing slightly away from it.

If she happened to be on the street in front of the house and met acquaintances who asked how General Fermin was doing, she pointed upwards and said: "As you can see, my Vladimir Fedorovich, the good man, is sitting there with his chronic gout; he can't leave the house or receive visitors."

Ulrich Becher

For years Lena's grandmother was thus able to lay claim to her husband's entire pension, which would have been cut in half if her widowhood had been known.

Lena's father, the descendant of a line of Teutonic Knights who had Christianized the Baltic area, was Imperial Gamekeeper, a quiet man who seldom killed a wild animal himself. Lena's childhood: journeys with her father in a horse-drawn sleigh over the huge Lake Peipus, behind them a pack of hungry wolves, in front of them the cracking ice, and yet they survived; family balls to which a hundred relatives were chauffeured from neighboring estates — a shoemaker was stationed all night in the little room beside the ballroom to repair the dancing slippers whose thin soles were worn through from all the waltzes, galops, mazurkas. Lena was the victim of girlish moon-madness (oh, cool-green Shakespeare moon of the North!); every evening she roamed through the woods of Tiflisana, riding sidesaddle with her face turned upwards toward the green gleaming light, which is why the Estonian peasants called her "Moon Maid." In those years Lena was secretly engaged seven times, earned a reputation as being a heartbreaking, bluestocking type who voraciously read the German and Russian classics, made worthless pledges of marriage to a series of rustic young Teutonic noblemen, and in the meantime dreamed of wedding a moon-bathed Knight of the Grail or a famous actor or an author or a musician from the outside world.

But instead, and before she knew what was happening, she fell prey to a frivolous young adventurer, the Baron Henricus Carlovich Henn, known at the University of Tartu as "that silly Henn"; at the age of barely eighteen she became the Baroness Henn-Kockspur. Her husband, equipped with an agronomist's diploma, made himself useless at Tiflisana, and when this — rapidly — became too boring for him, he persuaded Lena to go with him on a series of honeymoon trips. At a gala summer ball in the gambling casino at Zoppot, the foolish, pleasure-mad little couple danced into oblivion the child that Lena was expecting (a miscarriage). In the next winter the second and the third blows struck them.

The Imperial Gamekeeper broke through the ice of Lake Peipus and disappeared together with his horses and sleigh. Now the Baron Henn was master of Tiflisana and in a short time gambled and jollied away the family fortune of his wife on feigned business trips to Saint Petersburg, Warsaw, and Berlin; in her innocence she didn't suspect a thing.

Suddenly the minions of justice descended upon the house like a plague of locusts and confiscated, literally, the couple's last nightgown. The wick of their last remaining kerosene lamp had gone dry.

"I'll go get some kerosene, Moon Maid, . . . some kerosene," said the Baron. With a tin can in his hand he walked out into a night dimly lit by the midnight sun and was seen no more.

The family council urged the abandoned girl to sue for divorce —just as the news came that Henricus von Henn had already taken care of the separation in his own way.

He was discovered with a bullet through his heart in the boudoir of a society lady of Riga.

The twenty-year-old Lena had lost everything: unborn child, parents, husband, money, and property. The balance sheet of her young life totaled zero. But she was a sturdy conqueror of sadness, and her inborn, flourishing optimism, which had nothing to do with reason and experience, remained intact. Completely impoverished, she moved to Berlin, got a job as a typist in a theatrical agency, where she became acquainted with a young actor who was later to become one of the greatest celebrities of the German stage. After two weeks he asked her to marry him. Since the czarists had mislaid Henn's death certificate, they were united in "informal" marriage, an unheard-of scandal in 1903. A year later they had a civil ceremony; upon which occasion the bride already had twins in her arms.

A half-century later—her famous husband had died shortly after the second World War—I met Lena in Berlin, where she had lived the entire time. She was in an artists' cafe in the western sector, in the company of several actors I knew well—a cheerful seventy-year-old, highly respected by her much younger friends, radiating an aura of constant adventure. She lived alone but not lonesomely in her bomb-proof fortress of limitless memories (her twins were influential middle-aged businessmen in North and South America).

"I am now seventy-four and just recently I've had to admit that my youthful days are over," Lena said gravely. Her table companions smiled. "Since you write short stories . . ." and then she told me very openly and frankly about her younger years and concluded: "You know, when that Henn told me, "I'll go get some kerosene, Moon Maid, . . . some kerosene" and walked out with his tin can into the bright night—you know the North? and its summer? and the midnight sun?—and I stayed behind in the house that our creditors had emptied, and I waited for him, all alone, and Henn never came back, never again—well, that's what we call a very Baltic story."

La Paloma, or the Food of Love

Hans Bender

In the brown, bare, and musty coaches of the local train that used to run from the county seat to our village, it sometimes happened in the evening that the recessed wall lamps would go out because their wicks would be drowned in their own kerosene from the jolting of the wheels over the rough rails. The passengers were left in their dark compartments. Somebody struck a match. Cigaret tips glowed. A worker who always got out in Rotenberg poked me in the face with his elbow.

Not everybody was bothered by the darkness. The boys touched knees with the girls. Some of the men pulled their caps down over their eyes, let their heads sink, and slept the few minutes until the conductor called out their station.

Sometimes it happened that someone started a song. The others would listen or would start singing along: "She was so fair, too fair from life to part; she loved a highwayman with all her heart."

Other passengers talked more loudly and boldly than usual, because the darkness hid their eyes and faces, and the singing loosened the atmosphere.

One woman said: "No, there's no song more beautiful than

Hans Bender

'La Paloma'! When Rosie and Leo play it, Rosie on the piano and Leo with his violin, I just can't keep from crying."
I knew Rosie and Leo very well. They were the children of one of our teachers, Ritzl, and had made appearances as popular local virtuosos at the modest village concerts, at founders' day parties of the clubs, Christmas and New Year celebrations, and also in the little hotel my family owned.
". . . and when I hear 'La Paloma' on the radio," the woman's voice continued, "I start dropping my dishes because I can't see them through my tears!"
When the conductor came to punch the tickets, the light of his carbide lantern, intensified by its concave reflector, fell upon the face of the woman who had just spoken. It was Sophie, a neighbor of ours. A year ago she had opened a laundry service, which at first wasn't used often by the cautious women of the village, who were attached to their washboards; but as their enthusiasm grew, it became a flourishing business. Sophie, who wasn't married, was considered in the village as a robust type of person, one who waded into her work with rolled-up sleeves, and one whom I wouldn't have expected to show such emotion.
A few weeks after that train trip a certain Ferdinand Schwarz took a room in our hotel. He was going to be here a few weeks substituting for the stationmaster, Gramlich, who needed a vacation. Every evening after nine o'clock Mr. Schwarz entered our dining room lounge, sat down at the table under the stuffed owl, ate his supper, lighted a cigar, and leafed through the newspaper.
One of the people who came for a quick visit to the bar was Sophie. She brought her own green siphon flask, pushed it under the beer tap, waited until my father had filled it, paid, and went out again with an abrupt "good-bye."
In those days I usually would be sitting at one of the tables doing my schoolwork. Because I was thinking about the confession Sophie had made in the train, I watched her more closely than before. I noticed she came more regularly after Herr Schwarz moved in. She would look over at him, and he would look back. Once he asked how she could drink so much beer alone. The regular customers turned their heads when they heard that. She said: "Why not?" took her siphon flask, and closed the door sharply behind her.
They got no closer than that. She retreated into her shell and he seemed to be shyer than usual.

WEST GERMAN AUTHORS

In *Twelfth Night*, one of Shakespeare's characters, Duke Orsino, says: "If music be the food of love, play on! Give me excess of it." At that time I didn't know Shakespeare and his words yet. I was ten years old, in the fourth class of the Volksschule, learning how to write compositions and dictations, recite poems, and do arithmetic, which was very hard for me. I daydreamed over the world atlas or read *Robinson Crusoe*. For a year I had been taking piano lessons from Miss Wagenseil and I was just at the point where I could play the first sonatinas of Dussek and Clementi.

The next time that I visited the county seat I went to the music store and bought "La Paloma: Tango and Song." It was a four-page piece of sheet music with a brightly illustrated cover: lemon-yellow houses with red tiles, green cypresses, a blue ocean, and above them a white dove with widespread wings. I showed Miss Wagenseil the music and asked if I could practice it. She said I was not advanced enough to master a tango, and besides it would make the rest of my playing sloppy, and my rhythm was not very good anyway.

So I practiced "La Paloma" by myself. It wasn't easy. My left hand had to search out black and white keys that seemed too close together, and keep up the tango rhythm, while at the same time my right hand played the graceful melody above it.

Our piano was not the best. It had once been a player piano run by electricity. When a hotel guest put a ten-pfennig coin in the slot, a cylinder with a punched paper roll on it started moving and actuated the felt hammers, which mechanically played "Sweetheart, You're the Light of My Life," "In Grunewald, in Grunewald," Prussian marches, or waltzes by Waldteufel, while the keys moved up and down as if pressed by invisible fingers. My older brother, Theo, who even at an early age showed other than musical talents, had discovered a small gear in the electrical mechanism over which a drive belt could be stretched. He connected it with the little butter machine, which had just made its appearance on the market and was actually supposed to be run by a handcrank. By the time the roll of music was finished—"The Goblins' Parade" was his favorite piece—the butter was ready.

Despite such a useful double function, my father had the electrical mechanism taken out. The piano tuner, Mr. Eder, who came every year at Easter time and gave me a red candy rabbit, had advised him to. He said it would have a richer tone this way, especially since the electrical piano had greater resonance than a regular one.

But it still had a dead sound. The low notes rumbled like potatoes rolling on a plank floor. The high keys made a dry clinking tone, as if their strings were covered with chalk. The semiquavered high F, which is used so often in this particular piece, got stuck sometimes, and the keys were yellow from the smoke in the room and the nicotine-stained fingers of the pianists who played programs of dance music for the customers, accompanied by violin and trumpet. One morning I was sitting at the piano — my father had left, my sister was waxing the rooms upstairs, and my brothers were in school—and after I had played the tango maybe fifty times in succession my gentle mother, who was usually the most patient auditor of my piano exercises, came out of the kitchen and cried: "I just can't stand that piece anymore!" I calmed her down with the allegro of the Clementi sonata in C-Major. When she had gone into the kitchen, I used the damping pedal and quietly started on "La Paloma" again.

If I had done my exercises and the unloved Czerny etudes with such perseverance I would have become a Liszt!

After three weeks of hard practice with one hand and with both hands, I was burning for a chance to play "La Paloma" sometime when Sophie was standing at the bar. But every well thought-out plan needs the help of a little luck. It didn't come, and one evening after the regular patrons had gone, I heard Mr. Schwarz tell my mother that tomorrow would be his last day with us. Mr. Gramlich had returned from his vacation earlier than expected; he was very sorry he had to leave us because he had really enjoyed his stay, the food was good and substantial, and he must have gained at least ten pounds, and if he ever happened to be in this area again . . .

I went to the piano, opened the lid, swiveled the stool up to my level, and, as I opened my music, thought I would play "La Paloma" for him, at least, to honor his departure. With a feeling of sad resignation I put my fingers to the keys and, with a languishing left hand and a weak right hand, which was fearful of the tricky semiquavered F, I played my "La Paloma."

In the meantime the door opened. I heard Sophie say "Good evening" and Mr. Schwarz answered "Good evening." I played "La Paloma" as I never had before and never would again. Behind me someone moved a chair closer. I did everything I could to make it exciting — a roaring pedal and a crashing fortissimo. I improvised, I sang, because the human voice, as Beethoven discovered before his death, surpasses the voice of the instruments. I finished with a brilliant accelerando, turned on my stool just in time to see Sophie take her hand out of Mr. Schwarz's in order to put her handkerchief to her eyes, and I saw how he straightened up and adjusted his tie. "Don't stop playing!" Sophie said. I played "La Paloma" until my mother dragged me off to bed. Mr. Schwarz did not leave on the following day. He kept on rooming with us although Mr. Gramlich returned on schedule. Mr. Schwarz sent in his resignation to the railway company, and four weeks later married Sophie, who had described to him her plans for a large-scale laundry business.

On the wedding day the school principal, Lämmlein, who was very fat and played the organ in church, came to our bar to bolster his strength for the long ceremony with a glass of choice burgundy. While I poured the wine I asked him whether he couldn't perhaps play a variation of "La Paloma" during the ceremony, using Celesta, Aeolian Harp, Vox Humana, and similar registers. "Whatever gave you that idea, Hans?" he asked. "That's just the way I feel it should be," I said and set the wine glass down in front of his bulging vest.

Who Am I?

Kurt Kusenberg

When Mr. Boras went downstairs at ten-thirty in the morning he felt as light as a feather and had a great urge to break out laughing. The night before he had had a drinking bout with a friend—first wine, then brandy, then beer, and then everything at once. It must have been a little too much, because he had no idea how he had arrived home. So what's the difference? He had found his way home, that was obvious and all that was necessary, and then he had gotten up late, and now his breakfast was waiting for him down there. Maybe he should say "break*slow*"! At this late hour was his breakfast waiting for him or was he waiting for it? Perhaps they were both lying in wait for the other. The idea that he was at the point of taking his tardy and devious meal by surprise made Mr. Boras cheerful, and he burst out laughing. It was his last laugh that day.

Having arrived downstairs, Mr. Boras decided to take a look at the garden. He heard his wife in the kitchen but he wasn't eager to join her. People who have arisen early have a high opinion of themselves and treat late-risers rather sternly and brusquely, or even with scorn. A garden, on the other hand, is pure kindliness; it does not look at you but rather lets you look at it. It is there, just there, and very green. Human beings need greenness because it refreshes them—to see green things is almost as healthy as eating green things.

Mr. Boras strolled around a little in the garden. When he came to the raspberry bushes he saw his dog busily digging a hole in the ground. He whistled to him. The dog stopped, looked at him, and came running. But instead of joyfully jumping up on his master he circled him threateningly, with an angry growling and barking.

He's mad at me, Mr. Boras thought. Maybe he smells the alcohol oozing out of my pores. "Come here!" he said and slapped his trousers in a friendly way, but the dog took it as a challenge—he snapped at the trousers and when Mr. Boras tried to push him away he bit him in the hand. That angered him and worried him at the same time. What if the dog had rabies? He started toward the house to speak with his wife about it. He made slow progress, however, because he had to keep his eye on the circling dog; he spun his way to the house like a top.

"What are you doing in our garden?" a voice screamed, and when Mr. Boras turned around he was looking into his wife's face. He couldn't look long because he had to protect himself from the dog, which was closing in on him.

"Martha!" he shouted. "Is everybody crazy?"

"If you call me by my first name once more I'll telephone the police!" Yes, that's exactly the way she talked to him. It was incredible; just because he'd been a little drunk she wanted to deny the fact that they had been married all these years.

"Who's that man?" a child's voice asked. This was especially hard on Mr. Boras because he loved his son. And now his son had been turned against him too!

"Get out of here!" the woman screamed.

"Get out of here!" the boy shouted, feeling courageous under his mother's protection and the dog barked the same thing. All three moved toward Mr. Boras. Then he gave way and left his own property like a thief.

At a loss to know what to do he walked down the street, turned the next corner, walked some more, turned again, and so it went for quite a while; he just could not put his thoughts in order. Suddenly it occurred to him that he had perhaps behaved so badly last night when he came home drunk that his family was simply disgusted with him. That wasn't very likely, to be sure, but possible. In a drunken condition a lot of things are possible—anything really!

Kurt Kusenberg

"Maybe Kilch brought me home yesterday," said Mr. Boras to himself, "and maybe he knows more about it. I'll ask him." His friend lived fairly close. Five minutes later Mr. Boras was ringing his doorbell. Kilch opened and looked at him coolly: "Yes?"
"Kilch!" cried Mr. Boras. "What kind of nonsense is this?" The other stared at him scornfully. "That's what I'd like to know!" he said and slammed the door.

Even his friend was against him! What could have happened to close all the doors for Mr. Boras?

It's beyond me, the poor man confessed to himself. I can't return to my own family, at least not today — they're too angry with me. But where can I spend the night? Oh, yes—at Carlo's, of course. He is a better friend, I should have gone to him first, we've known each other since school days, and that brings you closer together.

Visiting Carlo meant taking a little trip, and actually that had been the reason the contact with his friend had gradually broken off. But on this particular day Mr. Boras conquered his inertia and rode a good half-hour before he arrived at Carlo's apartment. Going up the steps he stumbled. That's bad, he thought, I've been stumbling all day.

He rang the doorbell. Footsteps approached, the door opened, and his school friend appeared. "I'm not buying anything!" he said gruffly. "I'm not ordering anything, I'm not signing anything, and I don't have any money. Good-bye!" The door slammed shut. As Mr. Boras went down the steps he once again had a feeling of feathery lightness, as if he were hovering. The urge to laugh returned too but it was different from the first time.

On the street Mr. Boras understood—finally, finally!—what had happened. To put it briefly, he had lost all similarity to himself. He had misplaced his past like a wallet and could no longer prove his identity. Odd! Mr. Boras thought, I am alive, all right, and yet it seems as if I never lived, because no traces remain. And all the time I was so firmly convinced that I did exist! No, it *wasn't* imagination. But how did I lose all that? Did I make a wrong move perhaps? That's it, I've just slipped out of the world's scheme of things and now I don't fit in anywhere. A comet is more a part of the plan than I am.

In the meantime one o'clock in the afternoon had come. Although Mr. Boras might not, as he thought, fit into the world anymore, he felt the pangs of hunger because he was in the habit of eating at this time—insofar as he could now speak of habits at all. He looked around for a restaurant, but the prospects were not good in this neighborhood; it was a remote suburb and completely residential.

Mr. Boras gloomily walked past many houses and gardens; a large number of them bore an amazing resemblance to the house that he had considered his own until now. For that reason he was not especially surprised when a woman leaned out of a window and called to him: "Well, it's about time you came! The soup is already on the table."

Without much hesitation, Mr. Boras opened the front gate and went in; he was hungry. At the door a boy ran up to him: "Daddy, we're having omelets too!"

"That's fine, my boy!" answered Mr. Boras. He wiped the dust from his shoes, hung his hat on the hook, gave the woman a quick kiss, sat down at the table and started eating his soup. During the meal he watched the woman and the boy—as unobtrusively as he could, since they obviously considered him to be the father of the family. The woman wasn't bad, and he liked the boy; the food tasted good.

What does it matter, he thought, family is family, and the main thing is that you have one. I can consider myself lucky that I found another place to stay; things looked gloomy for a while. It's true, I didn't choose these two people but what choices do you have anyway? You always choose what you have to. "Yes, it's a good exchange, it looks quite promising, and at least it's different."

"Why are you looking at us that way?" the woman said. "Do you have something to complain about?"

Mr. Boras wiped his lips with his napkin. "No, just the opposite, everything is fine." He reached into the fruit bowl, took an apple, and began to peel it. He knew he would soon get used to living here. Maybe he had always lived here and had just imagined the other existence. Who knows so exactly whether he is dreaming or living?

The doorbell rang. "I'll take it!" said the woman, and she got up and went out. Since she left the door ajar, he could hear very clearly what went on in the hall.

"Where? What is that supposed to mean!" the woman's voice said sternly. "Get out of here this minute or I'll call my husband!"

Kurt Kusenberg

"You must be out of your mind!" answered a man's voice. "Stop joking, I'm hungry." "This is no soup kitchen. Out! I'll teach you to talk to me as if you'd known me all your life!" And so the battle continued, but not for long. The man retreated and the door slammed after him. The woman returned, her face flushed. "What nerve!—And naturally you didn't come and help me out."

"I felt sorry for the fellow," replied Mr. Boras. "He must either be very hungry or he mistook our house for his own."

"Mistook?" cried the woman. "That man has no house and no family—you can just be sure of that!"

Mr. Boras rose hurriedly. "And that's the very reason why I'm going to treat him to a lunch. I'll be right back." He ran out and caught up with the stranger at the front gate. The man was distraught and pale; his eyes had a confused look.

"I can imagine how you feel," said Mr. Boras, "and I want to help you." He pulled out his pocket diary, scribbled a line, and tore the sheet off. "Here is a good address, my friend. Go there but make it fast, otherwise the meal will be cold."

The man took the note but could find nothing to say. He wouldn't have had an audience anyway because Mr. Boras was already hurrying away.

"You're much too soft-hearted," said the woman when he walked in. Mr. Boras sat down and started eating his apple again. "Not at all, I just made a wise investment. What happens to him today can happen to me tomorrow."

The next day Mr. Boras went into town and visited the street where he had lived. As he walked past his house he saw his wife sitting in the garden with the other man. His wife was knitting and the man was reading the newspaper; both had a satisfied look on their faces. Then Mr. Boras was satisfied too.

The Fat Child

Marie Luise Kaschnitz

It was in January, soon after Christmas vacation, that the fat child came to me. This winter I had begun to lend the neighborhood children some of my books, which they were supposed to take out and return on a certain day of the week. Naturally I knew most of these children, but sometimes there were strangers who did not live on our street. And although most of the children stayed just long enough to exchange books, there were a few who would sit down and start reading right away. Then I would sit at my desk and work while the children sat at the little table next to the book-shelves, and their presence was welcome and did not bother me.

The fat child came on a Friday or Saturday, in any case not on the day set aside for borrowing books. I had planned to go out and was about to have a small snack in my room first. I had just had a visitor and he must have forgotten to close the house door. So it happened that all of a sudden I saw the fat child standing before me just after I had set the tray down on the desk and turned around to get something else out of the kitchen. It was a girl about twelve years old, wearing an old-fashioned woolen coat and black knitted leggings and carrying a pair of ice skates on a strap; she seemed familiar to me and yet not really familiar, and because she had walked in so quietly, I was startled.

Marie Luise Kaschnitz

Do I know you? I asked in surprise.

The fat child said nothing. She just stood there and clasped her hands together over her round stomach and looked at me with pale, watery blue eyes.

Would you like a book? I asked.

Again the fat child did not answer. But I was not too surprised. I was used to the children's shyness and was used to helping them. So I pulled out a few books and put them down in front of the strange girl. Then I started filling out one of the record cards for the borrowed books.

What's your name? I asked.

They call me Fatty, said the child.

Shall I call you that too? I asked.

I don't care, said the child. She did not return my smile, and I seem to remember now that her face became painfully contorted at this moment.

But I paid no attention.

When were you born? I asked.

In Aquarius, she said softly.

This answer amused me and I entered it on the card, half-jokingly, and then I turned back to the books.

Would you like something in particular? I asked.

But then I saw that the strange child was not looking at the books at all. Her eyes were fixed on the tray where I had my tea and sandwiches.

Maybe you'd like something to eat, I said quickly.

The child nodded, and in her assent there was something like a hurt surprise that I had taken so long to come upon this idea. She went about devouring the sandwiches one after the other, and in a particular way which I was not really aware of until later. Then she sat there again, casting indolent, cold glances around the room, and there was something in her character that filled me with anger and revulsion. Yes, of course, I had hated this child from the very beginning. Everything about her repelled me—the heavy, slow way she moved her arms and legs, her good-looking but fat face, her manner of speaking, which was lax and presumptuous at the same time. And although I had decided to give up my walk on her account, I did not treat her in a friendly way at all, but rather cruelly and coldly.

Or was I being friendly when I now sat down at my desk and began working and said over my shoulder "Start reading now," although I knew very well that this strange child did not want to read at all? And then I sat there and wanted to write and accomplished nothing, because I had an odd, tormented feeling, the kind of feeling one has when he is supposed to guess something and can't, and when he knows that if he isn't able to guess it, things will never be the same again. And for a while I held out, but not for very long, then I turned around and began a conversation, and could think of only the silliest questions.

Do you have any brothers or sisters? I asked.

Yes, said the child.

Do you like to go to school? I asked.

Yes, said the child.

What do you like best?

What? asked the child.

What subject, I said despairingly.

I don't know, said the child.

Would it be German? I asked.

I don't know, said the child.

I twisted my pencil between my fingers, and something rose up in me, a terror which had no relationship to the child's appearance.

Do you have any girl friends? I asked tremulously.

Oh yes, said the girl.

There's probably one that you like best of all? I asked.

I don't know, said the child, and the way she sat there in her fluffy wool coat she looked like a fat caterpillar, and she had eaten like a caterpillar too, and now she was sniffing around again like a caterpillar. You aren't going to get anything more, I thought, filled with an odd vindictiveness. But then I went out after all and brought some bread and sausage and the child stared at them with her expressionless face and then began to eat the way a caterpillar eats, slowly and steadily, as if from an inner compulsion, and I watched her in hostile silence.

Because now the time had come when everything about this child began to disturb me and annoy me. What a silly white dress, what a ridiculous stand-up collar, I thought, as the child was unbuttoning her coat after the meal. I sat down at my work again, but then I heard the child licking her lips behind me, and this sound was like the lazy lapping of a black pool somewhere in the woods; it recalled to my consciousness everything that is soggily dull, and ponderous, and melancholy in human nature, and it put me in a foul mood. What do you want from me, I thought, just go away, go away. And I felt an urge to push the child bodily out of the room, the way one gets rid of a troublesome animal, but instead I just went on talking to her in the same cruel way.

Are you going down to the ice now? I asked.

Yes, said the fat child.

Can you skate well? I asked and pointed to the ice skates that still hung from her arm.

My sister can, said the child, and again an expression of pain and sadness appeared on her face, and again I paid no attention to it.

How does your sister look? I asked. Is she like you?

Oh, no, the fat child said. My sister is very slim and has black curly hair. In the summer, when we are out in the country, she gets up at night when a storm comes and sits on the railing of the highest balcony and sings.

And you? I asked.

I stay in bed, the child said. I'm afraid.

Your sister is not afraid, is she? I said.

No, said the child. She is never afraid. She jumps from the highest diving board too. She dives head first and then she swims way out . . .

What does your sister sing? I asked curiously.

She sings what she wants to, the fat child said sadly . . . and she writes poems.

And you? I asked.

I don't do anything, the child said. Then she stood up and said she had to go now. I held out my hand, and she touched it with her fat fingers, and I am not sure what I felt at that moment— something like a challenge to follow her, an inaudible, urgent call. Come back again sometime, I said, but I did not really mean it, and the child said nothing and looked at me with her cool eyes. And then she was gone, and I should really have felt relieved. But almost before the apartment door had closed I ran out into the corridor and put on my coat. I went quickly down the stairs and reached the street at the moment the child disappeared around the nearest corner.

I just have to see how this caterpillar looks on ice skates, I said to myself . . . I have to see how this lump of fat moves on the ice. And I walked fast in order not to lose sight of her.

It had been early afternoon when the fat child came into my room, and now it was getting dark. Although I had spent a few years of my childhood in this town, I didn't know my way around very well anymore, and in my efforts to follow the child I soon had no idea which direction we were taking, and the streets and squares that we came to were completely strange to me. I also noticed suddenly a change in the air. It had been very cold, but now a thaw had obviously set in and with such strength that the snow was already sliding off the roofs and warm clouds were moving across the sky. We came past the edge of town, where the houses are surrounded by large gardens, and then there are no houses at all; then the child suddenly disappeared from view over an embankment. And although I had expected to see an ice rink with warming shacks and arc lights and a glittering surface full of shouts and music, I was confronted now by a completely different sight. For the lake down there, the lake whose shore I had thought would be covered with houses, lay in complete loneliness, surrounded by black woods and looking exactly as it had in my childhood.

I was so shaken by this unexpected scene that I almost lost sight of the strange child. But then I saw her again; she was crouched on the bank, trying to cross one leg over the other and to hold the ice skate on her foot with one hand while she turned the key with the other. The key fell several times and then the fat child got down on all fours and slid around on the ice and searched, looking like a strange toad. Meanwhile it was getting darker and darker; the steamboat dock, which jutted out into the lake just a few yards from the child, was very black against the broad surface, which had a silvery gleam, but not uniformly—it was a bit darker here and there, and in these darker spots the effect of the thaw was evident. Hurry up, I cried impatiently, and the fat girl actually did move more quickly now, however, not because of my urging, but because out there on the ice at the end of the long dock someone was waving and crying "Come on, Fatty" — someone who was skating in loops, a light and bright figure. It occurred to me that this must be the sister, the dancer, the singer to the storms, the child after my own heart, and I was immediately convinced that nothing else had lured me here except the wish to see this charming creature. But at the same time I was aware of the danger that the children were in. Because now, all of a sudden, the odd groaning sounds began, those deep sighs which the lake seems to emit before its ice cover breaks. These sighs ran through the depths like a fearsome lament, and I heard them, but the children did not.

No, they certainly couldn't have heard them. Otherwise the fat girl, that timid creature, would not have started out, struggling farther and farther out with awkward, scraping strokes, and the sister out there would not have waved and laughed and whirled like a ballerina on the tips of her skates before making beautiful figure-eights again, and the fat girl would have avoided the darker spots, which she hesitated in front of but crossed anyway, and the sister would not have suddenly straightened up and glided off, far away toward one of the small and lonely inlets.

I could see that all very clearly, because I had started walking out on the dock, farther and farther, one step at a time. Although the planking was icy I could make faster progress than the fat child down below, and when I turned around I could see her face, which had a dull and yet yearning expression. I could also see the cracks which were now opening everywhere, out of which driblets of frothy water were pressed like foam from the lips of a madman. And then I also saw, of course, how the ice broke under the fat child. For that happened at the spot where her sister had just been dancing, only a few armlengths from the end of the dock.

I must hasten to admit that breaking through the ice was not mortally dangerous. The lake freezes in several layers, and the second layer was only a meter below the first and still very solid. All that happened was that the fat girl was left standing there in one meter of water, in icy cold water, to be sure, and surrounded by crumbling ice floes, but if she waded only a few steps through the water she could read the dock and pull herself up. And I was there to help her. But despite that my first thought was, she won't be able to, and it also looked as if she could not do it, as she stood there, frightened to death, making only a few random movements while the water flowed around her and the ice broke under her hands. I thought to myself: Aquarius, the water man, will pull her under now; and I felt no emotion, not the slightest pity, and I did not move.

But now the fat girl suddenly raised her head, and, since the night had come and the moon had appeared from behind the clouds, I could clearly see that something in her face changed. They were the same features but still not the same. They had been forced into wakefulness by will and passion as if now, in confronting death, they were drinking in all of life, all the warm life of the earth. Yes, I believed, in this moment, that her death was near and that this was the end, and I bent over the edge and looked at the white face beneath me, and like a mirror image it looked back at me from the black water. But then the fat child reached the pilings of the dock. She stretched out her hands and began to pull herself up; very adroitly she grasped the nails and hooks which protruded from the wood. Her body was too heavy and her fingers bled, and she fell back, but only to try again. And it was a long battle, a terrible struggle for liberation and transformation, like the breaking open of a shell or of a chrysalis of which I was able to be an observer; I would have liked to help the child now but I knew I did not need to help her anymore—I had recognized that.

I don't remember my return home that evening. I only remember telling a neighbor I met on the stairs that there is still a stretch of lakeshore lined by meadows and dark woods. She said that was not true. And I remember that I then found a pile of scattered papers on my desk and somewhere in their midst an old snapshot of myself in a white woolen dress and stand-up collar, with pale, watery eyes, and very fat.

Traffic Accident

Heinz Risse

Hagerland[1] entered the café at the same time as always. The clock was just striking four. The editor, who had just wrapped up the evening edition, was already sitting in his corner reading. He did not look up as Hagerland walked past.

Hagerland was a very busy man: there were morning deadlines to meet at court, then a half hour for lunch, after that, meetings lasting into the night, legal documents, telephone conversations, and a resounding flow of small talk—Hagerland brought it all off diligently and expertly. Even the old man of the firm had recently called him "one of the best of the new crop of lawyers." What the Old Man did not know was that what he considered most essential was just a side issue for Hagerland. If Hagerland had told him that the hour from four to five in the dimly lit café was his attempt to rescue himself from a whirlpool that was incessantly pulling at him, the Old Man would have recommended that he go to a psychiatrist.

Hagerland imagined the possibility of such a conversation with the old lawyer, while the waitress brought him coffee—he didn't have to order it for he came here every day to find the same unvarying and beneficial dosage of complete irrelevance. This word had scarcely come into his thoughts before it took on weight and unsuspected significance for him. It's like a signal flag of my life, thought Hagerland: loneliness, emptiness, undiscovered wreckage; I have parents but neither father nor mother, and I have only a roundabout relationship to my brother and sister. That was actually the case. His mother had died at his birth and his father had remarried; later, when his father died without any children from the second marriage, the stepmother took a second husband —and the two children of these strangers called themselves Hagerland's brother and sister. The lawyer thought suddenly of the word "divine justice"—he now realized that he had long since believed in it. If the Old Man had any notion of that, he thought to himself—in fact, if any of us knew what the other is really like . . . but perhaps the Old Man has a weak spot in his armor too.

He tried to recall a single case in his legal practice where the unknown human element had triumphed; for its sake alone, millions of false judgments might be forgiven—he did not find it. But he discovered that this unknown human element could not be grasped; it lay somewhere in the depths, existing for its own sake, and nobody could know for sure whether it was more than superstition or fiction. Chaos covered everything, and nobody was strong enough to clear away its debris. He could feel that he was moving toward the brink, but that was his right in this twilight hour, a kind of game between cat and mouse—someone had told him once that this was a sure way for him to reach a goal, namely the door of the insane asylum.

Not I, thought Hagerland, not I. This saves me from death in the whirlpool of everyday life—some day I will stand here and see myself walking along on the other side and under my feet the rubble will turn into glass, into transparent glass.

He looked up and saw that two boys had entered the room; shabbily dressed and shy, they went from table to table. Is begging allowed here? thought Hagerland. Probably not. He looked at the waitress, who was standing at the bar and acting as if she hadn't seen anything; she probably pitied them. He watched the boys as they approached his table. Apparently it had begun to rain, for the boys' hair hung in wet strands over their foreheads.

"Well?" asked Hagerland as they reached his table.

"Mother is sick," answered the one and stretched out his hand; the other said nothing. He at least *has* a mother, thought Hagerland; I don't have one and never had one. A flow of small talk, that's my nourishment. This boy is lucky.

"How old are you?" he asked.

Heinz Risse

"I'm ten," answered the boy. "He's nine."

"Does your mother know that you go begging?" The boy did not answer. He was probably trying to figure out which answer would do him the most good.

"What does your father do?"

"He's at home. He can't find a job."

"Now listen to me," said Hagerland. "It's possible of course that what you said is true—your mother is sick and your father can't find a job." The boys nodded. "But it's just as possible that you lied to me. Oh yes, you shake your heads, but I don't know you. So tell me where you live and I will see what I can do for your parents."

"Yes," answered the older boy and mentioned an address. Hagerland wrote it down.

"It's also possible," he said, "that you gave me the wrong address, isn't it . . . because what you told me isn't really true, after all . . . ?" He reached into his pocket and took out a rather large bill. "Here, take this," he said to the older boy. "Naturally you don't understand why, do you? You think it is a reward for having lied to me—in fact, it does look that way. But it just looks that way to you now, when you're nine or ten years old. Later, when you find out what a feeling of shame is like—but maybe you never will find that out . . . and as for me, I'm concerned about something else too—my own self, for example, but you understand that even less. So, get along now."

The boys had listened uncomprehendingly to what Hagerland said. When he was finished they turned around and went straight to the door without stopping at any of the other tables. They even forgot to thank him. Hagerland sat for a few more minutes. He was thinking: Would the Old Man understand my words?—or why I did that just now? But it's all a searching, an attempt, and a temptation—yes, this too. Only the person who purposely goes astray reaches his goal. He laid a coin on the table and left.

He stood outside, still protected by the entranceway to the café and turned up his coat collar. It was raining hard and the lights were mirrored in the shiny asphalt. In the darkness of the entranceway he heard two quarreling voices beside him: "No, let me!" "Give it here—I'll take the money home to Mother, and you can follow me." In the same instant one of the two boys ran out of the shadows into the rain, and the other hurried after him. Hagerland sensed what was coming—the cars on the slippery street, no chance to stop. He leaned helplessly against the wall—there was a screeching of tires; one car skidded sideways and the next one rammed into it with a little boy between its wheels. The grand illusion, thought Hagerland, and I only wanted to do something good — my God, who can forgive me now? I will ask the Chief Justice myself. He ranks higher than the Old Man—maybe they've told him that the verdict against me has been carried out. But I'll have to take the boy with me.

He pushed through the crowd which had collected immediately. The people may have assumed that he was a relative of the boy because of the excited haste with which he pulled the bleeding child from under the car. They let him have his way, and some of them helped him. He took the boy in his arms, and then a policeman walked up: "You want to go to the doctor?" he asked. "There's one that lives on the other side. I'll go with you."

Hagerland laughed. "To the doctor? Why should we go to the doctor? I'm going to the Chief Justice. It's the wrong verdict even though I'll accept it. But I'm not afraid to explain that it is wrong, and the Chief Justice will tell me whether it can be nullified or whether I at least have the right to demand that it be nullified, even though this may never really happen. Because I will be sentenced . . ."

"You're right," the policeman interrupted him. "We'll go to the Chief Justice—but first give me the child; it's a long distance and he could get too heavy for you." He took the boy out of Hagerland's arms and walked calmly across the street. When he was about to enter the doctor's house, Hagerland tried to stop him. "Not here," he said, "there are no towers here, this is not the house of the Chief Justice."

"Yes it is," replied the officer, "but you won't come in with me. I will tell you afterwards what the Chief Justice decided."

As the officer disappeared in the house, Hagerland, to his surprise, felt his wrists being grasped by two men. He made no attempt to defend himself. "The mistake was," he said, "that for years I ignored the verdict." The men didn't answer. They had stationed themselves next to Hagerland in such a way that they had a view of the street, the wet asphalt, the flashing lights; the car that had skidded was being pulled aside.

After a quarter of an hour the policeman came back: "No danger of dying," he said. Hagerland did not move. The two men released his wrists.

"Listen," the policeman said and touched Hagerland's shoulder. "The boy's injuries are not too serious. But he will have to be taken to the hospital right away."

"You keep talking about the child," answered Hagerland, "but that is not the point. It has to do with the verdict in my case— the grand illusion is what you should have discussed with the Chief Justice. Only that—everything else is unimportant."

"I'll do that later," said the officer and walked away. Hagerland watched him until he disappeared behind the people milling restlessly around in the darkness.

When his attack of illness was over, he had the feeling of having walked over not glass but across a field of rubble whose size made mockery of all known measurements—to be sure it might be consistent with those that are unknown, otherwise Hagerland could have not borne its sight.

Notes

[1]The name suggests "barrenness" or "wasteland."

The Left-Handers[1]

Günter Grass

Erich is watching me. And I'm not taking my eyes off him either.
Each of us has a weapon in his hand and we intend to wound each
other. Our weapons are loaded. Our grip slowly warms the cool
metal of pistols that have proved their reliability in long practice
sessions and have been carefully cleaned each time. As far as
its length is concerned, such a gun looks harmless. Can't a
person just as well hold a ballpoint pen or a large key this way
between the fingers of a black-gloved hand and make timid souls
scream? But not for a moment can I allow myself to think that
Erich's weapon could have blanks in it, or be a harmless toy. And I
know that Erich doesn't doubt for one second that mine means
business too. Besides, about a half hour ago we took the pistols
apart, cleaned them, put them together again, loaded and cocked
them. We're no dreamers. We picked Erich's weekend cottage as
the location for our unavoidable encounter. Since this one-story
building is located a good hour on foot from the nearest highway,
thus is very isolated, we can assume that no undesired ear will
hear the shots. We have cleared out the living room and taken all
the pictures from the walls—mostly hunting scenes and still lifes
of dead game. After all, the shots are not intended to hit chairs or
polished dressers or elegantly framed paintings. We also don't

want to damage the mirror or any porcelain. Our targets are each other.

We are both left-handers. We got acquainted with each other at the Club. As you know, the left-handers of this city, like all those who suffer from a common defect, have organized a club. We meet regularly and try to train our other hand, which is unfortunately very clumsy. For a time a kindhearted right-hander gave us instruction. Unfortunately he doesn't come anymore. Our cabinet officers criticized his teaching methods and felt that the club members should relearn on their own initiative. So now, in mutual and unforced cooperation, we combine social games of our own invention with tests of skill such as using our right hands for threading a needle, pouring liquids, unbuttoning and buttoning. The constitution of our club states: "We shall not rest until right and left are one."

However beautiful and strong this statement may be, it is nevertheless pure nonsense. Because we'll never reach our goal this way. And the extremist wing of our organization has been demanding for a long time now that this maxim be replaced by the words: "We will be forever proud of our left hand and unashamed of its native endowments."

But this slogan is certainly not right either, and only its fervor and a certain nobility of sentiment prompted us to choose it. Erich and I, who both belong to the extremist wing, know only too well how deeply rooted our shame is. Neither family, nor school, nor later our military service has been able to teach us how to bear this small abnormality—small at least in comparison with other widespread abnormalities—with dignity. It began with the handshaking ritual in childhood. Those aunts and uncles, those female friends of mother, those colleagues of father, that frightful, inescapable family photograph which darkens the childhood horizon. Everyone of them had to have a hand to shake: "No, not the naughty little hand, the good little hand. Will you *please* hold out the proper hand, the nice hand, the clever, the skillful, the one true hand, the right hand!"

I was sixteen years old when I held a girl for the first time: "Oh . . . , you're a lefty!" she said disappointedly and withdrew my hand from her blouse. Such memories are lasting and although we intend to enter the new slogan—which Erich and I drafted—in our bylaws, we will have to realize that it is only the attempt to express an ideal which certainly will never be attained.

Erich's lips are tightly pressed together, and he is watching me with narrowed eyes. I am doing the same. There is a play of muscles in our cheeks, our temples are taut, our brows are furrowed. Erich now resembles a certain movie actor whose features are especially familiar to me from so many adventure-packed scenes. Can I assume that at this moment my features also have a fateful similarity with one of these ambivalent heroes of the screen? We probably look ferocious and I am glad that no one is watching us. Wouldn't this undesired witness assume that it's a duel between two young men with overly romantic tendencies? They both love the same gunmoll, or one of them insulted the other. A family feud that has lasted for generations, an *affaire d'honneur*, a bloody game of life and death. Only enemies look at each other this way. See those narrow, colorless lips, the implacable brows. How they relish their hate, these suitors of death!

We are friends. However different our professions may be (Erich is section head in a large department store, and I have a well-paying job as a precision tool mechanic) we can list any number of mutual interests that insure a lasting friendship. Erich has belonged to the club longer than I. I can still remember clearly the day I entered the favorite restaurant of "The One-siders"—I was shy and dressed much too formally—and Erich came up to me as I stood there hesitantly, showed me to the cloakroom, looked at me intelligently and without embarrassing curiosity, and said: "You want to join us, don't you? Don't be bashful; we're here to help each other."

I just mentioned "The One-siders." That's what we call ourselves officially. But I consider it as inadequate as most of our bylaw provisions. This name doesn't express clearly enough what should unite us and actually even strengthen us. It would certainly be more appropriate if we were simply called "The Lefties" or, more sonorously, "The Left-handed Brotherhood."[2] You can perhaps guess, of course, why we had to forego registering ourselves under these names. Nothing would be more unsuitable and, in addition, more insulting than to compare us with those certainly very unfortunate people whom nature has denied the very human capability of doing full justice to love. On the contrary, we are a very heterogeneous society, and I may say that our ladies are equal in beauty, charm, and manners to many a right-hander; indeed, if careful comparison were made, they would disclose a model of morality that might cause many a worried pastor to call out from the pulpit to his sinful parishioners: "Oh, if only all of you were left-handers!"

That silly name of the club! Even our first president, also one of the higher officials in the city government — department of revenue—who thinks and unfortunately also leads in a somewhat too paternalistic fashion, has to admit now and then that we shouldn't give the impression there is anything wrong with "left," admits also that we are not "one-siders," and do not think, feel, or act one-sidedly.

Political considerations were, of course, involved when we rejected the better proposals and adopted a name that we never should have had. Ever since the seats of the parliament members have been arranged on one side or the other so as to indicate their position relative to the Center, with the result that the mere grouping of the seats reveals the political situation of our country, it has also been the custom to ascribe dangerous radicality to every document or speech in which the word "left" appears more than once. But enough of this topic. If there is any club in our city which gets along without political ambitions and exists only for mutual assistance and for sociability, it is ours. And to put an end once and for all to any suspicion of erotic aberrations, let me say briefly that I found my fiancée among the girls of our youth group. As soon as an apartment becomes available we will marry. If some day the shadow disappears that was cast over my psyche by that first encounter with the female sex, I will owe this blessing to Monica.

Our love was confronted not only by the well-known problems described in many books; our manual difficulties had also to be overcome and almost transfigured before we could establish our modest happiness. After attempting in our first and understandable confusion to do justice to our love in right-handed fashion and after being forced to observe how insensitive this, our dull side, is, we started to caress each other the skillful way, that is, the way the Lord created us to do it. I am not betraying too much and also trust I am not being indiscreet if I mention here that it is always Monica's beloved hand which gives me the strength to persevere and hold my promise. Immediately after we first went to the movies together I had to promise her that I would respect her maidenhood until we were already wearing a wedding band — unfortunately yielding to and thus reinforcing a natural inequity—on the ring finger of our right hand.[3] In the southern, Catholic countries, by way of contrast, the golden token of marriage is worn on the left hand, which may well be due to the fact that in those sunny climates the heart prevails over relentless reason. With the intention perhaps of rebelling in feminine fashion against such attitudes and of proving how clear the arguments of women can be, when they feel that their concerns are in jeopardy, the younger ladies of our club worked very hard after hours to embroider on our green flag the motto: "Our hearts beat on the left."

Monica and I have talked so often about the moment when we will exchange rings and we have always come to the same conclusion: We cannot permit ourselves to be considered as an engaged couple by an unknowing and often malicious world if we have long since been intimate with each other and shared everything, the big and the small.[4] Often Monica cries over this problem of the rings. And however much we look forward to that day, there will probably be an aura of sadness hovering over all the wedding presents, the sumptuously laden tables and the solemnities of the occasion.

Erich's face has regained its good, normal appearance. I am relaxing a bit too, but I'm still feeling a temporary cramp in my jaw muscles. In addition, my temples are still twitching. No, those grimaces certainly didn't flatter us. We're looking at each other more calmly now and therefore more courageously; we are taking aim. We are both aiming at a particular hand. I am very sure I won't miss and I can depend upon Erich too. We have practiced too long, almost every free moment, in an abandoned gravel pit at the edge of town, to fail today, when so much is at stake.

You will exclaim that this borders on sadism, or indeed, self-mutilation. Believe me, we know all the arguments. There is nothing, no crime, that we haven't reproached ourselves for. This is not the first time that we have stood in this empty room. Four times we have held these pistols in our hands and four times, frightened by our intentions, we lowered them. Today for the first time we are completely clear in our thinking. The most recent events of a personal nature and also those involving the activities of the Club confirm our intentions—we have to do it. After much doubt—we examined critically both the Club and the intentions of its extremist wing—we have taken up our weapons irrevocably. As regrettable as it may be, we can no longer go along with the others. Our conscience demands that we disassociate ourselves from the conduct of our fellow members. Factionalism is spreading through the Club, and even the most rational elements have been contaminated by more zealous types or even fanatics. Some sing the praises of the right, others champion the left. And a thing that I never believed would happen: political slogans are shouted from table to table; the disgusting ritual of hammering nails into the table with the left hand as a kind of loyalty oath is so common that many of the cabinet meetings of the Club resemble an orgy in which the purpose is to reach a state of ecstasy by means of violent, wild hammering. And also, even though no one says this out loud, and even though those who are known to have fallen into depravity have so far been unceremoniously expelled, it cannot be denied that that misguided type of love, which I find completely incomprehensible, between persons of the same sex, has found proponents among us. And the worst of all is that my relationship with Monica has suffered. She spends too much time with her girl friend, an unstable and flighty creature. She accuses me too often of weakness and a lack of courage in that question of the wedding rings for me to believe that we still have the same trust in each other and that it is the same Monica that I hold—more and more rarely now—in my arms.

Erich and I are trying now to breathe together. The better we do this, the surer we will be that our actions are guided by the proper feelings. You should not think that we are obeying the biblical commandment to cast out that which offends us. It is, rather, the burning, unending desire to achieve clarity and even more clarity, to know how things stand with us, whether fate is unchangeable or whether we hold in our hand the power to intervene and give our life a normal direction? No silly prohibitions anymore, or bindings, or such tricks. Straightforwardly and by free choice, no longer separated from the mass of mankind, we will begin anew, and lay a happy hand to our tasks.

Now we are breathing together. And without a signal we have fired at the same time. Erich hit his target and I too did not disappoint him. As we had foreseen, each of us severed, as planned, the crucial tendon so that the pistols, no longer firmly gripped, fell to the floor, and any further shooting was superfluous. We laugh and begin our great experiment by applying—clumsily to be sure, because we have only the use of our right hands—the first-aid bandages.

Notes

[1]This is a satire focused mainly on the problems (internal divisions, weaknesses, compromises) of the leftist factions, particularly the Social Democrats, in West Germany during the long period in which the Right was dominant under the Christian Democrats and Konrad Adenauer.

[2]Grass uses the term "die linken Brüder," which suggests more clearly than my English not only the idea of left-handedness but also of homosexuality. Grass would seem to be alluding here to the Left's inability to be accepted as a normal and coequal element in German political life.

[3]In many parts of Germany it is customary for both partners to exchange wedding rings and wear them on the right hand.

[4]The problem seems to be that if they exchange rings and wear them on the left hand rather than the right they will be regarded as only engaged and not married.

The Swan

Gabriele Wohmann

This summer the hedge outside the room she shared with Anna had grown as tall as a man. The new clothes cupboard also blocked a part of her view through the tiny window, at least from the bed she had to sleep in because Anna and the whole family insisted that this was the bed she had slept in every year. The sea was not running very high this summer. The sandbank stretched close to shore, and a lazy, low surf crawled over it; maybe that was why the water no longer made her hair look pretty and the sand didn't feel good on her feet. *Milene is in a bad mood. This was her sullen summer from beginning to end.* Her breakfast face reflected dreams, dreams of Herman. Of course she heard what the others were saying, but every time a lull came she asked with the hint of a sigh: What was that? Did you say something to me?

But the worst thing was the swan. All the other summers he had recognized her. After their arrival, when supper was over (they talked of nothing but the swan) all of them, her father and Anna, Arthur and the little one, she and her mother last, with their hands still wet from washing dishes, had always run down to the fish pond—a short distance that seemed so long. She herself was soon ahead of the others, very excited but never really doubting. And the swan had always recognized her. The others thought it strange that the swan's slanting, sharp eyes looked only at her, only at Milene. It was toward her that he glided and for her that he etched his slender-wedged wake through the dark water.

Was the swan now her enemy too, like everyone else this summer? *Watch out, there goes Milene, don't get too close to her. Milene with her Herman-face. I miss him so and you treat me like dirt.* She had depended on the swan to stand by her, he would still like her best and would approve her choice. The swan and Herman and she.

The swan turned his head away from her—"in a comical but haughty way" seemed to be the family's verdict as it analyzed this movement with screeching amazement. The swan turned his neck and they immediately called him "majestic." And they cried: Just look, Milene, he is rejecting you, he isn't paying any attention to you! The swan, unembarrassed, splashed up on the bank, lost his seignorial charm, shamelessly showed his thick warty legs, his black flat feet, and his fat bulging belly, deformed by his gluttony; but they cried out: how wonderfully white! And: Milene, he doesn't like you anymore, isn't that funny? He poked around with his bill in his flea-ridden feathers and looked at them now and then. The father said, with a jovial tone in his voice, accompanied by the babbling of the child: We'll have to examine this matter thoroughly and find out what's at the bottom of it. Milene was the first to throw her handful of bread crumbs among the droppings that covered the swan's muddy terrain: he didn't touch them.

While they were all sitting at the round table after supper, making a big fuss about the fact, Milene, who was wedged in between Arthur's garlicky smell and the perspiring Anna, and across from the wide-eyed, lip-smacking child, was writing her imaginary, endless letter to Herman, in large and clear characters so that those next to her and across from her could read it easily: *This swan affair disgusts me more than anything else, as you can imagine.* A large, very clear "disgusts." And: *Swan. It is the dullest vacation without you and without your wonderful love . . .* Again and again with large letters, round and thick. *Love, your love, otherwise I could not stand it!* When she wasn't writing her letter to Herman she was sitting there with a face that said: *She is thinking of Herman.*

But she wasn't at all successful in keeping her thoughts on Herman, not even in the evening or lying in bed in the morning. The swan, again and again only the swan. The indifferent, disdainful, horrible swan. This was not her year for the swan; this year Herman was supposed to take his place. But this year the swan went so far as to waddle right up to the house door begging —and the rest of the family found nothing disgraceful about that; the swan made unpleasant wheezing noises like an old hag—but they liked that and took snapshots: Anna and the swan, Arthur and the swan especially close together, the child and the swan eating the leftover salad, the swan playing ring-toss with Father, Mother feeding the swan. In this summer, *dull, dull without your love,* her hopes had not been fulfilled, for example, that the little one would finally be nice. Or that Arthur would decide to take off his shirt in the sun. Or that Mother and Anna would say with less sarcasm: Oh, I'll go get the milk today, you others don't need to bother. *Unbearable without your love* (extra large letters). None of her hopes were fulfilled. Anna and Arthur right and left every night at supper, and right and left there were eyes, and curiosity, and a family betrayed. The swan. His faithlessness encouraged the betrayal. Every day *wasted without your love!* But she couldn't think of Herman the way she wanted to, even when she was lying in bed in the morning and evening. *Noisy, restless family* —they should read her letter and finally find out why they had to be betrayed. Every morning the metallic voice of the child recited his dream—embellished by lies—and every morning the dream had to do with the swan. The swan, always the swan, who spoke through the ugly, monotonously loud, bleating voice of the child. *You have to care for that child like a little baby. He's always close to the grown-ups. Stuffed with food, always a piece of cheese in his fingers.* Mornings were the most unpleasant; in the morning the swan stood at the kitchen door, lazy and misshapen. *Milene, he's already been eating and eating for about half an hour. He didn't wait for you.* This summer, with all their feeding, they forced the swan to start dropping the green-laced, ugly products of his digestive processes right in front of the kitchen door, and Milene, just like the rest of the family, had to follow the contented glutton around with a little shovel in her hand. This summer the iridescent and mysterious jewels, which were found bedded in splendid proliferation in the coarse dune grass, turned out, under closer inspection, to be piles of swan dung from which a diamond setting of sparkling carrion flies swarmed away as you approached; this summer the sand stayed clumpy because the sun never ventured out of its sultry hiding place in the clouds. Milene's hair hung matted together over a forehead occupied with thoughts of Herman and the swan. *But only one love.* This summer there was a completely different type of jellyfish at the high water mark, which seldom reached the fortress wall and consisted of a rust-colored, uniform, boring chain of jellyfish that roasted in the heat of a hidden sun and etched for a time the unclear pattern of their flat-roasted shields in the sand.

This summer . . . Only later did Milene find out that the changes and her annoyance with them had brought her satisfaction. *She is a pessimistic type.* Things had turned out all right, she could see now, on the last day before leaving, now when her hand was still warm from reassuring clasps. *You see, Milene, it really would have been odd. And so . . .* Now, afterwards, she felt ashamed to have had such dramatic intentions at times. Like killing the swan. Now, afterwards, she trotted along with the others, lethargic from supper, down the path to the fish pond. She saw the swan gliding, and the flecked dark water curling in his wake. It was sultry, this last day was sultry, and this last evening sultry too. The family's arms, and Anna's and Arthur's eager, warm hands caressed Milene's shoulders, the child was chattering at her, father and mother stood behind her; she was accepted again, her betrayal meant nothing. The piercing voice of the child was bright and clear. He looks completely different now! *Dear Herman, you see it wasn't even the same swan that was here last summer. You see how everything has changed. Oh, these dull, dull vacations!* They all were laughing, they all took Milene warmly and gaily into their midst. They held her firmly in their warm, relentless attachment. They looked at the swan; he seemed to take pleasure in gliding past them. Proud neck raised high, sly and elegant charm. *Everything has changed . . .* large, thick, round letters for those on the left and on the right, across from her, and all around her.

A Handful of White Daffodils

Luise Rinser
(Translated by Annette Bauer)

ANGEL: What are you looking for?

WOMAN: My bell. I have to wake up my children. I don't want to do it, they need their sleep, especially during harvest time. But who knows what can still happen tonight. The early morning wind is sweeping the dry leaves into the ditches as if they were nothing. Many die in the hours before sunrise. If I only had my bell . . .

ANGEL: Forget that. It's too late.

WOMAN: Who's talking to me?

ANGEL: The Angel.

WOMAN: I have a fever again. I hear talking and there's no one here to speak with me now, in the middle of the night.

ANGEL: You don't have a fever anymore. I am speaking and you hear me.

WOMAN: You say you're an angel. I've never heard an angel, not with my ears, perhaps deep inside, as a child, when I wanted to do something bad.

ANGEL: Soon you will see me.

WOMAN: I'm afraid of you. You have to understand, I never wished for anything like this. Such a thing only happens in legends about saints. But I'm a farmer's wife. For me it is enough to see and hear what is happening on earth. I don't want to see you. Maybe this is just a trick or a temptation, things like that happen, and you can easily imagine something like that, especially if you are sick and often alone and you think about dying. Perhaps he will go away if I make the sign of the Cross before him.

ANGEL: Here is the bell.

WOMAN: You're still here. Well, a lot of things happen that I don't understand. The bell, you say. Yes, give it to me. It feels good to hold something real, something solid, something familiar. But what's wrong with the bell? The clapper strikes but the metal is silent. And my voice is too weak. How shall I awaken my children?

ANGEL: I told you, it's too late.

WOMAN: Why do you say it's too late? I can speak, I hear, I can move. Why shouldn't I talk to the children? Do I have to leave without saying good-by?

ANGEL: You're already on the way.

WOMAN: What way, and where to?

ANGEL: To HIS presence. Why are you shouting? No one can hear you except HIM and me.

WOMAN: It's easy for you to tell me not to shout. I'm afraid.

ANGEL: Why? Haven't you thought about your death for years without fear and haven't you looked forward to meeting HIM since childhood?

WOMAN: I'm looking for sleep, a deep, good sleep for all tiredness. So put me to sleep, Angel, bring me rest. Sing to me the song that my mother and my mother's mother sang. I will close my eyes and leave them closed forever.

ANGEL: It's not time for sleeping. Listen! HIS doves are flying out. Day is beginning and it is time. Get up and come.

WOMAN: I can't, I'm tired, I'm sick. If I could get up, do you think I would be lying here now, when harvest time is beginning? We don't have enough hands for the farm and I can't pick apples or even cut carrots anymore. And you say I should get up and go with you.

ANGEL: You are expected.

WOMAN: By whom?

ANGEL: You know. Come. You've been ready for a long time.

WOMAN: Listen, Angel, to what I say. I'm not asking you for my sake, you can believe me. I'm only asking you for the sake of my farm and the children: leave me here a little longer. What will happen if I go now? My son is strong and does the work of two farm hands, but he is too young, just too young, and it is no small thing to take over a farm as big as this one. Experience is needed. And even if I have to lie here, I still can do some things, and give advice, and prevent trouble. My daughter, she's about to get married and nothing will come of it but misery. The fellow is good for nothing, everyone can see that except her—her eyes are blinded, and if I go now, her life will be ruined.

ANGEL: You should consider now what is more important.

WOMAN: That *is* important, Angel. A good housewife takes care of her own. That is her duty. She doesn't abandon her oven when bread is baking, or her cow when it calves, or the children before they have their own children. But perhaps someone like you doesn't understand that.

ANGEL: The bread is already baking without you, the cow is already having the calf without your help. Follow me.

WOMAN: The way you say that! It's not so easily done. Go through my fields sometime, after it has rained. You don't know how heavy the soil is. Clay soil. It's fertile, but when it's wet, and you walk on it, with every step you take you think the weight of the whole earth is clinging to your shoes.

ANGEL: You're talking a lot.

WOMAN: Whenever I'm afraid, I do that.

ANGEL: Listen!

WOMAN: Did someone call?

ANGEL: You tell me!

WOMAN: Who? . . . Is it that urgent? Well yes. What must be, must be. But tell me one thing: how should you act in front of HIM, when you come to HIM as a stranger? Should you throw yourself to the ground? Should you kiss HIS ring, as you do with a bishop, or HIS feet, as you do a crucifix on the steps of the Altar on Good Friday? And what should you say? Is it like confession? Will I be alone before HIM? Do I have to tell HIM all my sins since childhood? But HE knows them anyway. All of them. HE knows . . .

ANGEL: Don't cry. Think of HIS mercy.

WOMAN: Oh yes, HIS mercy which HE gives to those who attract HIS attention by force. He gives HIS mercy to great sinners. You have to do great things to feel HIS generosity. But me, I haven't done anything that could make HIM remember me. He can't say: Oh, she's the one, I know her, she did this or that good deed and this or that bad one. I wasn't hot and I wasn't cold. But HE doesn't like the lukewarm ones.

ANGEL: Leave the judgment to HIM.

WOMAN: The judgment, oh Angel . . . HE will look at me with a bored glance and then look away and won't recognize me. Am I not, for him, like a sewing basket full of odds and ends? The little worries day in and day out, and the work, and the children's sicknesses, and even in church, in the middle of praying, I would begin to figure crop prices, farmhands' wages, and taxes, and my head was like a mill wheel, and gone was my devotion. I don't have anything about which I could say: now look at this and that, it's bright and shiny from all my efforts. If there are cobwebs in the corner, you sweep them away. Good riddance! Believe me: when you are as old as I am, then you know where you belong and where you don't, you know very well what the proper thing is and what justice is and you like to save yourself the trouble — as well other people.

ANGEL: Where do you want to go?

WOMAN: To purgatory, where else? I'll find the way myself. All alone. I'm sure you can hear them crying from far away, those poor souls in the fire.

ANGEL: You were already in the fire.

WOMAN: Me? I wasn't in any fire. Aren't you confusing me with someone else?

ANGEL: Turn around. What do you see?

WOMAN: Do you mean that little girl in the white dress? It's probably her first communion.

ANGEL: What is she doing?

WOMAN: She is placing white daffodils on the altar in a church where she is completely alone. That's all I see.

ANGEL: The fragrance of the daffodils rises sweetly to HIM. And a vow was offered with the daffodils.

WOMAN: A childish vow, nothing more. My oldest sister took the veil of the Dominicans at that time and it made an impression on me and I wanted to do the same.

ANGEL: Why are you crying?

WOMAN: I broke the vow.

ANGEL: You renounced, and HE saw your renunciation, just as one sees a fire on a mountain top at night.

WOMAN: One more disgrace to add to all the others . . . If I had only been half as stubborn as a calf, they would have let me go. I should have pouted or twisted and turned like a cat. But the farm was in debt, my brother was dead, my parents were old, and so it meant that money was needed for the farm and I should marry someone with money, and that was the way it was, and no more dreams about a cloister and such things.

ANGEL: He counted your tears, and HIS thirst was quenched by them.

WOMAN: With us farmers, the farm always came first, and everyone of us would do the same if it was necessary. If there was any virtue in that . . . To raise objections, you have to have courage, that would have been a virtue and would have pleased HIM.

ANGEL: Your standards are not HIS. Turn around again. What do you see?

WOMAN: A woman peeling potatoes, nothing more.

ANGEL: What else?

WOMAN: One who is planting cabbage in the garden.

ANGEL: And what else?

WOMAN: One shearing a sheep and one weighing grain, and one feeding the chickens and one sewing, and one hanging up clothes, one dying wool, one bent over the bills to be paid, and one in a kitchen filled with smoke and steam.

ANGEL: Are they unhappy? Look carefully.

WOMAN: No, not one of them. As far as I can see, they are happy.

ANGEL: Do you know them?

WOMAN: They all look exactly alike.

ANGEL: It's you—your daily work, your life and your smile.

WOMAN: If it's supposed to be me, Angel, then I can only tell you: that is the daily work and life of each of us, and each of us does what is necessary, and as for the smile, we learn that in marriage.

ANGEL: You smiled when no one saw you.

WOMAN: You never know for sure that someone isn't there who might be watching you. It's best not to be seen in a bad mood.

ANGEL: For HIM your smile was like the fragrance of myrtle in the midst of the odors of envy and unhappiness which rise from the earth.

WOMAN: The way you talk! I'm a farmer's wife and such words embarrass the likes of us and make us a little suspicious. We don't know what to say to such things.

ANGEL: Then be quiet and accept it. What kind of scar is that on your forehead?

WOMAN: This one? It's not from anything special. A stupid fall on a damp cellar stairs, or from running into a rafter in the granary in the dark, or when a cow kicks you while being milked. You forget it later.

ANGEL: Someone hit you with his hand.

WOMAN: It's not our custom to talk about something that is better forgotten.

ANGEL: Think back.

WOMAN: My mother had a saying which was: "Remember the good things that happen to you for as long as the roads to Rome, and remember the bad things that people do to you for the length of a little lamb's jump."

ANGEL: HE wants you to remember.

WOMAN: What is there to say? The men in our country are quick-tempered, especially when they drink. They are terribly sorry about it afterwards. But that's the way they are and you have to take them the way they are.

ANGEL: Your man was never sorry.

WOMAN: Who knows what it's like for someone else? It was hard enough for him to lose a child.

ANGEL: Wasn't the child yours as well?

WOMAN: My youngest and my dearest.

ANGEL: Who moved the oak cover from the well, so that it was open, and when the child bent over it . . . ? Don't cry. You didn't cry then either. Who opened the well? HE has removed the seal from your lips. Speak!

WOMAN: No.

ANGEL: Then turn around a third time and look. Two people are standing in front of a dead child. What is the man shouting?

WOMAN: "Whoever opened the well, I'll make a cripple out of him!"

ANGEL: Why did you keep silent?

WOMAN: The way you ask! Should I have pointed with my finger at our oldest child, who wasn't much older than the dead one, and say: "That's the one, he did it." Do you think there is one mother in the whole world who could say those words, which would have made an innocent child his brother's murderer for the rest of his life? How do you think the father would have felt about his son? I could have just as well set fire to the granary with my own hand. There must be peace between the farmer and his heir so the farm can prosper.

ANGEL: Why did your husband hit you?

WOMAN: That's easy to understand. It was harvest time, just as now, with everyone in the field, and I was alone at home and there was no one else except the children, and strangers didn't come into the garden because of the watchdogs. He didn't really say that it was me. He meant I should have kept an eye on the well and that was true. It wasn't his fault. He was a good farmer, fair and hard-working.

ANGEL: You kept your eyes from weeping on that day and your mouth from speaking, and forced yourself to bear your burden. But you didn't let your heart become hard. You saved your tears, as the earth collects and saves rainwater until it becomes a spring. Cry now. Cry the full measure of tears that you have earned.

WOMAN: You say nice words to me and they are starting to please me. I could really almost cry. But I'll have time enough for that when I finally get there. Let's go.

ANGEL: You have a stubborn spirit. Why do you want to suffer in purgatory? I tell you—the sufferings of that place are as familiar to you as old sickness. They are behind you now.

WOMAN: Why do you tempt me? You wouldn't talk this way if you really knew me. What is not so good remains not so good in spite of fine words. I know my faults as well as those of horses, and no trader could ever talk me into buying a calf or a heifer that wasn't worth its price. I have eyes to see, Angel. And if someone would come to my farm and praise it to the skies, saying it's a model farm, then I would also think of the cracks in the brick wall and the rat poison set out in the cellar and the termites in the woodwork, and I would shrug my shoulders. I don't like undeserved praise.

ANGEL: Enough. We are at the end of the journey. Your words have passed through HIS sieve. Judgment has been made. Lift up your eyes. Have no fear. HIS face is still hidden to you behind a handful of white daffodils, fresh with dew.

WOMAN: Why are you touching my eyes? It burns like fire.

ANGEL: Look now!

Diary of A Dayfly

Wolfdietrich Schnurre

Zero hours, 1 minute, 17.7 seconds.

There is no doubt: I am alive. Just straightened my feelers and tried to figure out which legs are which. My God, how is all that supposed to work! And besides, these funny transparent things on my back; after all, I'm no mannequin. Really not much fun taking on a life I didn't ask for. Twenty-four endless hours! Wouldn't two or three be enough! Heaven knows what the world-spirit was thinking of, to put this burden on me. (Nothing, I suspect.)

1 hour, 27 minutes, 34.4 seconds.

Allpowerful One! I can fly! Still numb from this discovery. Now the world belongs to me! If I only knew where I've landed or where I am at all. I feel as if I'm on a runway: it's swarming with moths taking off and landing, and all sorts of ground personnel are bustling around me. I can recognize the glow of a satellite above me. Maybe I will soon be landing on it.

2 hours, 19 minutes, 1.2 seconds.

Just took a brief flight over my world. It is square and—to be perfectly honest—insultingly small. I probably won't be paying attention very long to the limits set for me. Just a little more train-

Wolfdietrich Schnurre

ing; after all, what are wings for! And so now I'm ready to have some experiences.

3 hours, 31 minutes, 4.8 seconds.

It's all over. I'm buried in a cloudy vault of the universe. At the border I spread my wings but then I plunged down into nothingness. Here I sit in deepest darkness and prepare myself for the end. Oh, this farcical existence! All this trouble because of a little bit of hoping; absurd. And oh, what couldn't I have done! Explored the satellite; discovered more planets; established my own route. . . . But no, the world-spirit is intoxicated with the powerlessness of his creatures; he creates us in order to see us fail. I am ashamed that I sacrificed myself to his wishes.

4 hours, 14 minutes, 33 seconds.

I am sitting in the glow of my satellite, leafing through my diary. Came upon the entry I made at 3 hours, 31 minutes, 4.8 seconds. For heavens sake, how arrogant I was then. To think that jumping off a desk (you see what my world turned out to be) means a lack of concern on the part of the world-spirit for his creatures; laughable! And how presumptuous I was! To fly . . . to get to know the world . . . to enjoy life . . . my God, the "world"! Where is it then, if not in me? And "enjoy." That simply means to observe how, second by second, the crystals of experience within me build upon each other:

I am the world; all things outside of me are mere sham-existence!

5 hours, 13 minutes, 13.3 seconds.

Something terrible has happened. The satellite has just been extinguished; my heart almost stopped beating. What now? Is it the end of the world? Shall I be forced to live in darkness? Why didn't the world-spirit consider me worthy of his grace anymore? Is it possible that I did something wrong (did I perhaps take myself too seriously?) In any case, I have the uncomfortable feeling that this is some sort of a trial.

6 hours, 12 minutes, 29.7 seconds.

What despondency the darkness brings. For over fifty (!) minutes I have been quaking in the universe's night of retribution. Under its merciless cloak I wander, quivering, groping with my feelers.

Really, I would gladly give up my pair of wings if by means of that sacrifice I could make the satellite shine again.

7 hours, 22 minutes, 17.5 seconds.

I'm standing here in dazzled and worshipful astonishment. A constantly growing brightness floods through the window and over the desk. Day is coming, the moths tell me disgruntledly. I don't believe that; my day began hours ago. No, what is out there can only be the world-spirit; he is descending to bring light to the satellite again. It's just good luck that I didn't give up my wings (as I seem to remember having offered to do quite a while ago) for that purpose.

9 hours, 49 minutes, 26.6 seconds.

Terrible disappointment. What I took for a satellite turned out to be a desk lamp. And worst of all, this terrible brightness! All my cozy security is gone; busy wasps and obtrusive blowflies are buzzing through the room, treacherous spiders lurk in fluttering webs, and leaning over my world there sits a creature who is reading the newspaper and who almost blows me down into the netherworld everytime he turns the page. Danger everywhere I look. And it's supposed to be worthwhile living in this world. Just to be a little safer, I have hidden under an "Income Tax Report"; here I want to work on myself and try to grow up. Oh, if it were only night!

11 hours, 28 minutes, 12.9 seconds.

A great restlessness has taken possession of me. I constantly have the feeling that I have passed up something of great importance. A short time ago two houseflies strolled past me, arm in arm. Was that the reason I felt this way? I am uneasy.

12 hours, 19 minutes, 15 seconds.

I'm shaking. I just proposed to a charming young dayfly lady.

But no luck. The ignorant girl asked for a full 24 hours time to think it over, and I didn't have the courage to correct her mistake.

14 hours, 54 minutes, 27.2 seconds.

Very amused. I was just reading my diary entry under 12 hours, 19 minutes, 15 seconds, which indicated I must have had marriage (!) in mind at that time. A dayfly with *my* wealth of experience! Grotesque!

15 hours, 36 minutes, 39.7 seconds.

I'm starting to show my age; had trouble raising my wings. But what's the difference, the main thing is that my spiritual wings do not grow weary.

16 hours, 20 minutes, 1.5 seconds.

There are only two traits that are worthy of attainment: kindness and composure; all other virtues are illusions.

Wolfdietrich Schnurre

18 hours, 58 minutes, 19.8 seconds.

My eyesight is failing; the evening is coming; soon the stars of my maturity will rise. Oh, how delightful it will be to wander without a goal and without desire beneath their gleam!

19 hours, 29 minutes, 7.9 seconds.

How strange; now that my eyesight is deserting me, the sky outside is also darkening; the world-spirit wants to make it easy for me; he seems to be unaware of my inner clarity.

20 hours, 41 minutes, 3.1 seconds.

It is night around me; my eyesight flickered like a candle a few more times and then was extinguished. Around me the swarming moths are still humming with velvety flutterings. They strike their heads against the desk lamp, which in their simplicity they take for a satellite. I do not try to deprive them of this belief; nothing is more undesirable than to shake prematurely a philosophy of life that is past its prime. Whether it holds true or not: the main thing is that it comforts you.

21 hours, 26 minutes, 12.4 seconds.

How rich my life was! I am almost bursting from memories. (I even seem to have a dim recollection of once having lived in a pond, apparently as a larva.) Writing is an effort. I wonder if what I jot down here will be read sometime? Odd, not even I can escape the unfortunate vanity of hoping that something I write will outlast me.

22 hours, 30 minutes, 3.8 seconds.

A delicate humming sound lingers in my brain; it sounds like a sustained tone from a violin.

I am beginning to get weary; my soul is ready to depart.

23 hours, 17 minutes, 31.9 seconds.

All is well; I am approaching the end without resentment. Perhaps I shall return as a mote in a sunbeam; then I shall fall upon this writing desk and ignite it into a sea of ecstatic flame—out of gratitude for its having taught me how to recognize the limits of my existence.

24 hours, 42 minutes, 9.5 seconds.

The humming sound in my head has swollen into a crescendo of music. I am sitting in the midst of the orchestra, awaiting the signal to join in. Which instrument shall I be playing? I do not know yet.

24 hours, 59 minutes, 57.3 seconds.

For the last nineteenth of a second there has been silence

around me, the silence of a leave-taking. And yet, whom am I taking leave of? Myself? But I am taking myself along. The world? The world will be *there* too. Life? It certainly does not cease. So I will go as if I have never come, or—and this is the same thing—as if I were staying, even though I am now going. Farewell!

Bleep, crash, zap, wow: Accidents in the Ruhr

Wolfgang Körner

wow, the fifty-three year old worker Erich G. carelessly walked across the Märkische Strasse into a car that was undoubtedly going too fast. He did this because he was thinking about how he could keep his job in spite of bad business and his age. bleep, an auto mechanic, who was either headed for home or a bar in a holiday mood, telephoned a report of the accident to police headquarters. From there instructions went to the emergency squad to remove the worker from the right of way and thus restore a condition of public safety and order, and that included getting rid of the pool of blood in prescribed fashion by spreading sand on it.

wham, the chief sergeant on duty was angry, this was already the third accident that evening and once again no chance to use the cutting torch that had been procured at his suggestion.

While the emergency squad was still busy under the revolving yellow caution light, and Erich G. still lay on the pavement, zip, a film was playing in the theater at the railroad station, showing how Doris Day takes Gregory Peck or Cary Grant or Rock Hudson into her arms, whump, the steel worker Georg Kacmarek was tapping a blast furnace, the furnace blew and poured a small part of its contents over K.,who had reacted a little too slowly, and whose widow was busy at that moment getting supper ready. The delivery of K. to the workers' first-aid center was carried out in pre-scribed fashion, purely a formality.

Note: The murdering of a laborer with the aid of production tools is recorded in the world of industry as an unavoidable work-related accident, which doesn't keep the chairman of the board from proposing new measures for accident prevention that involve at the same time appropriate justification and no extra production costs.

click, Channel Three, program of the WGR (Institution for the Blind), scenes from the studio of the fashion photographer Charlie Feld-mann. Over-all shot. Feldmann's house. Model in a model's coat, taking model's steps, walks up to the house in model's shoes. An-nouncer. Here's where Charlie Feldmann lives, who has the well-deserved distinction of being the busiest fashion photog-rapher of this country. Cut. Close-up. Feldman with his Hassel-blad. Announcer. Mr. Feldmann, photography can be art; do you agree with that statement, or what can you say about it! Feldmann. Well, you know, when you ask me so directly, I don't really know. wow, lost the picture. This loss of picture, and I have to mention this, is a real, actual and undoubtable one; the program director firmly asserted that Feldmann's statement didn't involve con-troversial opinion, since it can be proven positively that he has never had one.

crash, Jack the Ripper steps out of a poster over the entrance to the Union Cinema, skillfully climbs a few yards over to the right (!), takes hold of a roof gutter, swings down to the sidewalk, slits open the uniform and stomach of a street cleaner and with an elegant slice into the larynx takes care of two miners who were standing around doing nothing but waiting for the streetcar, and he thus makes the first effective contribution toward solving the unemployment problem in the coal mines, and then, having received no recognition for these achievements, disappears in the waiting room for first-class passengers and starts looking for a lady traveling alone. oh, oh, in the atomic reactor, Jülich II, a small quantity of fissionable material goes critical. The assistant in charge gets it under control again. Lethal doses of 800 roentgens. Nausea and vomiting after an hour, lessening of nausea, no symp-toms for a week, then vomiting, diarrhea, fever, rapid weakening, death in the second week.

heil, twenty-four neo-fascists, under the protection of the consti-tution, are rehearsing in a backroom of a restaurant for a take-over of power as soon as the democratic games are finished. They re-

Wolfgang Körner

hearse carefully—that is, quietly, for they know there's only trouble if they disturb the meeting of the Organization for an Undivided Germany that is meeting in the next room.

In a seminar in the School of Education a visiting pedagogue (or demagogue) is explaining his personal opinion, which he holds independently and under nobody's influence, namely that there is no class struggle in Germany anymore because differences of class have been completely eliminated. As proof he can cite once more the 312 Marks minimum wage law, the washing machine, and the vestiges of self-governance.

vroom, a student ventriloquist, and thus without fear of possible reprisals, delivers from hip level a contribution to the discussion, to the effect that the worker is, if at all, only of interest as the provider of one element of production—labor—, which cannot yet be completely dispensed with. Uproar, uproar.

bleep, the emergency squad, which was mentioned at the beginning and was still occupied with removing the remains of the store employee Erich G., gets the radioed order to proceed to a certain point close to the Ruhr Expressway and to present the next accident to the public. That despite the fact that the accident photographer is still photographing, the accident reporter is still reporting, and the accident investigator is still investigating. The sergeant on duty and in charge has a conflict of conscience and asks for clarification from central headquarters. Headquarters answers: wow!

The Amusement-Doctor

Siegfried Lenz

Nothing gives me greater concern than cheerfulness. **For three** years now I have been making my living from it; for three years I have been getting paid to care for the human needs of the foreign customers of our firm. When the exhausting negotiations of the day are over, the wearied gentlemen are turned over to me, and it is my responsibility to infuse them with invigorating pleasure which will relax them and make them receptive to further business dealings. "A happy man makes happy deals"—these were the words my first manager used to summarize my duties, which I have been attempting to perform adequately for three years now. Today I could no longer say what made me seem particularly qualified for this job. A decisive factor at that time, of course, was my graduation with a degree of Doctor of Laws, and, to a lesser degree, my joyous North German temperament, which was naturally also taken into account.

So I began my work as a specialist in gladdening the hearts of important customers, placing my talents at the disposal of a firm which produced fish-processing machines—filleting machines, bone-removal machines, first-class guillotines which beheaded the fish with a type of round cut hitherto unknown, and then, too, a model which could turn a two-meter-long tunafish into filets in four seconds with such sure and impeccable slicing action that we called it the "Robespierre," without the slightest fear that we were being too bold in our promises. In addition, the firm manufactured conveyor belts for fish, equipment for disposing of the remains, and spare parts in impressive quantities. Since these were highly specialized and complicated machines, we had customers visiting us from all over the world—no trip was too far. They came from Japan, from Canada and Hawaii, they came from Morocco and the shores of the Black Sea to negotiate their purchases personally. And, after the negotiations were over I had the task of cheering the whole world up so to speak.

On the whole I can say, with all due modesty, that my endeavors have worked out to the firm's advantage. Chinese and South Africans, Koreans and Norwegians, and even a psychologically withdrawn individual from Spitzbergen—all of them experienced, with my help, the refreshing power of good cheer, which dissolves every stress that business dealings can produce. Our evening excursions through the entertainment section of the city generated so much good cheer that they could be regarded as a kind of massaging of the heart, or, as the case might be, of the wallet. By paying attention to national temperaments, and igniting, as it were, different fuses of joy for every individual, I have succeeded without special difficulty in caring for the human needs of our customers, or, if we want to use a modern expression, in producing *good will*. I led the gentlemen into the land of pleasure by the shortest route. Humor became my business, and I was even able to find amusement for the psychologically withdrawn person from Spitzbergen. I submerged myself in my profession, indeed, I loved it, especially after they promised me a healthy salary increase.

And yet for some time now my love for my profession has been beset by moments of doubt, and if not by doubt, then by a particular anxiety. I am afraid that my security is threatened, and, above all, I have the impression that I am definitely underpaid for my job, because never before did I realize what a risk I run at times, what a danger. This insight came to me only recently. And I think I know now what prompted it.

The person to blame for all of this is Pachulka-Sbirr, a gigantic customer from the distant island group of the Aleutians. I can still remember how he looked when I saw him for the first time: the yellow-skinned, fierce face, the bearskin hat, the crinkled boots; and I can still hear his voice too, which sounded the way I imagined that the surf on the shores of his homeland would sound. When he was referred to me by our executives and made his first fierce entrance into my office, I was a bit startled, but soon I was confident enough to think that I could loosen up the psyche of even a Pachulka-Sbirr with cheerfulness. After giving him a water glass full of cherry brandy to warm him up, I got the gloomy customer into a car and drove him to our entertainment quarter— firmly convinced that my experience in the production of joy would suffice, even for him.

We didn't go to the shooting galleries—which had already been enough to make our Japanese customer jabber happily— because I felt that Pachulka-Sbirr had to be more substantially diverted, more solidly, so to speak. We went straight to Fiete's place, in which, from time to time, three ladies were wont to disrobe in artistic fashion. I know the ladies well; they had often helped to transform stolid Scandinavian customers, who couldn't get their minds off business, into a state of bubbling good cheer, and so I had given them a word in advance this time too. They had promised to help me.

The moment came. The ladies artistically removed their clothes, and then, as is customary at Fiete's, a guest was sought who could play the role of a modern, civilized Paris and hand one of the ladies an apple. As arranged in advance, Pachulka-Sbirr was selected. My giant customer walked to the center of the room, was given an apple and stared at the undressed ladies in such a grim and threatening way that a look of anxiety appeared in their faces and they instinctively drew back a few steps. Suddenly, in the painful silence, Pachulka-Sbirr stuck the apple into his own mouth, the crunching, grinding sound of his massive mandibles was heard, and then, to the speechless amazement of all, he came back to our table, sat down, and stared dourly at the floor.

I didn't give up. I was aware of my duty to the firm and, indeed, to myself, and I told him funny stories from my most tried and true repertory, the effects of which had been successfully tested on taciturn Finns, on Irishmen, and close-mouthed Faerøe Islanders. Pachulka-Sbirr sat there in an attitude of grim attentiveness and dispassion.

Irritated, I left Fiete's place with him and went to Max's; I found our reserved table and ordered a bottle of cherry brandy. At Max's, if not before, I'd been able to get even the grumpy Americans and still grumpier Alaskans into a good mood. Because, in Max's place there was an orchestra that chose its conductors from among the guests. Americans and Alaskans are used to being masters of a broad domain; the world of music is also a broad domain, and as soon as our customers had a chance to have it under their command, the tenseness from their business dealings dissolved, and they were filled with joy, pure joy. Since the Aleutians are not far from Alaska, I believed that I could make Pachulka-Sbirr happy in the same way, and so, following my secret prearrangements, he stamped up to the orchestra leader's stand wearing his bearskin hat and his crinkled boots. They gave him the baton. He swung it through the air like a whip, and the musicians spontaneously ducked their heads. Then he casually stuck it under his shirt and started to scratch his huge back with it. But then, without warning—I don't know how it happened—he pulled the baton and broke it—apparently it wasn't long enough to reach his itchy spot—then threw it into the orchestra. With a gloomy look on his face, while the individual trumpets tentatively and anxiously began to play, he returned to our table.

I looked at Pachulka-Sbirr in despair. No, I was not yet ready to give up. My ambition, my professional pride, was challenged, which anyone can understand, and I swore to myself not to take even this customer back to his hotel until I had succeeded in getting him into a happy mood. I reminded myself that I was known in the firm as the "Amusement-Doctor," and not without respect, and I wanted to prove that I deserved this name. I decided to try everything. I told him the jokes that up to now I had only dared to tell to a customer from Siberia—as a last resort more or less. Pachulka-Sbirr maintained a gloomy silence. However hard I tried, I could not remove that dourly silent look from his yellow-skinned face; a ride on a mule, a visit to a fun house, erotic films, and a few more bottles of cherry brandy—nothing seemed to be able to raise his spirits.

I'd saved Wanda to the last. After everything else had failed, we went to Wanda, who publicly bathed twice every night in a very large goblet of champagne. I put my last hopes on Wanda. Her children and my children go to school together; occasionally she exchanges plant cuttings with my wife for her indoor garden. She is like a member of the family, and so it was easy for me to take Wanda into my confidence and to tell her what was at stake. And Wanda promised to help me. When she was looking for a customer to help her climb out of her champagne bath, she chose, with charming innocence, none other than Pachulka-Sbirr. I thought I had won, because Wanda had already helped me once to thaw out an especially icy customer from Lake Baikal in Siberia. This time she would have to be successful too. But to my horror, the attempt failed. Yes, I was horrified when Pachulka-Sbirr walked onto the stage and stood in front of the very large champagne goblet in which Wanda was suggestively wriggling—which as a refugee you wouldn't expect of her. She smiled at him. She held out her arms toward him. The spectators clapped and clapped. Then Pachulka-Sbirr fell on his knees, bent his head over the champagne goblet and began pantingly to drink from it—with the result that Wanda in a short time was on dry land, so to speak, and didn't need any more help. She gave me a look of despair which I returned with equal fervor. I was ready to capitulate.

But toward morning my chance unexpectedly came. Pachulka-Sbirr wanted to see once more the machines that had prompted him to make the long trip. We drove to the factory and went to the showroom. We were alone, because the gateman knew me and had seen him before, and he let us pass without hindrance. In somber contemplation Pachulka-Sbirr laid his hand on the machines; shook them, looked inside them, had me explain the mechanisms to him once more, and meanwhile took notes in his pocket notebook. All the machines interested him, but the one that interested him the most was our "Robespierre" model, which is able to slice a two-meter-long tunafish into filets within four seconds, and indeed, with a fascinating technique. As we stood in front of the "Robespierre," he put his pocket notebook away. He started a thorough examination of our masterpiece. Occasionally he whistled through his teeth in admiration, clicked his tongue, or made hissing noises, and I could clearly see that he was becoming more and more fascinated by this model. But he apparently could not bring himself to make the final decision to buy the "Robespierre," and, in order to make this decision easier for Pachulka-Sbirr, I jumped onto the machine and lay down on the spring-mounted metal cutting pan. Personal observation, I thought, should hasten his decision, and I stretched out and lay there like a tunafish that is going to be processed into filets within four seconds. I glanced up at the specially tempered blades which glistened gaily over my neck. They were very heavy and were held only by narrow supports which could be moved aside by simply pressing a lever. Smiling, I twisted back and forth in the cutting pan, because I wanted to demonstrate clearly to Pachulka-Sbirr what a nice feeling it must be for a tuna to lie on our machine. Pachulka-Sbirr did not return my smile. He asked me which lever

Siegfried Lenz

had to be pressed to release the knives. I told him. And, as I was telling him, I could already see the supports releasing the blades with lightning speed. The blades were free. They plunged toward me. But just before reaching my neck they jammed and sprang back with a gnashing sound; the cutting-pressure attachment was stuck. Shaking, frightened to death, I pulled myself out of the pan. I sought out Pachulka-Sbirr's face, and yes, there was now a contented smile on his lips. He was smiling, and at this moment nothing seemed more important to me than that.

Today, of course, our "Robespierre" model is even more highly developed. The cutting mechanism never jams, and I ask myself how far I dare to go if another Pachulka-Sbirr from the Aleutians comes to us. He made me aware of the constant risks I am taking and of the fact that a professional purveyor of good cheer cannot be paid too much. I believe I have fully realized my danger, since nowadays, when I think of good cheer, I see specially tempered, gaily glistening blades hovering over my head.

Part Two

EAST GERMAN AUTHORS

The Reed

Anna Seghers

The little farm next to a lake outside Berlin had belonged to the Emrich family a long time before the war.

They planted mostly vegetables. Their one-story house was separated from the shore by a narrow lawn, the only bit of uncultivated land. The shore was flat and sloped very gradually; the reeds grew thick, as they did almost everywhere around the lake. From the boat landing a gravel path led to the windowed veranda which had been added to the house during a period of prosperity. From the small entranceway there were doors to the living room as well as to the kitchen, and there was a trapdoor between the kitchen and the cellar. The cellar door on the side toward the lake wasn't used anymore; it was blocked by all sorts of supplies, as was the cellar window, so that it let hardly any light in.

The Emrich family had formerly owned a second farm property in the next village and the blacksmith shop across from it. They had shod horses there and repaired plows and farm equipment.

Shortly before the war Father Emrich had died from complications after being kicked by a horse.

They say "Misfortunes seldom come alone." Maybe he had

been a little less cautious than usual because he was so shaken by the recent and unexpected death of his wife.

The two sons had been drafted. Their service was extended indefinitely by the war. One took part in the march into Poland and the other in the landing in Norway.

In the meantime, distant relatives had bought the other farm and the blacksmith's shop. The only daughter, Martha Emrich, took care of the land that was left. Her ambition was to do all the work by herself if possible. But now and then she hired somebody by the day, for example, to paint the house so that it would look decent when the brothers came home on leave. She not only did most of the vegetable gardening, but she papered the rooms and caulked the boat, which lay at the dock most of the time, unused. From the lake the white house with its hedge roses had a friendly and inviting look.

Martha worked very hard, from dawn to dark, not only to save money and avoid debts, since her brothers had lost their income from the farm and the blacksmith's shop, and not only because she said to herself, "That's what I'm here for," but also in order to forget her loneliness.

A farmer's son from the nearest village, her second cousin, who had been considered to be her fiancé, was one of the few soldiers who died in the attack that broke through the Maginot line. Through him the farm and the smithy might have been re-united with the Emrich property. To be sure, they hadn't been publicly engaged, but when the news of his death came, Martha felt herself abandoned and almost without hope. She had never talked much and now she became even more taciturn.

She was very healthy and used to managing by herself under all sorts of conditions. She was twenty-six years old in the third year of the war. She was big-boned, with a broad, plain face. She kept in touch with the world through the letters her brothers sent by army mail and through various events that she attended in the village. She raised the flag after every victory just like the neighbors.

Her younger brother died on the eastern front. Although he had been her favorite brother, more good-natured than the older one, she didn't feel this death as strongly as that of her fiancé. It was more as if he just wouldn't come home on leave for a long time.

In the late summer of 1943, on a rainy, misty evening, she was in the cellar, sorting out potatoes and beets as food for the next day.

She suddenly heard a soft, unusual sound in the reeds and then in the hedge. It seemed as if a shadow had flitted past. The thought flashed through her mind that a person would consider the house empty because no lights were on except the tiny lamp in the cellar. She called loudly, "Who's there?" Since no one answered she climbed through the trapdoor into the kitchen and went outside by way of the small room and the veranda.

On the narrow strip of land between the lake and the house stood a stranger, a young man; he was, as well as she could see, dressed quite well. She couldn't distinguish the features of his face in the twilight. He quickly asked: "Does a Frau Schneider live here?" Martha answered: "Not here," and she added: "Not in the village either." She looked closely at the unknown man and asked: "How did you get here?" He answered: "With the boat." "What?" asked Martha, because she could see through the dim light that there was no second boat at her dock. "Oh," said the stranger, "I came ashore quite far from here. I was expecting to find her house two villages away, and by asking several people I've gotten this far."

They heard a motorcycle coming down the road. He seized Martha's hand and said softly but firmly: "Don't give me away, if somebody asks."

Martha pulled her hand back and said angrily: "Oh, so you're in trouble."

The motorcycle didn't stop, and was already far away. The stranger took her hand again, and said quickly with a quietly vehement, urgent tone: "I did not do anything wrong. Just the opposite."

Now they heard the sound of a motor on the lake. The man continued: "Do I look like a dangerous person?"

She tried once more to see his face better, as if a face could vouch for the man it belongs to. She knew it was possible, because she had lived alone long enough and had had dealings with all kinds of people. But this face seemed to be a type she had never known before.

The motorboat was already gone. "Why are they looking for you if you haven't done anything?"

He spoke without hesitation, very fast, in the same vehement tone of voice: "Pamphlets against the war were distributed at the place where I work. And today they came for me." "Well, listen," said Martha, "if that's true, then you really deserve to be locked up."

The stranger poured out his words excitedly, interrupting anything she said. His voice was at the same time pleading and threatening. Maybe she had never lost anybody in the war and never waited for someone until the news came: "Killed in action." Martha had an answer for that, and the two of them went at each other. She said he should be locked up for such talk, yes, locked up, if not in prison then in a mental hospital. He asked whether people are supposed to wait until all the soldiers are killed; well, *he* didn't wait, and now they were looking for him. He said: "Have a heart! At least let me rest here by the hedge; you don't have to know about it."

She hesitated slightly for a moment. "Go back into the house, go on!" he said. "You haven't seen me at all. You don't know me. Go on!"

Then Martha turned and walked away as if they hadn't spoken a word to each other, and she went about her work.

That was the way it began. The next day she got up earlier than usual to see if he was still by the hedge. She vaguely hoped he had gone away in the meantime. She could even have talked herself into believing, on this first morning, that nobody had come by. But he was there, crouching in the same place. Without saying anything, she went into the house and brought him something warm to eat. She watched as he ravenously ate the food and choked on it, and then, shaken by coughs, bit his hand to keep from being heard. Then he looked up at her; it was light enough now to see his face. He said nothing, he just moved his lips a little and looked at her with his determined glance. She said nothing; she went back into the house as if she'd seen nobody and went about her work as she did every day.

This summer she had a boy helping her by the day. He was from the village and had a limp from an earlier attack of polio. He told Martha the police were looking for a pickpocket; they had left a warning in all the villages around the lake. In the afternoon—it had gotten misty early—Martha told the stranger to follow her through the cellar door. She had already put in her winter supply of wood and coal. She now made a tiny hideout for him, she said nothing, as if her doing or not doing it would only be real if she said something.

Her young helper was disappointed when the month of August was over and Martha didn't hire him for September. Yet no one was surprised—it had long been common knowledge that Martha Emrich could do all sorts of things by herself, in fact, that she was determined to do them by herself.

The small, quiet tasks, such as peeling and slicing food, and some of the repairs, were done by the refugee—his name was Kurt Steiner—in his hideout between the piles of wood. Sometimes Martha left the trapdoor open and turned on her radio. Gradually she got up enough courage to climb down and talk with him. He told her many things that had happened in the world and in his own life, which helped her understand what she was hearing now on the radio. They seemed like fairy tales and legends to Martha, who only knew of her own existence. At the beginning she was completely confused by his urgent manner of speaking, then she started paying attention to what his words meant and she contradicted him and asked questions and thought things over.

Once, in the night, when everything around them lay benumbed in winter hibernation, in ice and snow, she brought him up into the house. He had a short glimpse by flashlight of her room that she was so proud of. And her bed was fresh and good.

Quivering, clinging to him in the night she watched through the cracks in the shutters as a bombing raid on Berlin took place.

Gradually Martha Emrich got used to the idea of Kurt Steiner as a lover. She was convinced of the fact that her actions were good and right. She would do the same thing again, willingly and knowingly.

She only had a guilty feeling because of a certain sense of relief she had when she heard the news that her older brother Karl had been taken prisoner on the eastern front. For she wouldn't have known how to hide Kurt Steiner if her brother had come home on leave. Karl was an especially crude and harsh person, even malicious. He was one of those who would be glad to get his hands on a refugee.

In the springtime a new and frightening danger appeared. Through the fence a farmer's wife told her that the villages around the lake were being searched for deserting soldiers. They weren't missing a single cellar or garden or bush, the woman said to her, half in fear, half in spite.

Kurt Steiner grew pale when Martha told him that. He blurted out: "Everything I did was of no use and now I'm finished." He pondered and then with empty eyes, said: "I have to go, otherwise they'll catch you too."

Suddenly Martha remembered a story that her younger brother, her favorite brother, had read once in a magazine and told to his sister and brother. In this story—she didn't remember anymore where it took place—someone had saved himself—she didn't remember from whom or why—by staying under water and breathing through the stalk of a reed while they looked for him. Kurt Steiner said it was only fiction and could not possibly happen in the real world. Martha said: "Oh yes, it might be possible, try it!" He said: "I can't do it, it won't work." Martha said: "You have to, you have to!"

And she urged him to try it out, right now, before they came; there was nothing else to do and it might work. She made him go into the water and she cut a good reed. And by noon their practicing was put to the test. The house next door had been surrounded and searched with no results; now they came to the Emrich house. They even climbed through the trapdoor into the cellar. Martha was terrified that they might find a trace, a piece of hair, the slightest thing, when they came to the open space between the piles of wood. But they just rummaged around wildly and furiously. "Whom are you looking for?" asked Martha, with a touch of irony in her voice despite her fear. "My younger brother was killed in the war, my older one is a prisoner of war." "Shut your mouth," said the policeman, "a woman doesn't have only brothers." Martha felt a deadly premonition and thought to herself: "Will he live through it, is he getting enough air?"

After they had looked in vain around the outside of the house, they moved on, cursing, to the next house. So finally Kurt Steiner could crawl back into his hole in the cellar, which now seemed almost comfortable to him. But they had to be constantly on the alert for another raid. He was in despair and said he would rather be dead than go on living in this terrible uncertainty. He couldn't stand another search and having to breathe through that reed. Martha tried hard to convince him that the end of the war was near, and that he had taken such risks just so he could live to see the end of the war.

Soon the two heard that the villages were being searched again; they had begun during the night. She pleaded with Kurt Steiner to try it once more. What hadn't he risked already for the sake of peace! And now he wanted to die in misery at the last moment before it came! And so, giving in to her urging, he promised to try, and when they actually came again and searched, he again survived by breathing through the reed.

In a few weeks Berlin was taken. The war was over. The two in the Emrich house cried and laughed; they ate a celebration banquet together, and they drank wine and lay in the white, cool bed like regular married people; no sounds of motors could frighten them any more.

The whole area was so flooded with refugees, and the houses were jammed so full that nobody was surprised at Kurt Steiner's presence; he was just one of many strangers who suddenly appeared. Now that her heart was calm and all the dangers were overcome, Martha rigorously guarded her garden plots from the soldiers and the children of the refugees.

Kurt Steiner smilingly watched her efforts to restore order to her domain in the midst of great confusion. He saw her now the way she looked every day, rawboned, with her broad and plain face.

After a week he said he had to go to the city now to visit his friends.

She kept doggedly at her work; that made it easier to wait, since he really did stay away too long. And finally, unexpectedly, she heard his voice again. He had come with several others in a Russian Army car. He had brought a few friends that he had rediscovered. There were also two officers. One spoke German very well, and he questioned Martha in detail. Apparently Kurt Steiner had told them a great deal about his escape and his hiding place, and when the officer kept asking if that was exactly how it had been, Martha answered curtly: "Of course that's the way it was." The officers looked at her in astonishment, with friendly eyes. Then Kurt Steiner showed his friends the hideout in the cellar and also the place on the shore where he had lain in the water and breathed through the reed. He did not try to conceal what he owed to Martha—she had not only saved his life but had constantly given him encouragement.

Martha listened silently to all that. She found his tone of voice strange. When she wanted to make something to eat, because, as she said, she had hidden away a few things, Kurt Steiner said: "Oh, we wouldn't think of letting you do that. There's a package of food we brought for you, but we have to drive back right now."

"You too?" asked Martha. "Of course; I have to," said Kurt Steiner. "I have a job in Berlin now, a good one, in the new government." He stroked her hair as if she were a child. As he was going out the door he called back to her: "You'll hear from me soon!" Martha listened to the car drive away. Her heart had grown lighter before when she heard the sound of the motor fading away; now it became heavier.

From childhood on she had always kept her thoughts to herself. She was really not able to express herself in words. The people she had to deal with in order to take care of her gardening and house knew how quiet she was. So nobody noticed that she now spoke even less.

One day Kurt Steiner returned and asked how she was doing and offered her all sorts of help. Martha answered the way she did with everybody: "I can get along by myself." And when he once again emphatically assured her of his gratitude, she said: "It's all right, Kurt." She stiffened when he tried to embrace her as he was leaving.

Her brother Karl returned from the prisoner-of-war camp. He was cruder and harsher than ever. He didn't have one good word for his sister; he was displeased with every change in the garden plots. He found the house in good repair, to be sure, although he had no praise, and he found it suitable to move into and bring his wife, who was from a good family, a farmer's daughter from the next village. Martha had to give up her room and got a small unheated one. The young couple took advantage of her. Her brother had a compulsion to change completely everything she had done with the farm in his absence. And he did it from anger against the government, to avoid production levels that would have meant higher taxes on any surpluses. Sometimes Martha would quietly recall what Kurt Steiner had told her—although she hadn't seen him for a long time. He had said that people who behave like that want more and more land; they want foreign land too and they need war.

One Sunday, as she was sitting quietly and alone on the little bench that her brother had put on the lake shore for his wife—the two of them had gone to visit her parents in the village—a motorboat came up to the dock. Kurt Steiner jumped out and helped a young woman get out. Martha understood immediately that this woman looked about the way Kurt would want his wife to look. He cheerfully greeted Martha and told her he was retracing his escape route and showing it to his lady friend.

"And here's Martha when we need her!" he concluded. This time he permitted Martha to make some coffee; he had brought some real coffee beans to grind. They sat for an hour together: "What we went through here, you and I," he said and took her hand, "I won't be able to forget as long as I live." "Of course not," answered Martha. Kurt said: "If you need anything just come to us," said Kurt and he wrote down their address in Berlin. When her brother and his wife came home they were annoyed because Martha had had visitors; they smelled the coffee. The sister-in-law scolded Martha for using the set of dishes from her dowry. Then they became curious and were eager to find out who could have visited Martha. Martha answered, "People I knew during the war."

In the meantime an organization called "The Farmers' Cooperative" had been formed in the village. The brother cursed: "They can go to hell . . . a man like me doesn't join anything like that." Martha said: "No, not a man like you." In the evening she bicycled into the village. Meetings were held sometimes in the restaurant that belonged to her relatives. She would listen and sometimes shake her head if something went against her grain.

Her brother said: "If you carry on like that, you'd better go and live somewhere else."

"You can't throw me out," said Martha, "Father willed it to us children. You can buy my share if you want to."

Karl had no desire to do that. He was angered and astonished. The way Martha talked these days!

From now on Martha was treated inconsistently—first in a slyly friendly way, and then like poor Cinderella. She felt relieved when she could get away and ride her bicycle to the farmers' meeting, although the trip back always frightened her. And in any case it brought her no real contentment. Her life was bitter.

She longed to see Kurt Steiner again. She couldn't keep waiting and waiting for him to come of his own accord. She wanted to look into his face, which seemed different to her from all the faces she knew, and to see his light brown hair and his determined glance, and to hear his voice. She had many questions to ask him. She felt that he would be able to explain everything. He was married and he probably had a child already. He could be annoyed if she suddenly appeared. But he had visited her himself with his fiancée and written down for her where he lived in Berlin.

An opportunity came, due to the fact that her brother was very inexperienced in anything having to do with official matters and documents, and Martha, on the other hand, had been acustomed for years to managing everything for herself. Martha offered to take care of some business for him at the Farmers' Bank in Berlin, but she gave no hint of how important this trip was to her. Her brother didn't object.

She knew her way very well and arrived on time. From the bank she rode to Weissensee, to the building in which Kurt Steiner lived. As she climbed the stairs she kept asking herself if she should really do it.

But the apartment door in the third story had the name of a stranger on it. She looked at the other doors with no luck. Finally she asked a woman who was just coming from the market whether Kurt Steiner lived here. The woman said: "He's been gone a long time." "Where did he go?" The strange woman shrugged her shoulders. When Martha continued to look at her with anxiously questioning eyes, the woman scornfully waved her arm in a broad circle.

Then Martha went to the bus stop. She was tired. Her mind was saddened. She thought: "He could have told me in a letter." As if suddenly overwhelmed by her disappointment, her shoulders were limp, and her face was drawn. The closer the bus came to her village, the more people she recognized. She pulled herself together, because it seemed as if they were staring at her. She heard how one said to the other: "She was there on the farm all alone." She thought: Yes, you people would have really taken care of Kurt Steiner; you would have gone straight to the Gestapo with him. Then she thought sorrowfully to herself: Now he's gone forever.

She walked home from the last bus stop. She kept clenching her teeth, so her sadness wouldn't get the best of her again. She showed her brother the papers from the bank, and since he didn't understand any of them, he had nothing more nasty to say than: "Why didn't you come back earlier?"

All of a sudden she had a feeling of inner satisfaction. She possessed something all her own, and she was not going to surrender any of it. What belonged to her and only to her, was not a thing but all that she had experienced. She had every right to be proud of that. She held her body straighter.

Next to the garden plots was a piece of land that had been neglected. The former owners had either died in the war or had been frightened away. The community had given the land to a displaced person named Klein. During the escape, Eberhard Klein had lost his wife. He was taking care of his only child, a son. He was feeling depressed and helpless. Formerly he had been a gardener, but he'd always had good soil to work with. He couldn't get used to this poor soil along the lake—nor to the personalities of these people, who were as niggardly as their soil.

Emrich had been eager to get the piece of land that Eberhard Klein was now in possession of. So he gave Klein the cold shoulder. And if Klein asked him a question, he would give him scanty or even false information. Klein believed at first that Martha was the same type. A lot of people had told him that she was sullen and rude. But once she had volunteered friendly advice about how to trim his tomatoes. And in the farmers' meetings, even though she was shy, she had sensible ideas. Eberhard Klein listened to her in surprise. He thought: That's exactly the way I feel. He also began to notice how good and calm her eyes were.

She soon became his wife and was a good mother for his child. They lived peaceably and shared each other's views of the outside world and of their own work and their small family.

Once Martha received a postcard from Kurt in Düsseldorf. He wrote that he would never forget her. Eberhard Klein asked who the man was that wrote the card: Martha answered: "We helped each other now and then during the bad times, during the war." She added: "Once he brought me some real coffee." Klein didn't ask any more questions, and she said nothing more.

When somebody asked about Martha, which rarely happened, the answer would be: "She is Emrich's sister. And now she's married to Eberhard Klein." And somebody who shared the Kleins' opinions in general might perhaps add: "She is a good person." What else could be said, since that's all that anyone knew.

Invention of a Language

Wolfgang Kohlhaase

Ten numbers have been called out on the loudspeaker—the tenth is his. Straat feels neither fear nor hope. He steps out of his row, stumbles between faces and backs to the end of his group, turns right, and walks with painful steps up to the man who called his name and who is standing on a platform behind a table with papers and a microphone on it.

It is April of the year 1944. Straat, the tenth in a line of men who take their places with their faces toward the wall, is dead-tired although it is early in the day, and although he is so young. The sky that he sees when he casts a glance over the roof of the guardhouse hangs low and wet. Farther beyond, past these clouds, a small part of the way around the world, is Holland. They brought Straat from there with five others a hundred days ago, a long, long time ago. Why? So that he could sweat, so that he could freeze, so that he could carry rocks, receive blows, lie in filth, sleep on boards, eat rotten vegetables, and finally cease to be. But before that, still breathing and still seeing, he would forget who he was. He has already almost forgotten. It is unbelievable that beyond that piece of sky there is still a place where he was born, and earth and water, his parents, evenings, the different smell of the girls' class in school, the scientific instruments behind the glass door of the cabinet, and physics—six semesters of it—unbelievable! Because the law of conservation of energy isn't really true anymore. It isn't true for those who carry rocks up the big ramps, guarded by clubs and sniper scopes from darkness to darkness. Six students of physics, five of them already done for. The last one, dead-tired, is Straat, who isn't going to the quarry today because his number has been called.

Ten men, but where are they going? To isolation cells? To the infirmary? Ahead of them is a Kapo[1] in a white jacket, and he leads them to the kitchen. A stone building, tiled on the inside. Six shiny boilers in which the stinking soup is cooked. But they haven't been brought here to make soup. They're here because of the potatoes.

The commandant is having a "comradeship evening." On such occasions the guards, the executioners, the paymasters, the work crew leaders, the supply officers, the torturers, the office personnel, and the doctor sit pleasantly together at long tables. And the evening has three main attractions: first the comradeship, second the beer, third the pork roast with potato salad. And that's the reason why ten stools have been put in the camp kitchen with ten baskets of potatoes next to them, ten basins for peelings in front of them, a metal bucket in the middle, and Straat on one of the stools.

It is warm and quiet in the kitchen. The nearby stone quarry seems far removed. In an enclosure next to the door an SS-man is sitting and reading. The Kapo comes and stands by the potato peelers occasionally and looks on. No malice, just professional interest. And yet, Straat's fingers begin to twitch, he's not used to this, his peelings become too thick, it's not easy for him in the shadow of a Kapo who has his eyes on him. The Kapo goes away and then returns. Straat works faster but it doesn't help, and he hears the question:

"You, what did you do before?"

"Student," says Straat and doesn't look up and doesn't stop peeling with his quivering hands. He expects a kick at anytime. The SS-man behind the pane of glass will look up from his book. And then? But the Kapo just says:

"Studies are over, huh?"

At noon they get a bowl of soup, steam rising from its surface where a few shreds of meat are floating. Then a second bowl, filled to the rim.

Straat is outside now, leaning against the wall of the mess hall with all that soup in his skeleton, contented. Suddenly no hunger any more. No stone quarry. No yelling. Far away, behind the electric fence, where nobody can go, he discovers a shimmer of green and he remembers that it's April. The Kapo watches him and strolls over and asks:

"Hey, what did you study?"

"Physics."

"I see," says the Kapo in the tone of somebody who knows what it's all about.

That afternoon Straat is less afraid when somebody comes up to him. A little sun slants into the kitchen, the potatoes plop into the water, the regular kitchen personnel, in white aprons, are slicing bread for the next day—who would believe that here and there someone is dying, now, in the sand, not far away? The Kapo is standing next to Straat again and feels an urge to talk.

"Damn it, when I get out of here," he said, "after the war, I'm going to Persia."

The Kapo explains that he has a brother in Persia who just got out in time, in '39, and now he's sitting there, a big businessman, while the Kapo sits here like an idot.

"You're a Dutchman," says the Kapo. "What do you think—is Persia a good place to be?"

"I'm sure it's good," says Straat. He peels and peels, but he isn't peeling so fast anymore. The Kapo, in the mild afternoon light, nods like somebody who feels himself understood, and he sighs.

"What a waste of time, precious time. If a person could at least learn Persian here."

He has a worried look, with an honest good-fellow frown on his face, a man close to forty and quite well-fed compared to those human wrecks sitting there in a circle. Fate had first thrown him down and then raised him up again, but he still gets crapped on. That's for sure. Then Straat suddenly hears himself saying:

"I know Persian."

The Kapo gives him a long look out of his pale eyes, first unbelievingly, then doubtingly, then almost tenderly:

"You know Persian?"

Straat nods with frozen features.

"Come with me."

The Kapo goes ahead; Straat stumbles after him into the little office enclosure.

Wolfgang Kohlhaase

"So tell me now how you came to know Persian."

There was no retreat now for Straat. You don't play jokes on a Kapo, especially when all you need is one more push to knock you over for good. And Straat doesn't want to play jokes either—he just doesn't want to go to the quarry anymore—that would finish him off—he wants to stay in the kitchen where he can sit on a stool like a human being and peel potatoes and where he can get soup to eat. Although he's afraid his voice will fail, it doesn't betray him—it's just very soft. He says:

"I was in Persia before the war."

"You know what'll happen to you if that's not true?"

Straat's eyes are so full of terror that the Kapo is convinced that he does know.

"All right, how do you say 'hello'?"

"*Dalam*," says Straat.

"And 'shit'?"

Straat ponders too long, and the Kapo immediately becomes impatient.

"But there must be a word for 'shit'."

"*Tupa*," Says Straat.

"*Tupa*," the Kapo says with feeling. Then he says:

"Now peel as if your life depended on it."

That's the gist of their conversation. It accomplishes a lot. For example, the Kapo Battenbach pays a visit to Work Crew Leader Roeder, who has returned from a lengthy stay at the dining table. He explains to him that he has long since needed another man in the kitchen crew and has never been able to find the right one, but that now someone has turned up who impresses him with his special aptitude. The crew leader nods in reply: He has no objection to taking a look at such an outstanding person. With Battenbach in tow he marches over to the potato peelers and examines the half-starved Dutchman, formerly a physics student, but of what interest is that to Roeder? What interests him can be seen at a glance and that is the fact that this man doesn't have the slightest notion of how to peel potatoes, however desperately he tries. But this is not the main point, because twice a week the crew leader gets to take some sausage along, and on Sunday a roast, and occasionally some margarine. All of which comes from Battenbach. So Roeder nods a second time and goes back to his office and writes a name and number on a card. And on the same day this name and number are added to the duty roster. From there to the labor supervisor, and, in the light of the next morning that shines damply upon the drill field, Straat is the only one of the ten potato peelers to be returned to the kitchen, where Battenbach gives him a friendly pat on the shoulder. For Straat is now Battenbach's man. He is not going to be burned to ashes, he's going to get soup and bread to make him strong again. "Such a mind should not be wasted," Battenbach says to himself, and rubs his hands together. "They locked me up for pimping—unpolitical—but they can't stop me from learning Persian." Of course, Roeder doesn't know that—Roeder, who hangs around Straat the first few days and tries to figure out what's going on—no, he can't know that the well-fed Kapo and the hungry Dutchman are joined together by a special language. But what even Battenbach doesn't know is that this language doesn't really exist. Only Straat. He alone determines the rules and the words. How many words will he need, for how many days?

At noon, as soon as Crew Leader Roeder has eaten and left, Battenbach calls Straat into the office and sits down calmly at the table with crinkled paper and a pencil stub in front of him, ready to learn some Persian. On the first day he wants general information about Persia. Straat says it's hot there, and the women beautiful, the poor are poor and the rich are rich. Battenbach is satisfied—that's the way he had imagined it. He himself is in the "entertainment" business, do they have that sort of thing there too? Bordellos? Straat isn't sure at first what he means, and Battenbach explains. Why of course, absolutely, says Straat. And Battenbach nods—that's what he thought. But now he wants to know some words: schnaps, police, thanks, please, table, chair, bed, canteen, cutlet. Straat doesn't dare to hesitate, not on the first day. He names them all in order: *alan, monato, laps, nam, toki, sol, oltok, runidam, kotelett*. That last one is a borrowed word, says Straat, it's international. With a clumsy hand Battenbach writes down everything.

In the evening, under his ragged blanket, lying shoulder to shoulder with the neighbor who shares the cot with him, Straat tries, despite a debilitating headache, to invent words and, above all, a system to help him remember them. The heavy breathing of exhausted men surrounds him, the one next to him groans in his sleep, Straat's lips form words that no one has ever heard: *or, tal, mel, met, meb*, which mean: I, you, he, she, it.

Now Battenbach is punching him in the face with his fist, kicking him in the shins, slamming him against the wall—Battenbach, who is quivering from rage and disappointment. It's all because of *runidam*, the Persian word for "canteen." Straat had made it up the first day; later, when Battenbach asked him for it, he couldn't remember. Straat was aware that something had slipped his mind, but Battenbach wouldn't let him look at the notes. Battenbach gave him two days, in the meantime writing down the next words himself and having them spelled to him so Straat couldn't look over his shoulder. Now Battenbach is flailing at him with his fists and is determined to turn in this swine of a Dutchman before the noon hour is over. Straat screams in despair that it's been ten years since he was in Persia, and he was still a child, and *runidam* is a very rare word, and it just occurred to him accidentally. "Canteen" is actually *mardam*, but if he doesn't get some paper and pencil, he can't refresh his memory after so long a time.

"I'll see that you rot," says Battenbach. Then they are silent. Straat leans against the wall and watches the Kapo with anxious eyes and Battenbach stares at the forehead of his "boy," whose skin is taut and pale; he sees the veins in his temples beating, he curses—if he could only look into that head. A doubt slips into his mistrust, a doubt that he would like to surrender to. Because already in just a few days, this language has won a place in his heart. During the empty evenings, when he looks from his window out over the drill field, filled with a dull hate for the world, tormented by memories of women, he has, with the help of the difficult Persian words, all at once become a man who makes use of the hours and looks forward to them and has his secret far-reaching plans.

"I just hope you aren't cheating me. If you really don't know Persian . . ." says Battenbach, and the enormity of this thought makes his voice quiver. "I know Persian," says Straat. "I do! It was just a long time ago." From then on Straat has a pencil and paper to use. These are valuable items that can put you in a cell. If they catch him with them, Battenbach will claim to know nothing. Straat hides the pencil in one of his shoes and the paper under his cap. He carries his language over his brain, between the shorn hair and the cloth of his cap. At roll call he has to be careful, especially at the command "Caps off!" His language might fall out. It can be discovered and taken away from him. Then he'll be done for, whatever happens; the guards or his student will kill him. Every evening he also hides bread or a few potatoes in his clothes and brings them to his bedmate, an electrician from Groningen, quarry detail—who weighs only ninety pounds.

Straat works on his language at night. He twists letters and syllables to make up words. The special German things that surround him find a place in his language. When he can give them a sound that carries him away, not to Persia but into a strange and quiet world—at such moments he can escape their horrible meanings. *Rium, rema, matori, muro, kemato, ikre, tame, muir, rotam, kretum, orite, mekor, kumo, emati, katu meri, tamku, taritora.*[2] All of these words come from the German *Krematorium.* And it's the same with "arrest" and "barracks," with "quarry" and "barbed wire," and even with the name of Battenbach, his protector, who in this fashion can learn from himself. From the fat, black smoke (*Rauch*) comes *hacur*, the wind.

Straat writes down words on his paper in the dark, as small as possible. He hides the paper in his cap and puts the cap under his straw mattress. He doesn't invent more than five words a night, thirty a week, which is also enough for Battenbach. They leave Sunday out. Straat eats two bowls of soup each day, he is getting stronger, he notices how summer is approaching, the smell of blossoming lupines comes from distant fields. Another Dutchman, from the work crew, is waiting for him in the latrine.

"What are you doing with the Kapo in his office every noon?"

"What business is it of yours?" says Straat distrustfully.

The other looks at him with forbearance. He says: "You didn't accidentally get the potato-peeling job. We put you down for that because you were the last of the students. So that you could rest for a day."

He pauses and says: "And then Battenbach made use of you. Why?"

Silence, except for the buzzing of the green-glistening flies. And Straat sees in the eyes of the other man a suspicion mingled with anxiety and sympathy, but also severity and hardness. He senses in this moment that the language which only he knows can not only protect but also destroy, because it raises him above those closest to him. But he is afraid to reveal his secret, not even to someone who might be a friend, because who is really his friend? Most likely the boy from Groningen, who shares his cot, and whom he provides with bread, potatoes, and courage, but he doesn't even tell him.

Summer 1944.

The bombers draw lines of silver across the German sky.

Wolfgang Kohlhaase

Straat makes a word for life, he calls it: *sawal*. And a word for apple tree, as a joke—*pollimolli*. But not as a favor to Battenbach, who, at his own request, is learning numbers and idioms and words having to do with the world of entertainment. When Battenbach has bad moods, Straat makes up words in revenge. One of them is *suliduladornatlam*. Battenbach doesn't want to accept that one, but Straat explains to him that it's the customary word of greeting in that country—no door is open for you in Persia if you don't say *suliduladornatlam*.

"*Tupa*," says Battenbach like a real Persian.

While Straat's mind, schooled on physics and no longer weakened by hunger or dulled by fear, invents the structure of a language, men are dying around him, about fifty every day, week after week, their flesh burned, their brains hissing into nothingness as their souls pass into the heaven of their religious faith. Before their death, their mouths have perhaps spoken a last word that then starts upon a long journey through lands and peoples, and finally may reach those who are waiting for it.

Straat's language will reach no one except Battenbach—it will carry no message and represents nothing but itself; it saves the one who is inventing it and makes another, who is laboriously learning it, more gentle—he is still a "dirty dog" but not a blood-hound. Otherwise the language is useless. But for it Straat needs the imagination to make great discoveries, the courage for great hypotheses, the ambition for great undertakings. And Battenbach, kitchen Kapo, pimp from Hamburg, needs to regain the eager simplicity which he once had, long ago, as a schoolboy.

One August morning they carry Straat from the drill field, where he had fallen, to the infirmary—his face is spotted, his tongue swelling out of his mouth. For three days he lies delirious on the straw and on the floor; the male nurses hear him speak a series of words without sense. Then it becomes apparent that he will pull through; he is stronger than others but is he still sane? The camp orderly goes through the rows with the needle. With an injection of air he heals all pains; after all, when you're dead you're no longer sick. When he hears Straat screaming he will declare him insane, will note his number, then push up his sleeve and look for the vein. The attendant pulls Straat by his feet into an adjoining room where the dead are lying; nobody will hear him or search for him there. Then Straat regains consciousness. In the warm sunlight that shines through the two windows he sees others of his own kind, rigid, in the ridiculous contortions of their last moments, the pupils of their eyes fixed forever, mouths opened wide without a scream. Is he himself alive? He has a voice with which he can howl like a wolf and with which he can say words which surprise everybody except his silent companions here. Does he belong among them?

Before the zinc-plated burial van comes and backs up to the building they take Straat, still thrashing around in his fever, and put him in a bed. The next day he is quieter. The nurse, a German, is watching him and shaking his head:

"Say, buddy, those were crazy things you were saying. We thought you'd really had it." And he taps himself on the forehead.

Straat is very weak and forgets to be cautious.

"It is Persian," he says, "but it is not actually Persian. I make it all up."

"What do you make up?"

"A language," says Straat.

But then the nurse thinks that this man is crazy after all; well, fate is blind, great minds go kaput—this Dutchman is lucky. And he really is lucky, because the Kapo uses his influence and sends him bread several times. Straat recovers, and, when the nurse asks him again about his language, he pretends that he remembers nothing. And Straat also conceals his fear, his fear over the fact that he has lost his cap. He goes back to his building like a man raised from the dead; he sees new faces, also a new man on his cot. He waits for the chief prisoner who comes and shakes his hand.

"Come along, I have something for you."

In the chief's room there's a floor tile that has been loosened, and from underneath it he fishes out a dirty piece of cloth—no, not a rag but a cap; Straat twists it in his hands and feels the pieces of paper that his language is written on.

"The man who shared the cot with you, the electrician, brought it back from the drill field."

"Where is he?" asks Straat.

"He got sick after you did," says the chief. "He's not coming back."

The chief breathes with a whistling sound, as if something in his nose were broken. He says:

"Keep bringing things from the kitchen. There are many men here who need them."

So the situation returns to normal. Straat goes back to the

kitchen detail, and Battenbach's blue eyes sparkle with satisfaction, and he refrains from sending anybody to his death. At noon when Crew Leader Roeder has gone, he sits down at the table, with the pencil stub in his hand, on his face the look of humility of a person who is learning something. The word for "learning" is *lifu*. And Straat smuggles paper and pencil and bread and potatoes through the bellowing of the rollcalls and, in the evening, shoulder to shoulder with another bedpartner, he thinks up idioms and sentences and constructs a conjugation and a declension. It's no longer just for Battenbach, for whom the customary assignment is enough. Now it is the language itself which drives him on. Once more he is threatened with exposure. Battenbach has found out that a Persian has been brought to the camp—a live Persian, of all things. For two days Battenbach prowls through the camp, trying with the help of all the tricks he knows, to find him. When he finally locates him, he turns out to be an Indian. Battenbach spends another whole day cursing.

"This is a lousy camp. There's not even one Persian in the whole damned bunch."

"The Fuehrer hasn't got that far yet," says Straat consolingly. And he thinks: 'That poor lonely man from India!'

Fall comes and winter. An icy wind blows over the drill grounds and whirls the light snow over the frozen ground. Columns of people in rags move through the gates, infinitely slowly, foot by foot, step by step; they come from other camps, have survived the march and now move into the tents, surrounded by barbed wire, to die quietly in the night under high, bright stars, or in the day under swiftly moving clouds—sometimes when the sun is shining.

Within the mess hall, where it's warm, Straat practices with Battenbach an imaginary scene in Persian:

"I am a gentleman from abroad. I am a business man. May I dance with the lady? *Ta muli asa okadir. Ta muli lem basarmelko. Neli ta ramadamda donga?*"

A day in May will come when the gates are opened, the chestnuts will be blooming in the streets, whoever is still alive will go where he wants to. Straat will return to Holland, will finish his study of physics and become a teacher. For the rest of his life he will become easily tired. Never again will he do anything as great as what he accomplished here: he invented a language . . . which he is gradually forgetting.

Battenbach will go to Persia, to the Empire of Iran, amazed at the strange language which is spoken there.

Notes

[1] Kapo: a prisoner put in charge of a work party composed of other prisoners.

[2] I have retained the original words, all formed, as the author says, from *Krematorium*. Some of them, at least, can also be seen as partial or complete anagrams of other words relevant to the times: *Ruhm* (fame), *Reich, Amt* (governmental bureau), *Mauer* (wall), *Mord* (murder), *Kretin* (cretin), *Terror, Amerika, Territorium* (territory).

A Certain Date[1]

Christa Wolf

Communists? If she knew one, it would be the shoemaker, Sell,
from the village of G. When she assigned him, or rather, his
wagon, to labor corps work just as she did with everybody else, he
came to the municipal office, threw his cap on the table and
shouted: Always me, that's strange, maybe the rich farmers
greased your palm, Fräulein? Then she took the list she'd made out
carefully and fairly, and threw it down next to the greasy cap and
started shouting too, and then Shoemaker Sell stormed away and
slammed the door behind him. But the mayor, whose term of
office was limited because the higher-ups wouldn't accept perma-
nently the fine distinction he made between being a member of
the National Socialist Workers' Party and being a Nazi—the
mayor taught her what fairness is: You see, it doesn't mean equal
treatment of all, but only privileges for those in power at the moment—it used to be the rich farmers like Otto Müller, nowadays it
was people like Sell, the shoemaker. A list is a list, she said, and a
horse is a horse; but the mayor said: You may be able to speak a
foreign language, young lady, but there are a lot of other things
you still have to learn.

Then there was the other one, a dead Communist, a driver of a
beer wagon, whose son turned him in to the authorities. Listening

to enemy broadcasts, said Kruger, the bookseller, the spreading of subversive propaganda—that will be his neck, especially if he's a Communist too. So there were still Communists in our midst—that surprised her, and she kept a close eye on all drivers of beer wagons. The one whose son had denounced him drove his wagon through her dreams, and she asked him why these Communists wouldn't stop listening to the enemy radio when it was forbidden and also unnecessary, because what did they want to find out that was worth such risks? She felt that she had to side with the son against the father, but the father had a certain expression in his eyes (that was the only part of him she could see clearly, because what do Communists really look like, anyway?) that put her defense of the son to shame over and over again. But her hyperactive imagination forced her to picture to herself again and again how the good son made that honest decision. And how he went about finding the agency to which such things are reported. What was the name of the agency? Then she thought of the name. But where was that located? People were right when they accused her of ignorance in practical matters. Now the good son is there, looking for the office that records especially the denunciations of fathers—of mothers too? What does the sign on the door say? Then the son goes in. Then he clicks his heels, thrusts his right arm upward in a "Heil Hitler" salute, and explains: I wish to lodge a formal complaint against my father, driver of a beer wagon. Then she was compelled to picture herself how the father was told about it: But it was your own son who felt duty-bound to inform us; are you accusing your son of lying? She pictured also how the father was probably dead by now, while the son still could wake up each day and have a life to live, and, without giving expression to it even in her thoughts, she had no great desire to meet this son who was thoroughly loyal to his duty. Although she might actually meet him, because there were more sons to be seen in the streets than there were drivers of beer wagons.

Then she broke the flow of her imagination and tried in vain to forget that man who drove the beer wagon.

The certain date mentioned here was accompanied by a day whose events did not appear remarkable. Next door, the widow Gideon was chasing her son Heiner around the table, this thief who had gobbled up her bread; she grabbed the rug beater, oh, didn't Heiner scream, the pig! His father was away at war. At our own table, separated from the two of them by a thin door, we are eating the two slices of the heavy black bread that the farmer's wife, in whose house our family lives, had managed to get for each of us on the weekend. We aren't hungry but we never have enough. In the big mirror of the washstand I see my face and behind it the end of a bed and faded wallpaper, and any connection that all these things might have with each other is difficult to see. I run down the four flights of stairs, through the gate, along Fritz Reuter Street, into the center of town to the school by the Pfaffenteich, where the English teacher, a local product, apologizes every morning with the same smile for having to search through the hair of adult students for lice, and if we are curious about anything it is to see how long the supply of these smiles will last. I have already had typhoid anyway—which could be mentioned offhand just to see whether certain people are still startled by certain words. Hildegard Pietzsch is absent for the third day in a row, perhaps one of the ladies knows . . .? One of us *does* know. Abortion. Miss Heymann, what's the English word for that?

By the way, *Don Carlos*[2] ("Grant us freedom of thought, Sire!") was forbidden reading, our German teacher remarked, in "those brown days that are behind us."[3] I can't let her get away with that statement—he wasn't forbidden here, it's an out-and-out lie to say that Schiller was forbidden reading. . . . Then we suddenly said to each other that we couldn't care less whether Schiller was forbidden reading or not, and we stopped talking. We'd just like to know, though, why our German teacher was crying in the street yesterday. During the noon hour we heard the embarrassed explanation that it was because she couldn't get potatoes any more, and her sick mother. . . In the margin of my essay about "Personalities who are building the New Order," the teacher had written "Unnatural style"; that doesn't say much, how could a person write any way but unnaturally about these things? Ruth gets an A, the teacher thinks her essay is convincing. Are you really convinced? She shrugs her shoulders. Are you bringing her forget-me-nots on May first, or not? Of course, what do you take me for?

There should be some way to get over the feeling that everything—including those stupid forget-me-nots—is meaningless to me. Ruth found a letter under her desk again; her boyfriend attends the class that is taught in the same room in the afternoon; she's going to marry him, and says that her mother, who is dying of cancer, approves. I never find a letter under my desk, but I can't let that mean anything to me either.

In the middle of the mathematics class, Elizabeth faints; the last few weeks her eyes have seemed larger than they should be for her small face. They drag her to the water faucet and hold her wrist under the water, that helps, she says with a weak voice, it was just too warm for me. Well, in April in an unheated school it can never be too warm, but Elizabeth comes from Königsberg and has four younger brothers and sisters at home. Somebody asks the embarrassing question whether anyone has something for her to eat, but Elizabeth violently denies she is hungry. During the noon hour her mother brings her a slice of bread that she got with her new ration card, and she eats it secretly. Ilsemarie has her fit of coughing, and two weeks later the lung specialist says to me: Of course you got it from her because she has a very virulent case. She's the one I sat beside, hunched over a Latin book. The Latin teacher is saying: Yes, now the times are brand-new, but the old texts remain, and I'm curious to know whether you are able to translate a simple sentence like the following: Tempora mutantur, the times are changing, as we Latinists say, and we change with them.

What do you think about that, we asked the German teacher when we visited her in the old parsonage, where she came to greet us with bare feet. The times are changing, she says, we are changing. Christ remains. Who do you think gave me the strength not to salute that flag, never, not a single time? Do you know Iphigenia?[4] Really not? Get it, read it. On my bed in Widow Gideon's room: All human weaknesses are made whole by pure humanity. Oh yes, of course, a person doesn't want to be impolite. Every noon the thin, black-dressed lady, who goes to the restaurant where half of the large arched windows are nailed shut, carefully bores out the eyes of four greenish boiled potatoes with the tip of her knife, then mashes them with their skins on in No. 2 standard gravy and eats them up. She never says a word, because she can't publicly eat potatoes with their skins on and at the same time chat with her friends as if nothing were happening. Outside, Ruth walks by with her boyfriend, he has curly black hair, hers is blonde, their fingers are entwined, they don't see anybody no matter how long you follow them, you've always wanted to know what that is, love.

You stare impudently into everybody's face, that's a game you play every day because there's no danger that you suddenly will recognize a face. Then somebody stops you and begins a cheerful wordy conversation, yes, this face is really Anneliese's, don't you recognize her? Time rolls back within you, another city, other streets, a schoolyard—oh yes, Anneliese. You act as if you're really

UNGAR

REVIEW COPY

TITLE   VOICES EAST AND WEST:
German Short Stories Since 1945

AUTHOR   Edited and translated by
Roger C. Norton

PAGES   200

PUBLICATION DATE   December 20, 1984

PRICE $14.95 Cloth
$8.95 Paperback

Twenty-six striking examples of
the artistic prominence of this
genre in East and West Germany.

*We would appreciate your sending us
two copies of your review.*

FREDERICK UNGAR PUBLISHING CO., INC.
36 Cooper Square   New York, N.Y. 10003

startled to hear that Anneliese got out with the very last train, the one that the tank column set fire to with its shells. Then recently she ran into Sieglinde, don't you remember, a leader in the Hitler Youth? Oh yes. This Youth Leader Sieglinde made a terrible scene once because the drama group cut tiny peepholes in an expensive stage curtain, that's something that German girls just don't do. So now she's all finished, the bigwigs of the district just left her sitting there and filled their cars with cartons of food; she had a crying fit right in front of me; she's lost interest in everything. As if it mattered the least bit to me what a leader in the Hitler Youth had lost interest in.

The idea[5] may have had its good side, says Anneliese, but the way it was carried out! I quickly say goodbye, give Anneliese a false address so that I can lie undisturbed on Widow Gideon's bed and read from Diedrich Speckmann's "The Holy of Heart": "O heart, if you wish to attain high goals, you must find within yourself the uplifting power" . . . "The greatest man is he who swears allegiance to no flag."

Now and then you tentatively walk to the window that reaches to the floor, and you look with a strange longing at the street far below and the crowd of people that means nothing to you, and which you can't enter. Then you have to hold fast to the bed or take refuge in the kitchen; there at least Heiner will be sitting at the table and watching as you cook yourself a watery bowl of oatmeal every night.

The truth is that it was not until two and a half years after that 21st of April 1946 that I read my first book on Marxism. It was a fine autumn day. I was eating great quantities of the small tart apples that my grandmother handed me through the window; in the evening I wrote the title of the book in my diary—incorrectly, as you can see: "Feuerbach and the End of Classical Philosophy."[6]

If this had not been the beginning, something else would have, I tell myself today, but in any case it did happen that way. "And so, in the course of development, all former reality becomes unreal . . ." If I had learned anything through experience, it was this: That which used to have reality gradually lost this reality, devoured by an incurable disease which easily spread to us ourselves. What people used to call "time" then moved past us like a hermetically sealed train which gave no indication of a goal.

What came after that day is a long story that many of our generation share. From time to time I have thought back to that beginning with no desire to change it. Just as I can't look at my penciled notes in the margin of that book by Friedrich Engels without being moved: "A new and vital reality appears and replaces the reality which is dying." That was to be the event that would fill my life. Did I sense it that evening? Not at all? I will try to be precise. I went outdoors that night. It was cool, autumn, and the air light and clear. We lived on the side of a hill. The stars above and the city lights below seemed to be, as always, reflections of each other. I walked up Thomas-Müntzer Street to the "Blutrinne," a swale in which the blood of the rebellious peasants is said to have flowed after the slaughter of May 15, 1525. The beauty of the night repelled me. The symmetrical crescent of the moon, this refined illusion, was repugnant to me. The leaning church tower, romantic landmark of the city, should long since have yielded in its obstinacy and collapsed. Everything should have been given relevance for us, whose indifference has now ended.

Notes

[1]The East German author is recalling a particular date, as well as the period in general, right after World War II when she and other East Germans were confronting on one hand, the ghosts of the Nazi past and, on the other, the realities of the present in their part of a divided country, under a Communist government.

[2]Famous play by Schiller on the theme of political freedom.

[3]"Brown days" alludes to the days of Hitler and his brown-shirted storm troopers.

[4]Refers to Goethe's drama, "Iphigenia in Tauris."

[5]The "idea" of Nazism.

[6]The correct title in English is *Ludwig Feuerbach and the End of Classical German Philosophy* (by Friedrich Engels). The German title is *Ludwig Feuerbach und der Ausgang der klassischen deutschen Philosophie.*

Someday He Really Will Come Home[1]

Günter de Bruyn

And one day Karlheinz, my big brother, really does come home. He has walked past the movie theater to the Litfass pillar[2] and crossed the street at the very same place we always did and I still do today; he is wearing a white nylon shirt, has his jacket over his arm, one hand in his pocket, and no luggage—two porters will bring it, or the baggage-express men. He walks to the exact place on the corner where the front part of the building once stood, which we always had to go through; he looks at the grass planted there and then glances up at our fifth story.[3] Sometime he's going to look at this rear building that now gets the light, and say: "It has its place in the sun; justice is finally done," or something like that, but now he is still too surprised and isn't used to the way things look now; twenty-two years are a long time. He is not confused, just surprised and at the same time calm and in charge of the situation as always.

His look says: So that's what happened to the house I was born in—I remembered it differently—but those times are over and done with. He walks across the street, which is empty and quiet because it's a Sunday morning in summer and I'm on my way to buy some milk, holding my little boy by the hand; for him it's an event to walk down the street with his father; and I hope he will never forget how it was when his uncle came home, in the morning, unexpectedly.

EAST GERMAN AUTHORS

And we approach each other, slowly, hesitantly, not at all the way a veteran moviegoer would imagine. Of course I recognized him right away, but still would have walked past him if he hadn't reacted, because, after all, he is prepared, he knows that he is coming home and can expect to meet his youngest brother, but I've just left the house to get milk for my children and can't suspect that my big brother is suddenly going to come across the street after twenty-two years without any news; so a person hesitates, although he has hardly changed or for that very reason, because it's so unexpected, but later I'll probably notice the wrinkles and lines in his face, the jaded look in his eyes, his jowls—now I only see the very familiar features, the ironically benevolent look, the delicate hands—compared with which my own hands always seemed so clumsy and peasantlike and a reminder that it was foolish for me to try to be as good as my big brother. Naturally, this painful impression of inferiority returns as soon as I shake his hand, and when I put my arms around him, a little tardily and not without a feeling of uncalled-for theatricality, and he laughs as always at my tendency toward sentimentality. And also, when I introduce his nephew to him he laughs a little, because it seems odd to him that his little brother has a family, and I immediately feel some of my old defiance: Yes, just go ahead and grin, but, you see, I don't want to do anything but stay at home and be average and normal. Naturally, I want to do that only because I realize that I can't do anything else; the only trouble is, my wife will suddenly realize it too, as soon as she meets Karlheinz. I'm a little ashamed, a little jealous, a little stubborn, but very very proud of my big brother and overjoyed at this homecoming, which I never doubted, but which now seems to be not entirely real because it has unexpectedly interrupted the pleasant monotony of my life.

It's my daughter who first conquers this impression. She listens impatiently as I tell about our last meeting, in '44—the destroyed railroad station, nobody allowed to leave the train, ten minute stopover, Karlheinz together with many others in the door of a cattle car, their mothers crowded around, a train whistle, a waving and crying—and then she impatiently asks her uncle how it happened that he didn't send word to his mother and brother for twenty-two years, and I'm afraid that now he himself will question the reality of his homecoming because of uncertainty and unclear recollection, and perhaps will not even admit that he is Karlheinz. But he immediately starts telling his story, confidently and in detail, and everything agrees with what we already know: St. Nazaire; the motors of the pursuing American tanks close enough to be heard; he says to his driver: we'll make our own armistice; they get out, run toward the Allied Forces; a hedge suddenly separates them and they never see each other again. Yes, that's true, we already knew that: in '47 the driver came and visited us. But then? What happened then?

We are all sitting at the kitchen table, he's across from me, filling his pipe with an exotically scented tobacco, his own blend; he doesn't smoke any premixed brands. Two minutes after he was separated from his driver, they caught him—interrogations, confrontations, brief retraining, and then a fine life in Luxemburg at the German Army radio station, but only until May '45, then PW camp, hunger, lice, he was ready for an offer from the secret service, twenty years duty—Switzerland, Austria, Tangiers, Greece, South Africa. He shakes his head. All over, finished! Afraid to come here? He laughs again at his younger brother, a family man, ignorant of the ways of the world. Don't worry, the switch was planned a long time ago, he's earned a rest here.[4] I find it hard to give an understanding smile because I'm thinking of Mother.

In our Trabant[5] we drive out to see her in the Rest Home. It's still Sunday. He's driving; I'm afraid of every policeman because I haven't dared to ask whether he has a driver's license. But he drives well, he learned that in the monastery with the French Trappist monks, the silent monks, who aren't allowed to speak or write but are allowed to drive cars. For twenty years he transported patients for an insane asylum. Right after the separation from his driver he saw some members of the French underground; he ran away and suddenly came to an endless wall, a white, high unscalable wall; he scaled it, the silent monks hid him; as early as the Battle of the Bulge he took the vows, in all sincerity, but some homesickness is so strong that all the vows in the world cannot cure it.

Then we walked up the landscaped path to the Home—he in front, holding my little boy's hand and arm-in-arm with my daughter as if she were his bride. When we point to Mother and her white hair at the window, he waves casually; he doesn't know that she can't see this far anymore. Then, of course, he also talks much too softly to her, but she doesn't scold him the way she always did with us: Didn't you children learn in school to speak loudly and clearly? She just keeps hugging him and talking to him the way she did with Father, whom I can scarcely remember because he was killed in Poland during the war; for me Karlheinz was always something like a father, and now he's here again, reassuringly familiar in his self-confidence but confusingly strange in his youthfulness; he's finally here again, in a white shirt, after twenty-two years. He couldn't have written without endangering his life. As soon as his driver had disappeared, he got back into the car and drove homeward at top speed; he had to hide two months near the Rhine before he could get across unnoticed, went into hibernation with a farm woman in the Harz mountains; on an April evening he finally reached the outskirts of Berlin and was in a barn near Schonefeld—in four hours he could have been home—when the Russians nabbed him, that is, a Russian woman, a major, nabbed him and kept him with her, wearing the uniform for four months although he didn't know a word of Russian; then Natasha's discharge from the Army, their return to Siberia, where he lives now as a fur hunter with three children; in four weeks he has to go back—the flight only takes a few hours but the trip by dogsled will last for days.

I am overcome by terrible grief when I think of the distance that will soon separate us, but he gives me an ironic glance from his place next to Mother, and I decide not to let my head sink onto his shoulder, because my wife is present and the children; the girl is already thirteen and I know that I have a fever, I can't sleep, and I have to lie quietly so I won't wake up my wife lying next to me; my head aches; I'm thirsty, but none of that is so bad, because after all, my big brother is home again, in his white nylon shirt, after twenty-two years.

Notes

[1]De Bruyn, in a manner reminiscent of Kafka, challenges the reality of experience and recollection in this story (or dream?) told by one brother about another who returns home with widely differing versions of what happened to him during his long absence.

[2]A round sidewalk pillar for advertisements, notices, etc.

[3]Many city dwellings in German cities consist of a "front house" and a "rear house," with a courtyard or passageway of some type joining them; poorer families have traditionally lived in the darker and less elegantly built rear part. In our story the war had destroyed the other half.

[4]His story, insofar as we can believe it at all, suggests that he was taken by the Germans on his way toward the American lines, was able to convince them that he was not a deserter, and then after being in Luxemburg and the prisoner-of-war camp of the Americans or English, he became an intelligence agent for them or the West Germans, and later switched, perhaps as a double agent, to the service of East Germany and thus was not afraid to return to the Eastern sector of Berlin.

[5]The brand name of a car manufacturered in East Germany

A Letter to Comrade Ernst L.

Uwe Kant

Dear Ernst,

I was intending to write you just a short letter to tell you that I wasn't at the funeral and *why* I wasn't. But it's going to be a little longer than that, after all. Not very long, but longer in any case.

Certain questions might be raised. For example, about good taste or basic philosophy of life. You know, of course, what I mean. And you say to me: Listen, none of that crap! But it isn't that simple. For you and me there's no problem. But it isn't just between us. Perhaps you've heard that I've become a public scribe (the second one that has lived under your roof), and, in fact, one of the simpler, fairly frequent type that writes for readers.[1] So, some of them will be reading this letter too, I hope. For that reason I'll at least mention those questions (without belaboring them further) before somebody gets the idea we hadn't noticed it at all, and considers us to be extremely tactless fellows or even characters with idealistic illusions, who cover our risks with double insurance.[2] Of course, that's ridiculous. Above all this last point. After all, you were the one who said to me: Listen, religion is the opiate of the people. I still remember exactly. I had just come back from harvest duty in Oderbruch.[3] That was practically part of our study program then. Nowadays they don't do it that way. And I told you about the driver for the cattle brigade, whose helper I was for three weeks. He always referred to his horses as the "oxen of Galilee" and every time he came to a big puddle he would call out: "Here comes another Lake Gennesaret." I thought it was funny. But all you saw was the "enemy" laying a hand on me in one of his many crafty ways, and so you spoke your words about "opiate of the people." I was familiar with them already, of course—I was in my third year of study. And in my case the idea came more from the printed word. On the other hand, you had gotten it personally from August Bebel.[4] Ernst, he had said, listen to me, my friend, I want to tell you something: This whole matter of religion, it's just an opiate of the people—nothing else at all. At least that's how you told it, because you always spoke about the man in a very familiar way. He was just a little fellow, you told me, and easy to lift on your shoulders (which was necessary if no desk or chair was there for him to stand on during a speech) but what a voice he had, and what a brain—he could really put hecklers in their place! I told other students at the University that I had a landlord who had occasionally held Bebel above the crowd when he gave a speech. But they thought we were liars because they only knew me and not you. When I first met you I knew you were a strong man. Your neighbor lady, that is, *our* neighbor lady, had told me that you spent a lot of your time in the grocery store. My first thought, of course, was that you were shopping for marmalade and sausage. But no, you were carrying the heavy cases of beer in from the street with such enthusiasm that the whole shop shook. A man well over seventy carrying a stack of full beer cases between his knees and his nose (I don't know how many fit in!). The brewery men would stay by their trucks smoking the cigars you had given them. Later, of course, I found out that it was just a sport for you. That was about the time the First Secretary had come out with his rhymed decree: "Everyone, in every port,/Once a week should play some sport!"[5] And your sport was slinging cases of beer because you were so used to it after forty years working for Schultheiss's Brewery. You took one of the cases under your arm and went to your house, which you had built yourself. To tell the truth, one of my friends at that time called your self-built house a ramshackle place. And we let *him* study architecture! Was that the right thing to do? On the way I gave you a sidelong glance. Your big bearlike figure, those broad sloping shoulders, the baggy work pants with the patches crudely attached to them. Your wife had been dead for ten years, and your fingers weren't very good at needlework. Fortunately, as you must admit, I soon learned about the practical method ("Duosan Rapid") of making patches out of adhesive cloth. That was a big help to us. The two old women in the neighborhood, who always wanted to marry you, argued against it, of course. But once again you proved to me that you were always open to new ideas! So, as I was saying, I gave you a sidelong glance and thought: What a giant! Oh yes, you looked at me sideways too. After all, a person notices such things. And I even know what you were thinking. Because you told me. It's really practical when a person says what he thinks. You said that I looked quite a lot thinner than the other man who had lived before I did in the self-built addition to your self-built house, but that otherwise the similarity between him and me was so great that we really wouldn't have to make up a new contract at all. And we never did, did we? When you put on your glasses there in the low-ceilinged room and opened the little writing desk, I thought for a moment you were going to put it in writing after all. But all you did was get out the chess set and say: I'm sure you know how to play chess, so let's go; I haven't played for at least three days. Naturally the three days should have put me on my guard, but—and I can tell you this now—I had the crazy notion that I could beat you, because you didn't look the least bit like a chess player. Of course, at that time I didn't know about your twenty years as a member of the Worker's Chess Association. I lost three times in a row in gruesome fashion. And at the time I was not amused by the fact that you accompanied our playing with couplets from Otto Reutter. As the sportcasters say, I wasn't in top form. Under such shattering circumstances, I wasn't able to learn any more chess but at least I learned about Otto Reutter and, later, Claire Waldoff.[6] Thanks for that, too. That sturdily built wallpainter who visited you sometimes was almost your equal in chess, wasn't he? You were sly and used your secret weapon on him. Oh yes, I saw it: the more he drank of your homemade fruit brandy, the faster he lost. Only your quiet and friendly son, the teacher, could beat you regularly. In a quiet and friendly way he would drink the brandy, and in a quiet and friendly way he would checkmate you. And when he left, in a quiet and friendly way, you watched him go and, half relieved and half shattered, you said, shaking your head: Oh, that rascal; that rascal is better than I am! But it was no wonder; after all, he had gotten everything from you. Nor was it a wonder that you sometimes came out second best in your contest with those weighty articles in the magazine *Unity*.[7] Sometimes in the evening I would come to borrow an onion or a bottle of beer, and I would find you bent over that difficult magazine, and your eyes had fallen shut behind the glasses you wore for chess and *Unity*. You would clear your throat mightily, shake your big head with the short gray hair, and then take on the next sentence. And you said: You know, if I don't understand this, what will the others say? Right! Because you were the Party Secretary for the homeowners' organization.

I lived in your house for three years. In the new wing with the separate entrance and its own porch. You had painted the porch red and yellow inside like a Minol gas station. Someone once called your self-made house a ramshackle place. Another wanted to find me a bed in the school dormitory. If they'd only known! As I already mentioned, I write stories now. Mostly for children. I've had a little practice at it, and now it's going quite well. I'm often invited to give readings. I like to go too. They let you know when they like something. I'm always a little afraid too. They aren't very respectful, and when they're quiet, it's from boredom and not rapture, and if they don't like your story, they just leave you standing there alone with your little sheet of paper; that can make you feel pretty foolish.

But recently they laughed a lot about a story that had been written to make them laugh, and they said nice things to me and asked a lot of questions, some of which I was even able to answer. This happened at the same time the burial was taking place, ten kilometers away. I hadn't noticed the time conflict early enough. That morning I debated a long time before making my decision. I imagined myself standing there, benumbed and powerless, in the cemetery and imagined myself throwing three handfuls of earth down upon you. I thought of you and of what your decision would have been. Then I went to the children. Right?

Notes

[1]A subtly ironic reference perhaps to the fact that he is an author who writes what his readers will like and not simply what is dictated to him (by public policy or whatever). This story in general is a testimonial to an admired friend who sometimes questioned or didn't understand governmental policies but who acted constructively and loyally, and who, for Uwe Kant, was an outstanding example of a rough and ready, but very intelligent "common man," united by friendship and deep sympathy with the author as representative of the intellectual element of socialistic society.

[2]This rather obscure passage apparently means that the author is afraid that his letter may be considered in certain quarters either as lacking good taste and tact, or in other quarters as being imbued with a spirit of idealism, or even religion. That is suspect in a society that does not encourage religious practice.

[3]Students in East Germany are often assigned during certain periods of the year to duty in various work brigades, for example, harvesting the crops.

[4]1840–1913. Leader of the Social Democratic Workers' Party, well-known and highly respected as a public speaker and parliamentarian in the Reichstag.

[5]A playful reference to the East German government's very strong emphasis on sports, competitive and otherwise.

[6]Otto Reutter, 1870–1931: Known for his public readings, chiefly in Berlin, of satirical and epigrammatic couplets which he himself wrote. Claire Waldoff, 1884–1957: Cabaret performer and singer of popular songs in Berlin.

[7]Periodical of the Socialist Unity Party, the single political party of East Germany.

Border Crossers

Rolf Schneider

Hanna's oldest brother had been working in West Berlin since the Spring of 1961. He had a contract as an apprentice machinist at the Borsig plant. Hanna was thirteen years old then. The large mirror in the hallway of their house showed her the way she looked: skinny, with a nose that was much too large. She made faces at herself. Even the summer dresses from Karstadt's[1] didn't help this reflection much.

Werner, her brother, whom she liked, wasn't home very much these days. He had the same time-consuming trip to work as her father. Many nights he didn't come back at all; he said he was spending the night at a friend's place in Wedding.[2]

In the newspapers that they read (except for the West Berlin *Groschenzeitung*, which her father brought home with him in the evening), articles began to appear against the border crossers. Hanna found out about that in her school classes. Border crossers were people who worked in West Berlin and lived in East Berlin. The radio station in Oberschöneweide broadcast editorials against the border crossers. At first, Hanna's father laughed when he heard of them; he laughed and then went to the radio and tuned in a station with music.

Hanna made the trip to Borsig's a few times. In the late afternoon she would stand at the big exit gate. The air was full of the sound of machines and motors. It tasted of soot. It tasted of dust and automobile exhausts, and smelled of sweaty bodies. Hanna waited until, in the midst of a crowd of employees, the small group of apprentices, including Werner, appeared.

During these weeks her father was becoming irritable. The attacks on the border crossers didn't let up. Her father suddenly found ridiculous excuses for fits of rage and shouting that would make the baby wake up and cry. In the evenings her father was drinking more and more beer.

One Sunday morning he quarrelled with Werner. The outward reason was that Werner had spent three nights in a row with his friend in Wedding, but his father doubted it was a male friend. Werner had also stayed away before for several nights at a time. But that had never caused an argument. Hanna cowered in the garden. She sat next to her little half-sister, who was putting wet sand into a plastic bucket and smearing her mouth with it. The pile of sand was on a neglected plot of grass where goldenrods were growing too. Hanna heard the voices of Werner and her father through an open window. She heard Werner laugh and ask why they didn't get away from this mess over here and just go over to the other side. The voices got louder and louder. They weren't listening to each other any more. It was a stupid quarrel. It ended with the sound of a hard slap in the face. After half an hour Werner came out of the house holding two bright-patterned travel bags in his hands. Hanna went to the streetcar stop with him. The path was dry and sandy as usual. Old cigarette butts lay scattered around by the tracks. They waited. The streetcar came and stopped. As Werner walked up the steps to the platform, Hanna told him she wanted to go on visiting him, she was sure of that. She watched the streetcar pull away, but she didn't wave.

The summer was very warm, but there was a lot of rain. On some afternoons Hanna rode her bicycle to Rahmsdorf, then through the woods toward Friedrichshagen. She went as far as the Müggelsee. A big public swimming pool was being built there. Right next to the construction site there was a free bathing area in the lake between the reeds and the shore. The water at the edge was muddy. Swans were swimming through the water, leaving their droppings behind them. With a few strong strokes, she swam through the muddy part. The water was warm. In the middle of the lake there were a few sailboats, and beyond them the

Müggel hills. The water didn't have a smell like the water of the Havel River, only some pale green algae floating beneath the surface.

One evening she listened to a conversation between her parents in the next room. Her mother mentioned Werner's name. She cried as she said it. But Werner is doing well, said her father, and anyway it was his own decision. Then they talked about what they should do now. Only in the worst circumstances would they want to give up the house they lived in. It belonged to them. Hanna's mother had inherited it from her parents.

On another evening two men rang the bell at the front gate. Hanna let them in. They said they wanted to talk with Hanna's father. One of them wore the oval metal insignia of the Unity Party on his lapel. Hanna led them into the house. Hanna's father was sitting at the kitchen table in his shirtsleeves, with a bottle of beer in front of him; in his lap was the spotted cat that everybody called simply "Mulle." Hanna was sent to bed. As she lay in her room she could hear the voices of the three men and the clear breathing of the baby, whose bassinet, covered with a brightly printed material, stood next to her bed. They were probably talking about the border crossers again.

In general it was a restless summer. In the railroad stations at the border of West Berlin, Neukölln or Gesundbrunnen, the colorful daily newspapers were displayed at the stands. Numbers, rounded off to the thousands and printed in huge type, showed the extent of the flight from the zone. Hanna read them as she walked past to buy coffee, bananas, and powered milk with the unconverted West German marks that her father had earned.

A dark-green sedan stopped in front of her parents' house. Two policemen got out, a third stayed at the steering wheel. This time it was Hanna's mother who went to the front gate when the bell rang, but Hanna was beside her and watched everything. The policeman showed her a piece of paper. Hanna's mother was frightened. With a confused gesture she motioned the men into the house. Hanna's father was in the bathroom; the sound of the shower could be heard, mingled with her father's voice: he was singing very unmelodically and loudly, singing a song which Hanna knew only from him, having to do with the erica, a flower that blossoms on the moors. The policemen sat down at the kitchen table. One toyed with a cigarette but didn't want to light it. Hanna's father came into the kitchen with wet hair, wearing a bathrobe. The policeman with the cigarette stood up and showed him the piece of paper. Hanna, who was watching it all, expected an angry outburst from her father, like the one that had driven her brother Werner out of the house. Her father just stared at the paper. Drops of water ran from his hair and splashed onto the paper; her father didn't try to wipe them off. He asked the policemen what the reasons were. The policemen answered in detail; they took turns explaining; the most important words, repeated several times, were "currency violations." Hanna's father did not shout. He only nodded. He said he wanted to get dressed. The policeman who had handed him the paper sat down on the chair after Hanna's father had left the kitchen; he took his cigarette again, played with it until it broke and crumbs of tobacco trickled onto the waxed tablecloth. Hanna's father came back, wearing a shirt, sweater, and pants. The two policemen stood up and went out with him to the waiting car. The broken cigarette was still there, lying on the flowered pattern of the kitchen tablecloth.

The next day Hanna's father came back. He had been at the district capitol, east of Berlin. The connections for the return trip had been very complicated—as bad as those to Siemensstadt. Hanna's father had drunk some alcohol on the way. He just said scornfully that he had been under investigation; he described the interrogation and said they had informed him that there would be a follow-up. He laughed. He took a bottle of beer out of the refrigerator and opened it. The next morning he glumly made the trip to his job in Siemensstadt, two and a half hours away.

Werner had not been back after the quarrel and hadn't even written a postcard. His mother baked a poundcake secretly and packed it in wax paper. On a Saturday afternoon, the twelfth of August, Hanna took the package with the cake and rode the Stadtbahn, transferring at the Ostkreuz, to Wedding. Werner's friend, an apprentice at Borsig's like Werner—Hanna had seen him a few times and knew his address—said that Werner was living in Charlottenburg now. The friend gave the name of the street and the building superintendent. Hanna went to the Stadtbahn again. She rode to Savigny Square, after transferring at the Westkreuz. She got out and asked a policeman where the street was, and found it. It wasn't very long; only one side of it had any buildings; on the other side was a park; beyond that, far away, were some tall buildings. Hanna found the house number. She stood and looked at the old-fashioned façade. It had figures and pillars made of sandstone; everything was dirty, and Hanna could see how the stucco was crumbling off the walls in mangy blotches. Hanna went into the house. The hall had a tiled floor with a pattern of green leaves. Next to the stairs was a black iron cage for the elevator. Hanna pressed all the buttons she could find next to the cage, but the elevator didn't come down. She went up the stairs. The stairwell smelled of hot cooking fat and freshly brewed coffee. On a tarnished bronze nameplate she found the name that Werner's friend had given her. Next to the bronze plate was a metal handle instead of a button for the doorbell. Hanna took it in her hand and raised it. Behind the door a dog immediately began barking, and soon a gray-haired woman opened the door. She had a cigarette in her hand. A dog was rubbing against her legs; it was a brown-and-white-spotted long-haired dog, wriggling and nervous, making short, almost squeaking, yelps. Hanna mentioned the name of her brother. The woman held the dog by the collar and let Hanna in.

The corridor was dark. The gray-haired woman had pointed to a door in the corner. When Hanna opened this door, she saw a high-ceilinged, narrow room with a bed in it, and Werner was lying on the bed. He jumped to his feet as soon as he saw Hanna. He was only half-dressed, but he put on a brightly patterned shirt right away. Hanna unwrapped the wax paper and took out the cake her mother had baked. Werner took only a quick glance at it. He said the landlady's dog liked cake pretty well.

He went with Hanna to the Stadtbahn and rode with her to the station at the Zoological Garden. He sat down with her in an inexpensive restaurant that had tables placed in a row along a passageway in front of a very large window; the window looked out on Joachimtaler Street; cars and people were passing by. Werner invited her to have a meal. In the meantime, he told her that he was no longer an apprentice—with that money he couldn't have paid for his room; he was a transport worker for a big construction firm in Charlottenburg, and that's why he lived in this neighborhood. As he talked he alternately drank cola and brandy. Hanna didn't eat much.

He went with her to a movie near the Gedächtniskirche,[3] where he'd never been with her before. He confidently reached into the right-hand pocket of his black leather jacket to get out some silver coins to lay on the cashier's counter. The film they saw had to do with rich people in Italy who passed their time with drinking, fighting, auto trips, and Catholic miracles.

Afterwards they rode back to Savigny Square. Werner said she might as well stay in his room overnight. Hanna was tired.

Rolf Schneider

Werner drank some more cola and brandy in a cheap tavern that was on their way. In his room he let Hanna sleep in his bed, and he made a place for himself by moving his two armchairs together.

It was bright daylight when Hanna awoke. She was alone in the room. Through the window she could see the sunlight. The door opened and Werner came in, balancing dishes, rolls, and a can of Nescafé on a tray; he put the tray down and opened the window. The air that came through was warm and tasted of sweetish auto exhaust fumes. Somewhere on the other side of the wall a radio was on, very loud; the hurried voice of an announcer could be heard, but they couldn't understand what he was saying. Hanna ate. Werner told her about his job, about the money he was earning; he proudly showed her the little portable television set he had bought.

He wanted to with her to Wannsee.[4] They walked down the street; Werner was carrying a bag with bathing gear. Many windows were open, and through all of them came the hurried voice of the announcer. They came to a street corner. The traffic light was red, they had to wait; next to them, also waiting, was a young man with a small transistor radio, and the hurried voice of the announcer blared from it. This time they could understand. The announcer was reporting excitedly that East Berlin had closed all the border crossings, and that construction workers were busy building a wall around West Berlin. The young man with the radio seemed to pay no attention to the news. Slowly and in a bored manner he was running his hand over his long slicked-down hair. When the traffic light turned green, he slowly sauntered across the street with his transistor radio.

Werner took Hanna's hand and said: Come on.

They turned around and went back to Werner's room. Werner turned on his television set, and a few seconds later the screen had pictures of the border on it. They could see the construction corps of the Army setting up concrete posts and stretching barbed wire between them. Other pictures showed a roadblock across a border street; behind it were men in uniform, and in front of it a crowd of people who were being asked questions by a television reporter; at the opened windows in the East, seen through shaky telephoto lenses, people were standing and staring toward the camera; some of them were waving white cloths.

Werner said: It's goddamned lucky that you're here!

Hanna didn't answer, she stared at the screen. A commentator appeared and, with a sour expression on his face, spewed out a great many malicious words. Werner got a bottle of lukewarm vermouth out of his cupboard; he screwed the cap off and poured glasses full for Hanna and himself. On the screen of his portable television set, the pictures began to repeat themselves. Werner drank his lukewarm vermouth and began to plan a future here for Hanna; she would have to go to Lichterfelde to the reception camp; there would probably be difficulties because she was still a minor; they would have to find some agency, probably a church organization, that could help her; Werner had a lot of practical ideas. Hanna was getting dizzy from the lukewarm vermouth and from Werner's words. Outside the window the sun was shining, and wind blew the curtains.

Of course, you're going to stay, said Werner.

I don't know, said Hanna.

You have to stay, said Werner; after all, you aren't stupid.

He suddenly got the idea of calling up the boss of the construction firm he worked for; the boss was a representative of the Christian Party in the City Parliament of West Berlin, and Werner said he would surely put in a good word for Hanna, especially since it would make a good impression; besides he had the necessary connections. Werner said: "I'm going to the pay telephone on the corner; pour yourself some vermouth if you want some more, and there's a box of candy too." He laughed and waved good-bye and hurriedly left the room.

Hanna sat huddled on Werner's bed. She felt sick to her stomach; besides, she had a feeling that was close to fear. She went to the window. She pulled the curtain aside and looked down at the street. Below there were a few cars parked at the curb. It was still windy and warm. Hanna didn't have a watch with her and couldn't have said whether it was already noon, or later.

She left Werner's room. When she was in the hall, the dog behind one of the doors started barking. She left the apartment. She went down the stairs. She was afraid she might run into Werner but she met no one. She went into the street. On the sidewalk a few children were playing with a red ball. She ran past the row of houses and turned into the first sidestreet.

She had West German money with her, a few silver coins that Werner had given her. She went to a bus stop and got into the first one that came along. She didn't know where she was going. She bought her ticket from a sweating conductor. There were parents sitting in the bus with children dressed in their Sunday clothes. Hanna left the bus after riding for about a quarter of an hour. She found herself at the edge of a public square that she didn't know.

Rolf Schneider

There were trees, bushes, grass; there were a few doves, and there were benches along carefully raked dirt paths.
She sat down on a bench. Up in the sky, several airplanes were circling. She felt like crying, without being able to say exactly why.
She walked through a lot of unknown streets. She soon felt dusty and tired, her feet were beginning to hurt. She finally happened to come to a subway entrance. She went down the steps. The familiar smell of the tunnels encompassed her. At the counter she bought her ticket. The next train that arrived was going north. Hanna checked her route on the map of this line, which hung next to the door. Without being able to give a reason, she wanted to go to Brunnenstrasse. She had to transfer there. She left the train and she left the station. She walked down the street. From far off she could recognize the border; people and vehicles were crowded together, filling the entire street. She went toward the border, walking more and more slowly. People were standing in groups and talking excitedly to each other; policemen with white caps moved among them. Hanna saw she didn't have a chance to get through these groups of people, and then she asked herself also if she even wanted to.

She was sitting on a park bench again, and it was already afternoon. She was hungry. She was wondering if she should go back to Werner. She thought of the narrow room with the blowing curtains and the portable television set. She still liked Werner.
She was standing at a sausage stand. A fat woman in a white smock slowly took, with wooden tongs, a sausage from the smoking grill and put it on a yellow plate; the woman squeezed ketchup out of a transparent plastic bottle onto the sausage, scattered curry powder over it from a can, and added a roll. The stand was under the tracks of an elevated train. The area around the stand was littered with bright yellow paper plates; the trash basket next to the steel pillar of the elevated was filled to overflowing with them. Hanna eagerly devoured the roll. The sausage burned her tongue as she bit into it.
She was sitting at a table on a terrace in front of an ice cream and pastry shop. She was leafing through an illustrated magazine she had bought. In front of her on the table was a glass cup with ice cream and fruit. She didn't eat much of it. She now had three silver mark pieces left. Subtracting the bill for the ice cream it would still be enough for her to go back to Werner.
It was evening when she bought a ticket for the Stadtbahn.

The ticket had red printing on a yellow background; now she had one mark and four pfennigs left, made of yellow metal. She rode to the Westkreuz. She left her train and got into another one in the direction of the Zoological Garden. The coach she sat in was empty, it smelled of stale cigarette smoke. The train entered the station at the Zoological Garden. She had been there with Werner yesterday: She remembered that, and now it seemed to her as if an unbelievably long time lay between. Still nobody came into the compartment. The train went on. It went past the zoo. Hanna saw the skyscrapers with their colorful façades. At the stations there were large advertising posters for ice cream and cigarettes, which she had seen often enough but which she would now be seeing for the last time, if she didn't change her mind. The train came into the Lehrt station. On the platform were some young people staring threateningly at the train as it slowed down and stopped. Hanna bent over so she couldn't be seen through the window. The train pulled out again. The young people on the platform shouted at the moving coaches. Hanna straightened up. Through the window of the moving train she saw warehouses and apartment houses with white walls. She saw the bank of the Spree River. She saw the bridge over the Spree. Her train roared over it. The sun was low in the sky. Hanna recognized the roofs of the Charité Hospital, before the dark mouth of the station entrance at Friedrichsstrasse swallowed the train. Perhaps she still could have turned back, even now—she didn't know. She also didn't deliberate. At the station she saw a lot of men in uniform; most of them were carrying weapons. The train stopped. Hanna pushed the door open. She climbed out, a thin girl of thirteen years, with shoulder-length hair and near-sighted eyes behind her glasses. Some of the uniformed men stared at her, surprised or smiling. She herself went up to the nearest man in uniform, she noticed he had a perspiring and fleshy face, and she told him she wanted to go home.

Notes

[1] A well-known department store chain in West Berlin and West Germany.

[2] A section of West Berlin.

[3] A famous church of West Berlin, left in its half-ruined condition as a memorial to the victims of World War II.

[4] A lake and recreational area by the Havel River.

My Richard

Stefan Heym

Nobody lives in the house anymore. I've heard it's going to be torn down; maybe even the whole street will be cleared—although the border, which comes in diagonally here and swings off at a right angle, touches only this one house.

They sent Richard to the reformatory. I'm allowed to visit him once a week; he tells me then that he's doing all right and that his teachers are satisfied with his work. He's not a troublemaker and never was, but there are hard lines around his mouth that were not there before.

And that hurts me. Because it's basically my fault—I admit that; I didn't bring him up right—I, a longtime party member and widow of a party member, who have always had a position of responsibility; how else could we have been permitted to live in a house right by the border? I didn't watch over him as my duty demanded. Today we have to keep a careful eye on our children; they have learned to say one thing and think another, and they have this distant way about them that's so hard to penetrate, and a smile as if they want to say: "You believe that, Mama, you actually believe those words you're reciting to me?" I should have noticed that he went out too often and came home too late with the boy from downstairs, who also happens to be called Richard—Richard

Edelweiss—and who is a year and a half older than my Richard, but looks younger because he is short and thin and has blond curls and porcelain-blue eyes like his mother. Richard Edelweiss didn't have to go to the reformatory; they took him out of school and put him in the Army. And his father didn't lose his job as manager of the export department of the cosmetics division of the People's United Chemical Works, while I lost a much more important position; but that can be explained by the fact that the divorce had become legal six weeks before our authorities discovered the repeated violations of the border regulations, and Herr Edelweiss was no longer responsible for the education and conduct of his son Richard. I should have been aware that my Richard, together with Richard Edelweiss, was leading a double life; I should have looked into his stories of how he passed his evenings. As the judge explained, parents, especially those who are party members of long standing, should always keep in touch with their children's teachers and also with the German Youth Federation at school; she told me that if I had done that, I would have soon found out that my son had not attended the Youth meetings as he should have and that he also was not in the Biology Study Group or the Russian Study Group, but somewhere else entirely.

I didn't investigate. I trusted Richard. Or, when I think it over now, with hindsight, I realize I didn't want to question him, for fear that I would make him have that certain smile and that certain tone in his voice which showed that a curtain had been drawn between me and my own child. When I think it over now, I feel that I had a sort of premonition when the young man walked into my office and said, "Frau Zunk?" In any case, I'm sure that I wasn't so surprised as I should have been. I guessed right away what office the young man had come from—it may have been also the way he held himself: he acted a little too casual.

"We don't want to worry you unnecessarily, Frau Zunk," he said, as he moved a chair in front of my desk and sat down. "But your son won't be coming home from school today."

"Where is Richard?" I asked shrilly and was startled at the tone of my voice.

"We had to take him into custody."

I thought of Richard when he was three years old and had diptheria and couldn't breathe and the doctor had to make an incision in his neck. My heart was convulsed now as it was then. "Has something happened to him?"

"Happened? Why?" He crossed his legs. "We had him taken

out of the schoolroom, and he went along very nicely. I can assure you he is doing very well under the circumstances."

"But what did he do wrong?"

He acted as if he didn't hear me. "Can you tell me, Frau Zunk," he inquired, "where you were the night before last, between 7 and 11 o'clock?"

"Night before last?" He had said "under the circumstances," but what did that mean? "Of course I know where I was the night before last."

"Well?"

There had been a Women's Alliance meeting on Monday; on Tuesday a Union leadership meeting—discussion of the contract for the industrial collective—evening before last, that was Wednesday . . . "Wednesday was German-Soviet Friendship Society, a film about the cotton harvest in the Soviet Usbek Republic, and one of our women told about her trip to Moscow . . ."

He was bored. "Did you come home from your office before you went to the German-Soviet Friendship meeting?"

"No," I said guiltily. "I went straight to the meeting. You see, there was an officers' meeting before the film, and I am vice-chairperson, and if I had gone home first I would have been late for the meeting. So I had already told Richard that morning that he should make his own supper and wash the dishes. Yes, that's what I told him."

"And did he tell you anything about his plans for the evening?"

"He said he might go down to see Richard—you know, the boy from downstairs, his friend, is called Richard too . . ."

"Yes, I know," he said, "Richard Edelweiss. And then you came home from your German-Soviet Friendship meeting—when was that?"

"Shortly after 11, I think."

"And when you came home from your meeting, where was your son Richard then?"

"In his room," I said. "He was just getting undressed. He didn't steal anything, did he?"

"Did he mention where he'd been that evening?"

"I assumed that he was with Richard, the Richard from downstairs; they often listened to records for hours—that terrible howling—but they like it, it's a different generation, sometimes I'm really frightened, but he didn't do anything, did he—anything violent?"

"It's not a question of wrongdoing of that type," said the young man and he emphasized "of that type" as if robbery and acts of violence were beneath him—small fry. Then he stood up. "Put on your coat." And when he noticed that I was opening a desk drawer, he said, "Please leave everything the way it was."

I was too numb to protest. He used my telephone, cupping the mouthpiece as he talked. Scarcely had he put down the receiver before the door opened, and Comrade Otter, the Party Secretary, and Comrade Dr. Wieland, assistant manager of the factory, hurried in, both rather breathlessly, as if on cue. Comrade Dr. Wieland said: "I am informing you, Comrade Zunk, that you are for the present relieved of your post as head of the purchasing department; your salary continues until a final decision is made." Comrade Otter looked at me with concern: I wished he'd had something to say—basically he was a well-meaning person who understood people's problems—but Comrade Otter just shook his head.

A car was waiting downstairs. A stranger got in and sat down next to me; the young man who had come up and talked to me sat in the front next to the driver. During the whole trip I saw only the back of his neck and his shirt collar, which was wet with sweat. I would have liked to know where they were taking me, but I didn't dare to ask; under the circumstances, how well could things be going for Richard where he was now?

The car stopped; they had brought me home. The men jumped out; the one who had spoken with me in my office took me by the arm as if he wanted to help me over the puddle that the rain had left in the street that morning; but he didn't let go of my arm even after I had stepped over the puddle. The entrance door was open; I got a very brief glimpse of Frau Edelweiss in front of her apartment door—her face was pasty gray, her eyes wide open from fear. The two men led me upstairs. Richard's room and mine were both full of people, several of them in uniform. The rooms looked as if they had been searched and then carefully put in order again. A photographer was taking pictures the way they do in the movies when there's a murder. A man who had a build like my Richard's took off his jacket and climbed through the window of Richard's room and jumped onto the roof of the garage in which Herr Edelweiss still kept his Polski Fiat and walked to the edge of the roof and acted as if he were going to jump over the barbed-wire fence into the Western Zone, and each of his movements were photographed. On this side of the fence several border guards were having their dogs look for scents. On the other side, clearly visible between the trees, the Western police were standing watching what was going on, and an American soldier kept look- ing at us through a telescope, and I thought: 'Oh, my God, they caught Richard trying to run away from East Germany, but why had the young man just told me that they'd had him taken out of the schoolroom and that he had gone along very nicely?' And then something began to hum in my head. I heard my own sobbing and my despairing cries: "I want my son! I want to see my son!" The young man who had talked to me in my office hurried to me and said: "Get hold of yourself, Comrade," but I sensed that he was bewildered because the representatives of authority are probably not used to being shouted at.

They had me lie down and rest on the couch in my room. I watched them through my half-closed eyelids; they were like fig- ures in a play, making odd motions, and I heard one of them say: "It's pretty clear now," and another answered pensively: "I'd just like to find out how long that's been going on," and a third voice prophesied: "It'll all come out, don't worry," and somebody handed me a cup of coffee and asked if I could answer a few questions for him, and I said I thought I could.

He was an elderly man with rather bent shoulders; the one who had come to my office treated him with deference. "You don't have to stand up, Frau Zunk, if you don't want to," the older man said. I took a swallow and said that I would soon feel better and wondered if I couldn't perhaps find out what my Richard had done that was so wrong that so many people had to be concerned about it.

He raised his graying eyebrows. "I can't tell you anything about that until we are through with the investigation and know who else is involved in the case and how far it's gone. They tell me you've been in the Party a long time. So you know that the antifas- cist protective wall which we had to build between our Republic and the territory of West Berlin is not to be taken lightly."

I sat up. "Has he—has Richard tried to get over . . ."

"Tried? . . .'Tried' is a very mild expression for what we suspect." He suddenly broke off; perhaps he thought he had al- ready revealed too much. "And now," he said coldly, almost with hostility, "What friends does your son have besides the boy from downstairs, this Richard Edelweiss?"

He questioned me for what seemed to be a very long time. The questions concerned many different topics. Often, as far as I could tell, they had no connection with each other and not even my life or Richard's or the crime that Richard was supposed to have committed. Twice I had to ask my interrogator to pause so that I could go to the bathroom; the second time I went I threw up and stayed so long that he knocked on the door and wanted to know whether something was wrong and whether I needed help. I said "no" and came out of the bathroom with thick beads of sweat on my forehead, and shortly after that he said that it would perhaps be enough for today, and that I should be ready in case they had more questions, and that I should also not leave the Potsdam district without informing them. The technicians had packed their things and had left; the young man who had come to my office gave me a telephone number "in case you wish to give us additional information if someone shows up who wants to get in contact with your son."

And then I was alone.

I went to the kitchen and forced myself to eat a piece of bread and butter. I went into Richard's room and stroked the teddy bear, with half of its hair worn off, that he had always cuddled when he was a baby. I went downstairs and out into the garden. They had trampled the grass and flower beds. A piece of rope hung from the steel hook at the corner of the garage roof. Frau Edelweiss saw me through her kitchen window and came out, her eyes swollen from crying, and embraced me; her Richard had also been taken into custody, and she was expecting the worst.

The arrival of the Polski Fiat interrupted us. Herr Edelweiss got out of the car accompanied by a chubby man with a rosy face. Herr Edelweiss immediately began heaping reproaches on his wife: The whole trouble was caused by her carelessness and flightiness—no wonder the boy was getting in trouble. "But I," he proclaimed, "am not going to be drawn into this! The court gave you custody of Richard, my dear, and it's all your responsibility." He became aware of my presence and quickly added: "That doesn't mean I'm turning away from the boy. I know what I owe our son, even if you, my dear, apparently don't." And with a gesture toward the man accompanying him: "That's why I asked my friend and lawyer, Dr. Kahn, for help."

Dr. Kahn shook hands with Frau Edelweiss and me and lowered himself into a wobbly lawn chair. With his somewhat bulging eyes directed at us he remarked: "I've had cases like this before. Ah, these young people . . ." He laughed abruptly. "Yearning for adventure, for new horizons . . ." and then, turning serious: "Unfortunately we can't do much until the official investigation is concluded and we know the charges against . . . What's the boy's name?"

"Richard," said Frau Edelweiss and I simultaneously.

"Frau Zunk is the mother of that other boy that I told you about," explained Herr Edelweiss, "who has this unfortunate influence on our Richard."

"He does not!" I protested.

Dr. Kahn broke out in laughter again. I found his noisy merriment uncalled-for, but when he casually brought up the question of whether I wouldn't like to entrust the defense of my Richard to him, I said "yes" with a feeling of happy relief; I warned him of course that I didn't have much money.

He dismissed this difficulty with a shrug of his shoulders: "Let's hear what the two ladies know about the affair."

It turned out that Frau Edelweiss knew even less than I. The authorities had stopped questioning her as soon as they discovered that her statements were wildly contradictory. At first they had tried to settle her down: "You didn't quite understand us," they said, and reformulated their questions, but that only made Frau Edelweiss more befuddled. Her poor brain was still in a whirl, and the reproaches of her divorced husband made things even worse now and brought more tears. "Leave her alone," said Dr. Kahn, and with a wink to me: "According to what you've told me, Frau Zunk, I gather that the authorities really believe they're on to something big. That's understandable too, considering the location"—he pointed to the garage and the fence—"and apparently they are wondering whether Richard 1 and Richard 2 might not be involved in some bad business."

"But that's crazy," I said. "My Richard . . ."

He folded his hands over his stomach. "You wouldn't believe how little the parents often know about their children."

"But I certainly would have noticed something like that," I said uncertainly.

"With your very busy social life?"

He left unmentioned precisely what type of social life might have kept Frau Edelweiss from being concerned with her son.

I led a strange existence during the weeks that followed. Fits of anxiety alternated with periods of complete numbness. I tried to read, but couldn't concentrate on anything. I left the radio on all day—East, West, no difference. In the evening I caught myself staring into space with no idea of what I was looking at. I could only sleep with the aid of drugs. I didn't have any family who might have helped; an old aunt inÜckermünde and a few distant cousins in Erfurt were scarcely people I could turn to. I discovered how few friends I had. At first Frau Edelweiss still visited me, but there was scarcely anything we could talk about except the case and about her Richard and mine, and both of us soon had the feeling that we were getting on each other's nerves. Twice I was visited by unobtrusive men who said they had a few more questions. The questions were more of a technical type and didn't permit me to draw any conclusions about the fate of my Richard or the nature of his offense. Once Comrade Otter, the Party Secretary at the factory, appeared, and asked how I was doing and whether I needed anything. He stayed about half an hour. The conversation faltered. Then he murmured an excuse and left.

The next day the doorbell rang again in the urgent way that I was already acquainted with, and I thought it was the investigators again, but it was Dr. Kahn. He laughed: "You probably weren't expecting me?"

"But please come in," I said.

"I have my car downstairs," he said. "Get ready, Frau Zunk—we're going to take a ride and visit your Richard."

The visitor's room was painted gray-green; a tinted photograph of the Council President hung on the wall. Richard sat across from me; he was pale and blinked nervously. The uniformed guard at the end of the table acted as if the matter had nothing to do with him. Dr. Kahn breathed heavily at intervals or laughed to himself.

"I'm so glad that you came, Mama," said Richard.

"Is it very bad?" I asked. "I mean—it all came so suddenly."

"You get used to it after a while," he said. "I'm in a cell with another boy."

"Not with Richard?"

"No."

"How's the food?" I asked. "Are you eating enough?"

"It's not like home," he said.

I felt stupid asking these questions.

"Mama," he said, "I didn't do anything bad."

The guard looked up. "You're not allowed to talk about the case."

"Richard," I said, "the Comrade here is Dr. Kahn, your lawyer."

"Everything will be all right, Richard," said Dr. Kahn cheerfully. "Just keep telling the truth."

"I'm sorry I'm causing so much trouble," said Richard. "I guess it was a stupid thing to do—but it was so much fun . . ."

"What was?" I asked.

"If you talk about the case," said the guard, "I'll have to take the prisoner back to his cell."

'The prisoner,' I thought, and asked: "Do you get enough sleep too, Richard?"

"Yes, now I do." He hesitated. "At first the light bothered me. It's not a strong bulb, but it's on all the time."

"You're not allowed to talk about the conditions of imprisonment," said the guard.

"I brought you a few pieces of cake, Richard," I said. "Strawberry torte, you've always liked that. And socks and underwear. They promised you can have them."

"Mama . . ."

"Yes, Richard?" Suddenly he looked so small, still so much like a child. "What did you want to tell me?"

He put his hands to his forehead, his shoulders heaved. Then he let his hands sink. "Do you know that I've learned to roll cigarettes, Mama?" He smiled. "Even with one hand!"

"Time's up," said the guard.

Richard stood up. He took a step as if he wanted to take refuge in my arms, but the table was between us and it's also possible that I misunderstood his movement. Dr. Kahn patted Richard on his back and said he would come to visit him soon and then they would talk about the case, and Richard said, "yes," that he would like to talk with Dr. Kahn about it, but he didn't know when he would be allowed to.

"Keep your chin up, Richard," I said.

He nodded and left through the door at the rear of the room.

I wonder where they get the light bulbs for the corridors of our courthouses. These bulbs light up little more than their own filaments, and the people in front of the doors to the courtrooms look like shadows of the dead who are waiting for entrance into some underworld. The typed notice at the right of the door could scarcely be read: "*Legal proceedings against Edelweiss, Richard and Zunk, Richard,*" I deciphered, "*because of repeated violations of border regulations.*" Frau Edelweiss gripped my hand, her fingernails dug into my flesh. "Violations of border regulations," she said, completely shaken, " . . . repeatedly." Herr Edelweiss was absent; he had to attend a management meeting of the cosmetics division of the People's United Chemical Works, and since he was no longer legally responsible for his son he had no valid reason not to attend his meeting.

The thought that I would see Richard again made me happy; he would look at us and I would give him an encouraging smile. But my worries were greater than my joys. As a longtime party member I knew how the Comrades react to things like repeated violations of border regulations by the son of another Comrade: We have our Workers' State and we demand that our laws and our borders be respected, especially by the children of Comrades; when a sixteen-year-old puts himself above the law, what—and where—will he be when he is twenty-five, and what kind of an example is he for other young people?

Then the familiar laughter. "Ladies," Dr. Kahn announced, "the waiting is over." The shadow figures in the corridor turned their heads. He lowered his voice. "I know the judge, she is a sensible person. If the boys just follow my advice and show a little repentance . . ."

The door to the courtroom opened. Frau Edelweiss went first, I followed her, then Dr. Kahn. Two little old women, dressed as if they were going to a funeral—probably retirees who spend their spare time on the visitor's benches of courtrooms—were just being ushered out by the bailiff. The prosecuting attorney, still youthful, hair thinning, nodded with a solemnly formal expression first at Dr. Kahn and then at two men who had sat down in the first of the four rows of seats for the spectators. I recognized the back of the neck of the one man and the slightly bent shoulders of the other. Dr. Kahn went to a small table at the left of the judge's bench and put down his briefcase; the prosecuting attorney was leafing through some papers. At this moment my Richard stepped through the narrow door behind the table of the prosecuting attorney. I could tell that he had seen me. He turned to Richard Edelweiss, who looked even thinner than usual, and took hold of his hand. I was so engrossed in this little gesture that Frau Edelweiss had to give me a push to remind me to stand up when the presiding judge and her two fellow judges entered. The judge glanced about her courtroom; she had a figure similar to mine, wore her hair pinned up in back like me, and her eyes had an expression which I had also noticed in myself—an expression of withdrawal which develops as the great hopes of youth gradually fade away. She looked at me briefly, then sat down.

There were lengthy introductory formalities. I had eyes only for Richard. He seemed to have grown since my visit—or was it because his face had lost all its childlike qualities in the few weeks? He reminded me of his father as a young man. His father and I had never had enough time for each other; his father dedicated all his energy to the socialist cause.

The reading of the accusation by the prosecuting attorney brought me back to the present. He mentioned our young people, of whom an overwhelming majority had a positive attitude toward the goals and achievements of socialism, and desired nothing more earnestly than to help in the attainment of still greater objectives. Then he spoke of the antifascist protective wall as a bulwark in the battle against imperialism, and how an overwhelming majority of our youth was proving by word and deed that they could completely understand and appreciate its importance— which, however, was *not* the case with the two defendants. He read off a series of dates, fourteen in all, on which the defendants, in full knowledge of the illegality of their actions, had crossed said antifascist protective wall in both directions, always at the same location, namely behind the garage that belonged to the dwelling shared by the respective parents. To do which they had to observe the guard who was watching this section of the wall, and had to, by stealth, avoid the technical devices which were supposed to alert the guard, and in such fashion deliberately violated paragraphs such and such of the penal code of the Republic. They had even gone so far as to boast of their deeds to the representatives of the capitalistic Western press, and in so doing exposed the laws and institutions of our Republic to ridicule and poured water on the mill wheels of imperialist propaganda, as apparent from Exhibit A of the prosecution. The youthfulness of the defendants—one not yet sixteen, the other under eighteen—did not prevent them from spinning a web of sophisticated lies in order to deceive their parents, their teachers, their German Youth officials. Further incriminating evidence was the fact that neither of the two ever thought of informing the appropriate authorities of the existence of the route used by them, which fact increased the danger that others who intended to cross the border illegally might employ the same tried and proven way—and who knows whether some had not already done so. In consideration of all of which, there was no doubt that the law must be applied in all severity. "Only thus," concluded the prosecutor, "can these two misguided youths again become useful members of our socialist society." And he wiped the perspiration from his nose and sat down.

Fourteen times—I thought—fourteen times into the West and back; that meant crossing the border twenty-eight times. *Twenty-eight times* my son could have been shot, I thought to myself, and could have bled to death in the no-man's-land between two worlds, and I had no suspicion of it. Frau Edelweiss, I could see, was tugging at her handkerchief. Perhaps a similar thought had gone through her mind; but I didn't have the heart to ask her, and in any case her thoughts were never very precise.

The judge called the first witness: the younger of the two men who had questioned me. He stepped forward and stood before the judge's bench, with his weight on his right foot, his left foot slightly forward. In this position, the perfect image of a detective from a TV show, he reported on the technical side of the repeated violations of border regulations. His testimony sounded very complex, and yet the point of it was that actually anyone who was young and nimble, and possessed a strong rope of the right length, and knew the intervals at which the guard passed, and avoided the field of vision of the man in the nearby watchtower, could have done the deed.

His superior, who followed him to the witness stand, spoke in more general terms: according to his experience, crossings of this type occurred only rarely as individual cases; the individual violator of border regulations was usually in contact with others who had similar intentions, and even when there was no organization involved at the beginning, groups and bands soon developed; and of course, as was well-known, the youthful thirst for adventure is often exploited by certain elements; herein lies the greatest danger, and therefore this case must be regarded in a much more serious light than might seem necessary upon superficial consideration.

Dr. Kahn's face beamed beneficence. "In your investigation, Comrade, you did pay special attention to this point?"

"Of course."

"And did you find any proof that the boys had such contacts or that such an organization existed?"

Richard raised his head. I wanted to smile at him, but my lips were frozen.

Stefan Heym

In the meantime an exchange of words developed between the witness and Dr. Kahn, which seemed to displease the judge. Finally Dr. Kahn pointed his fat finger at the witness and said with a short laugh: "Is my finding correct or not, that you did not become aware of the matter at all until the West Berlin newspaper clipping, which now has been presented to the court as Exhibit A of the prosecution, reached your desk?"

The judge cautioned that the witness could not be compelled to reveal the investigatory methods of the agencies concerned.

"Comrade Judge," said Dr. Kahn, "could we have Exhibit A read aloud?"

The judge turned to the prosecutor: "Do you have any objections?"

I can still see the prosecuting attorney taking the piece of printed paper out of its cellophane wrapping. I can still hear the voice with which he read the excerpt, and his repressed anger, but also the mocking undertone of the article itself. Richard E. and Richard Z., it said, both sons of Socialist Unity Party functionaries, both residents of the small city of D. near the border of West Berlin, had made a habit of crossing the border to visit the West. Richard Z., 15 years old, said it was child's play to cross the wall where they did; Richard E., 17 years old, added that they had first been a little afraid, but now it was "like climbing over the fence into the neighbor's yard." They indicated that the life in West Berlin pleased them, but that they didn't intend to stay in the West. They said that their parents knew nothing about their excursions over the border; shrugging their shoulders the boys had explained: "They wouldn't understand, of course . . ."

'Wouldn't understand, of course,' I thought. Hadn't I always patiently answered Richard's questions? Hadn't I always explained everything to him—how he was born from my body and how he got there, about history, about the origins of human society, about revolution, about Germany, and about the barbed wire fence that stood behind our house? And he had listened to me. But in the course of the years his way of listening to me had changed, and that certain expression of his face had appeared and that curling of the lips, although he still answered: "Yes, Mama," and "Of course, Mama."

"Well, Richard?" said the judge.

Both boys stood up.

The judge specified: "Richard Zunk."

The young Edelweiss sat down again, visibly relieved.
"You knew, of course, Richard, that it is against the law to go over the Wall into West Berlin?"
Richard lowered his head.
"Then just tell us once in your own words why you two did it."
"We wanted to go to the movies."
"And did you go?"
"Yes."
"Fourteen times?"
"Yes."
"Go on and tell me what else happened to you over there."
"When we went over the last time, a few Western Police saw us and wanted to know whether we came from the East. And we . . . we said "yes." They asked us whether we wanted to stay in the West, and we said "no," and then they asked what we wanted to do, and we told them . . ."
"Yes? Go on."
"Then they laughed. And then one of them said he knew somebody who undoubtedly would like to hear our story, and when we came out of the movies this man was there and asked us questions and treated us to curry-sausages and cola, but we didn't really trust him and we didn't tell him much."
The judge played with her ballpoint pen.
"Richard!" said the prosecutor.
Richard gave a start.
"So you two went over there fourteen times and fourteen times you went to the movies. Always in the same theater?"
"Yes."
"How did you pay for the tickets?"
"When we said that we only had East German money, the cashier called her boss, and he looked at our identification cards and said we didn't need to pay."
"And did you enjoy it?"
Richard distrustfully kept silent. He had recognized the trap which the prosecuting attorney was setting for him. If he answered with a "no," then how did it happen that we went to the movies in West Berlin again and again?—and if he said "yes," where did that leave the repentant attitude that he was supposed to show?
Finally he straightened up. "Yes, we did," he said very calmly, "it was fun for us to go over the Wall and to look around

Stefan Heym

over there. It was so . . . I don't know . . . different . . ."

'O, my God,' I thought, 'the boy is talking himself into disaster.'

The judge announced the verdict.

The defendants were led away, first Richard Edelweis, then my Richard. The judge stepped down from the bench and came to me and Frau Edelweiss and spoke about the guilt that we also shared, and hesitated a moment and then said something about time passing of course, and about how the experience can only be beneficial to our sons, whether they go into the Army or the reformatory. The prosecutor, I saw, walked up to Dr. Kahn, and they shook hands like two professional boxers—it has been a fair bout, no hard feelings.

The judge found nothing more to say.

Then suddenly the familiar laughter, and Dr. Kahn's somewhat rough voice said: "If I had been in your place, Comrade Prosecutor, I would have requested a medal for the two boys."

"Why should you do that?" said the prosecutor.

"Because, as is now officially established in the court record, they proved their absolute loyalty to our Republic not once, but fourteen times."

The prosecutor smiled wryly. Then he turned and left.

How the Jungle Soldiers Became Sons of Heaven

Eduard Claudius

It was a pleasant evening on the veranda of the newly built bungalow hotel of Dien Bien Phu and the wind was like a soft hand on our faces. The flow of words had slackened. We were tired from all the things we had seen during the day—the new rubber plantation, the planting of ricinus seedlings so that we in the German Democratic Republic would have enough of the medicinal oil from them, the many stables, the pole villages of the Tho with their banana-leaf roofs—and the conversation wasn't very lively.

Near us were some goats, quite small and dark brown, hopping around and adding their bleats to the increasingly loud evening chorus of the cicadas; we were suddenly curious because we remembered having seen large number of goats all day long—a rarity for Vietnam—and asked: "Is the People's Army starting to raise goats?"

The Commissioner of Military Property, a former officer—slim, emaciated, with thin lips and slanting eyes—smiled, and the soldiers sitting around also couldn't suppress a smile.

"They are raised for the gods," said the Commissioner.

"Oh, I see . . . for the gods."

We apparently looked dumbfounded, because he laughed loudly and continued: "If anything unexpected happens, a misfortune or a disease, they get their heads chopped off and are sacrificed to the gods at the house altar, and, according to the old ritual, people jump between the horns as part of the ceremony.'' ''And that's supposed to help? It's just mumbo jumbo; such things go on, even nowadays?''

The Commissioner's face became serious and he asked: ''Can a person change by words what only life itself will change by its wisdom?'' He obviously did not expect an answer. But suddenly the humorous twinkle was in his eyes again and he said: ''Listen . . . I remember a story . . .''

One of the soldiers with a rather grumpy look said something in Vietnamese, but the Commissioner just laughed and said in French: ''Why shouldn't we tell him? After all, he's our friend!'' Turning to me he continued: ''Ah, yes . . . superstition . . . None of us would have believed that it could go so far, and nobody would have imagined even in his dreams that superstition would become a political weapon of the enemy. Listen . . .

''When we came out of the mountains after our first victories over the forward positions of the French and moved down the valleys, it was mainly the Tay who fled from their villages.[1] And it wasn't an isolated case. Every time we came to a village it was already empty, although the fireplaces were still warm and the chickens, pigs, and goats were still running around. It was not a simple problem. We needed rice and meat. But what had we done wrong; what could have made them so afraid of us? We hadn't done anything wrong, not a thing! We were strictly forbidden to touch even a stalk of grain in the fields or steal a chicken, let alone have anything to do with the girls. As the gods are my witness, that would have meant a dishonorable discharge from the Army. Our soldiers were disciplined; they didn't chase the chickens, even in the empty villages, and they couldn't look at the girls, since they had left the villages and there was just no opportunity. So there had to be a different reason. But what was it?

''One day we came upon an old Tay, a gray-haired, dignified man, who was perhaps too proud to run away from us in such haste. They brought him to headquarters. He held his hands in front of his eyes, peeked through his fingers, and only after we had given him tea and tobacco and a glass of brandy did he dare to say a word.

'' 'Sons of the Devil,' he said and repeated: 'Sons of the Devils.' Then he asked for a second glass of brandy and continued more courageously: 'You are devils—devils from the underworld . . .'

''We listened attentively. There was and still is much superstition here. You've already seen the large number of goats. We went to a great deal of trouble before we finally got the old man to tell us what was really wrong. Then we started laughing, and laughed until our stomachs hurt, although it was a bitterly and desperately serious matter, since an army just can't live in a hostile vacuum. Our good behavior toward women, the strict orders against all excesses, and our soldiers' close adherence to these orders, had been used by the French for a clever propaganda campaign against the army of liberation.

"The old man—more talkative because of the liquor—stammered out the words: 'Between your legs . . . there isn't what all normal men have—nothing . . . nothing . . . You are sons of the Devil and you come to destroy us . . . If you were human beings, how could you scorn our pretty girls this way?—and also the old rule of hospitality that says that the guest should spend the night with his host's prettiest daughter.'"

"Does this rule still hold good today?" we quickly asked.

But the Commissioner didn't answer and went on with his story: "It was hard to find a way to show them that we were normal human beings. We would have preferred to work out a regular battle plan. We thought and thought and finally found a way, or so we believed.

"It wasn't far to the next village. A unit was ordered to sneak up to the village, guided by the old man, and at dawn to take a bath in the brook close by, in full view of the village. Naked, of course!

"And that's what they did. It must have been a funny scene—this company of naked, skinny soldiers, splashing like puppies in the brook, each of them convinced that the whole village was watching from the bushes around them. The girls too!

"But what did we gain from this? Not very much. When the soldiers, dressed and sparkling clean, walked up to the houses with big smiles on their faces, they found them all empty. Except for the chickens and the slowest pigs.

"It was like a slap in the face for us, and the old man grumbled: 'What did that prove anyway? Of course you looked like other men, but . . . can't that be a trick of the Devil too?'

"We thought it over again, and realized that we had to really bite into this sour apple. We picked out a young man from the delta region who was quite handsome and decided that he would be asked to court and marry a Tay girl in the conventional manner.

"He said he was willing: 'I'll do it . . . I'll do it!' After all, the Tay girls are very pretty.

"With the help of the old man the necessary steps were taken and the young man certainly contributed his part since he was really a good-looking, energetic type. It's also possible that he just happened to pick the village girl with the greatest curiosity and perhaps also . . ., but be that as it may—on the morning after the wedding night the couple's hut was surrounded, and when the young woman came out, she was bombarded with questions. She answered blushingly that everything was all right, really all right, and that even if the young man turned out to be a son of the Devil, she wouldn't care.

"Happy and relieved, we teased the young man and asked him how sour his apple had been, and he laughed and answered that it wasn't sour at all, but a sweet, really sweet apple of paradise.

"But everything was not really settled until the news spread through all the Tay villages that the girl was pregnant. Of course, our order to avoid the Tay girls had to be reaffirmed and repeated again and again, because the battle against the French had been won."

"And the soldier," we asked, "did he get a decoration? He was worth more by himself than a whole division!"

At first the Commissioner looked at me in a perplexed way, but then he laughed heartily and answered: "No, not yet! But we should really correct this oversight, although you have to admit that it wasn't hard for him to win the battle."

The soldiers around us—all of them still in uniform the way they had come in from the jungle, with dark brown faces, broad cheekbones and lips, wiry black hair, wearing sandals made from old automobile tires—all of them laughed. Only one looked sourly and disapprovingly at the Commissioner.

We pointed at him and said: "He seems unhappy that he didn't get that battle assignment."

When the interpreter had translated, the soldier laughed too, and I added: "I don't mean because of the job, but because of the decoration, which he certainly would have been glad to get!"

Then he reverted to his glum and disapproving tone, and said: "That's nonsense! What a crazy story, anyway! By the gods, such stories are almost always just a pack of lies!"

Notes

[1]The events of this story take place at various times during the period of 1946–1954 when the Vietnamese fought against the French occupation, which ended with the defeat of the French at Dien Bien Phu. The Tay mentioned here are tribesmen living in certain border areas of Vietnam.

A Judgment Worthy of Solomon

Karl Mundstock

The amiable Guy de Maupassant, in one of his masterly short stories written a century ago, told a tale of entanglement like the one reported here. There are stories that repeat themselves in every new period but under circumstances that are different in every case. Although I do not by any means pretend to equal the charm of the Chevalier de Maupassant, I still feel compelled, for the sake of truth, to record these occurrences. I am no more than their chronicler, and though French *esprit* is lacking, I think a touch of German buffoonery will suffice.

In a villa of old Pankow[1] that lies nestled between a bushy lawn and an arbored area, there lives, in the second story on the right, a young mother who is single and who is never going to marry. Every morning we can see Fräulein Viola leading her four pixies to kindergarten and see her return in the evening like a good mother hen with her brood. She works as a seamstress in the nationalized domestic service organization and earns good money since she, like many not-too-bright people, has skillful fingers and has developed an elementary cleverness in the conduct of her own affairs.

Fräulein Viola's boyfriends are of the type that spend most of their time in high-security national sanatoria.[2] When they are released they pay discreet visits to the homes of fellow citizens during the nighttime hours when these citizens are absent, and they manage to take with them some very expensive items as mementos of the hospitality they have enjoyed. Usually there would be one of Fräulein Viola's admirers living outside the sanatorium gates while the others were restoring their damaged nerves under the care of attendants skilled in curative treatment, in well-kept cells. Altogether there were three who regularly, insofar as their schedules permitted, bestowed their favors upon the Fräulein, and with substantial success, as the first three baby boys proved. Our chronicler does not relate whether any other patients had a share in the successes of these three. Fräulein Viola has a rather blank face that was not pretty and not ugly. She has broad, soft, full lips and broadly-spaced, slanted, moist eyes over prominent cheekbones. Perhaps that is what did it.

The three boyfriends specialized in different branches of their many-faceted trade. They knew each other but only superficially, as is common in the widely scattered membership of a tradesmen's guild. They would meet each other occasionally in the treatment rooms and on the grounds of the sanatoria and would discuss their professional experiences insofar as the strict program of treatment would allow. Fräulein Viola was also a topic of discussion. Each one expressed his admiration for her qualities but carefully concealed the fact that he himself had the benefit of them. She had convinced each of them that he alone was the chosen one and that he mustn't say a word if he didn't want to endanger her love for him. Because—and she would say this with a lisping voice and downcast eyes—she was very shy and sensitive and would never recover if her intimate feelings were whispered about and if a malicious tongue should report them back to her, perhaps even with all sorts of embellishments. He should also not forget how such gossip about the secrets of love can make people angry and envious, and how he might unwillingly create rivals and thus be responsible for tearing down the relationship with his own hands or, rather, with his own tongue. How much happy love has already been destroyed by thoughtless men, Viola said with a sigh.

As long as only three tokens of requited love were present, and each of the three fathers could definitely say which one was his, the affair continued without complications. The Fräulein knew how to reconcile each one with the other two strangers by assuring him that her true love belonged to him and to no one else. Only her longing for him during his long absence had caused her to go astray. In her imagination, he had been the one sleeping with her, and it was just as if he had also planted the seeds that produced the other offspring. Even if he wasn't their father in the flesh he was so in spirit. The three were satisfied with this; they enjoyed their blissful state without the pangs of jealousy and cared for their family with the money that they got from the sale of the property they acquired, and left something for Viola to use during their abstemious periods of straw-widowhood. As sensible men, each forgave her in advance for her subsequent amorous indiscretions, but each pleaded with her to cherish him as her dearest and to avoid mistakes that might bear future consequences. Everything would have been settled and in the best of order, but then all three got a leave at about the same time from the P. P. Pen,[3] as these state-run curative institutions are officially called.

Through an exchange of letters that was regular but very limited due to curative constraints, Fräulein Viola found out the dates on which she could expect her husbands to return, and made the necessary preparations. She knew what would happen because she knew her men. Although otherwise weak in mental arithmetic, she now made exact calculations and set up a calendar of events. After their release, each of the men took a job for the sake of appearances but devoted himself at nights to his old profession; after all, he wanted to be sure the family was provided for when the time came for him to return for another cure. Fräulein Viola had to take care that her men's professional activities were coordinated in such a way that, robust as she was, she would be able to satisfy all three without any of them discovering his cuckoldry. So each of the three considered himself the rightful lord and master. The fruit of their mutual endeavors was soon evident. All three believed themselves to be the father of the future little girl or boy, whom they saw pressing against the walls of its tiny dungeon, before, one after the other, they had to leave once more to take up residence in their accustomed hostelry, and thus freed Viola from her predicament for the moment.

The resident physician prescribed for them, in order to strengthen their nerves, the pasting together of paper bags. The activity brought them together in the same room during the day. Their locations permitted them to exchange glances and signals and occasionally to whisper a few words unobtrusively. For in the treatment rooms of those sanatoria, the attendants pay strict attention that no one talks, because too much talk is dangerous for the health. But the three eventually had a chance to draw closer to each other in sorrow and joy, and one of them began to tell about his present and past delights as a father. After all, such reveling in former and future amorous exploits is often the only consolation during the rigorous program of rehabilitation. In order to dramatize the number of his successful forays on the day of conception the narrator had to call upon the fingers of both hands. His two co-fathers grew pale, they felt dizzy, and the floor trembled under their feet. After they had gotten hold of themselves, they reported their own procreative exploits, and they too needed more than one hand. Each time a finger was raised, the rivals felt a pang in their heart. None believed the others. They accused each other of lying; they were at the point of coming to blows. Yet, in these institutions, whose hospitality is extended to a negligibly small, select group, the wisest of laws prevail and hinder jealous people from cutting each other's throats. One can indeed say that the life of our citizens is nowhere better protected. But for an ordinary mortal it is almost impossible to gain access.

Writing, which truly has caused enough misery for mankind, is also restricted there to such an extent and so wisely regulated that any harmful effect is practically out of the question. The first of the three who had his turn to communicate with Viola used the opportunity to beg her to announce straightforwardly who the father of the child was. She was gracious enough to admit what this *Dummkopf* wanted to hear; in detail and touchingly she reminded him of the circumstances under which he had become a father. He could scarcely wait until he could meet his companions again and hold the letter under their noses and overwhelm them with the truth. But both of his accomplices in fatherhood had nothing on their minds but extracting the same admission from their dear Viola when they in turn had permission to write. They too received such gripping reminders of the day and hour, as well as the circumstances, of their fatherhood, that no doubt remained whose child it was. The three fathers requested paper and ink and wrote to the appropriate court of law. The magistrate who got this case, which was unique in the annals of the court, visited the Fräulein, spoke earnestly with her for several hours, but discovered only that any of the three could be the father. He would have had to get blood tests made and have a legal investigation, but he saw that if he did he would be getting into a rat's nest of charges and mortal hostility among the expectant fathers. Upon his advice, the council of judges referred the case back to the director of the sanatorium with a request that he clear up the matter peaceably in socialistic fashion by means of an arbitration procedure.

A commission was formed, consisting of two patients known for exemplary adherence to institutional rules and two attendants who had a reputation for fairness, as well as the Party Secretary[4] of the sanatorium, who acted as chairman. All documents were conscientiously examined; the case was discussed from all angles, and finally a proposal by the chairman was unanimously accepted. The three fathers and the mother were summoned to a hearing for which the Director had given his permission. They were asked whether they would accept the judgment of the Commission, and, when all agreed, the fathers were reminded several times that they could still withdraw their claim to paternity. Each remained steadfast in his opinion.

"Good," proclaimed the chairman, a modern-day Solomon. "All three of you have, according to your own testimony, enjoyed the pleasures of becoming a parent. All three of you, for identical reasons, claim fatherhood in this case. So the Commission has decided that it be granted to all three of you in equal portions, with equal rights and duties. Let each one accordingly contribute a third to the care of the new citizen of our Republic and receive in return a third of the paternal pleasures."

The three fathers considered the fact that they would only rarely be intruding upon each other's domain and that, if such should occur, Viola would be entirely capable of giving each his due, as she had indeed proved. So they agreed, shook hands with each other and with the members of the Commission, and took their leave after receiving a sanctioned kiss from the communal mother of their children.

Notes

[1]Suburb of East Berlin and seat of the East German government.

[2]A playful reference to penitentiaries as "curative institutions" run by the East German government.

[3]"People's Party Penitentiary." Original is VEB (Volkseigener Betrieb) "Knast," which means literally an industrial or business enterprise (in this case a "Knast" which is slang equivalent to "pen" or "clink") run by the people, thus a nationalized operation in a country run by a one-party government. Mundstock seems to be satirizing the clash between public enterprise and private enterprise

under this form of government. Later in the story, it will become clear that he includes writers, not just thieves, among those who have somewhat ambivalent professions.

[4] The Party Secretary is the leader of the local member unit of the SED (Socialist Unity Party) within a given enterprise or work cadre.

Hic sunt leones

Joachim Nowotny

Bruno is talking about Domel. Here's how he got on that subject:
First there was the coffee—that makes you feel like talking—
and then the brandy—that gives you a cozy feeling—and then the
woman—that raises the level—and finally that sorry story about
the man who suddenly ran away from his family. This last is what
really started it all.

Look here, says Bruno, a man lives his life a certain way. And
nobody notices anything. Suddenly he goes berserk and starts
hitting at everything. He used to be gentle as a lamb, now he beats
his wife. Or strangles his kid. Or throws himself out of the tenth
story onto the pavement. And he used to ride the train into town
in proper fashion, with a good suit on and a ticket that's punched.
So. . . How do you explain that? Don't bring in any psychologists.
They don't explain anything. Or if they do, it's after something's
already happened. But how do you check up on them? Well, anyway, here are . . . some of the details. Maybe I won't have to tell
any more. To your health!

Take Domel for example. All right? Do you see anything
wrong with him? . . . You don't see anything strange. He's a decent person, you know, thirty-five, wife and child, an income; so
what's wrong? Just wait, my dear, just wait and drink your tea. No

thanks, no more coffee. Or maybe half a cup, if that's all right. Now don't expect anything sensational! Everything you say about Domel is really true. And I'll even add some more. He doesn't drink, has no affairs, drives a taxi. No complaints in five years. That means something! At the wheel every day, a fare here, a fare there, and fixing the car himself—just try doing that for five years. After all, a crate like that doesn't get any younger. It needs things. And the traffic nowadays—you know something? I wouldn't want to do it. That takes nerves and steadiness, and calmness. And it's only the beginning. The driving starts early and ends after dark. And in between, all the fussing around with gadgets. For gauging and controlling and regulating. I know, you've heard all that! All the miserable little farms in the district, the factories in every dumpy town want to look big these days. And that leads somehow to gauging and controlling and regulating, I'm told. And not only that—they just instituted a uniform quitting time. Anyway, Domel had the electronic things installed. Now he has to service them. And repair them. Then they put a telephone in his house as something extra. With an overhead line from the sawmill into town. Probably wasn't cheap, but it'll pay for itself in the long run, because now good old Domel can be phoned directly, he doesn't always have to go back to that place whatever it's called, where his headquarters is. Saves time, saves gas—what more do you want? So, all in all, everything seemed all right. Ah ha!

At the beginning, you know, it must have been quite exciting. He didn't know where the troubles would come from yet. Every defect was new. So he had to putter and putter, and feel his way until—whoops!—he spotted the trouble. We would be sitting in Habedank's bar with the cards already dealt. And the one who didn't show up was Domel. He would be hunched all alone over his gadgets in some garage. Looking for the trouble. Looking until the man on duty lost his patience and turned the lights out on him. Well, Domel drove there right away the next day. In the early morning, before his workday started, he was looking. And he got rings under his eyes, he got thin and grouchy—but why do I need to tell you that? Now that's all in the past. Domel knows his way around now, sometimes he can tell what's wrong just from hearing about it over the telephone. He's gotten to be a smart fellow. And he has the time to show up for Skat[1] every Thursday.

Ah ha, you're thinking he's having problems with his wife because of that. Not a bit! They're beyond such things. I'm positive. They're sure of each other and don't get excited anymore. You know what I mean? I don't mean to suggest that they don't care. Far from it! You know, she's one of those types, if you'll permit the expression, who give what a woman should be able to give. And the children and the house—everything in good shape. A man would have to be a real idiot to be indifferent to that. And yet . . .

You know, sometimes I watched him at cards. Let's say he's playing a Grand Solo.² And I'm the fourth man, so I sit and have time on my hands. Well, I'm used to Domel knowing what he's doing. Understand? He plays with all his might. He's happy about every good trick, he's mad when he plays the wrong card. He forgets that he's biting his lip and afterwards he's surprised when it bleeds. And if he actually makes the Grand he casts a triumphant look around the table. Something like a top-rooster that has just crowed.

That's the way it used to be. But lately . . . Oh, he still plays. He even comes regularly. But that look, that top-rooster look after he's made the Grand, he doesn't have it anymore. He tosses his aces and jacks down, cashes in his points and makes a face as if to say: Is that it? Is that all there is?

And now I ask you to follow me in your imagination. Think of this same kind of look in another place. Let's say on a road between two little towns in the middle of a wooded area. It could be around noontime. Domel has already done a few things: Kissed his wife in the morning, took a quick look at the children before he left (you never know, do you?), put a good 50 kilometers on his taxi, delivered a load of passengers who had their efficient gauging and controlling and regulating to do, and so now he's standing here behind a tree doing what comes naturally . . . after all it's only human—when you have to go . . . And then he's finished and he looks through the trees into the woods. And sees pines and more pines, a few birches between, maybe some tall grass and beetles, and he knows that behind these pines there are even more, with birches between and tall grass and beetles. And it's very quiet all around him, there are clouds in the sky, there's a soft breeze, and that inspires Domel to take a look at himself and at these days with all their driving and puttering and eating in factory cafeterias, and his wife's watching him leave and the children romping around (which is getting on his nerves recently), and suddenly he asks himself the same question: Is that all there is?

You have to admit: This time everything's at stake. Even if the

Joachim Nowotny

effects are relatively minor. Of course, there's nobody telling him
he has to deal the cards, or telling him about the old woman who
mixed herself a fatal dose at the drugstore; so he would have time,
Domel would, time to think about it and ponder it, and, of course,
even if he should realize that the life he still has before him is
pretty empty and dull—even then he would have to get back into
his taxi sometime (and quite soon too) and drive on. Because his
headquarters in whatchamacallit is waiting for him, isn't it? Waiting impatiently, too. And here comes a big truck and trailer that he
has to move over for, and then a milk truck, and finally there's the
column of army vehicles that takes some clever passing to get
around. And that puts Domel back into it. All the way into it. And
he feels the car and the road beneath him as always, but also a sort
of dull and shaky after effect in his arms and legs. Maybe he'll
never think about it again. But do you think that's likely? Don't
you feel that such moments can return? That they get stronger and
more frequent, and that they can paralyze a person like Domel,
don't you feel that? Until a certain moment arrives, and he suddenly starts beating the drum, breaks loose, does something crazy,
wants to show the world: Here I am, I'm not finished yet, I'm
ready for anything that comes. That top-rooster look, you know.
  Now I have to emphasize that this is a guess, based on the
worst that can happen. In most cases it might be different. No so
exaggerated and with a different result. When I think of Domel
and the years that he has lived through and still has before him.
Then I can understand some of it. But now I'll probably have to tell
you what happened. You'll keep it to yourself, won't you? Domel
told me in a weak moment, over quite a lot of beer. And a person
really shouldn't pass such things on. But that's the way things turn
out: you want to tell what might have happened and you end up
telling what really happened.
  So . . . everything happened differently. Domel had driven a
load of passengers to their destinations in a little town and was on
his way home. Early for a change. Maybe he'd clean out the rabbit
hutch. Nothing else to do today. But now something incredible
occurred. His taxi breaks down. Maybe Domel had hit the brakes
too hard some time. Maybe. At any rate, the right front wheel is
jammed. And even though he usually fixes everything himself,
Domel shies away from the brakes and steering. He'll have to go to
a garage. It's half past three in the afternoon; the only one that
hasn't gone home is the grouchy old service manager. He listens,
not very patiently, and keeps nodding his head as if he knows it

all, and says: Tomorrow, mister, tomorrow. Can't do it today. Leave your car here, we'll take a look. And come back tomorrow. There's nothing Domel can do. He walks away with drooping shoulders. Locks up his tools, takes his old briefcase out of the trunk and looks for a bus stop. Studies the schedule, notices to his surprise that the next bus in his direction doesn't leave until five. All of a sudden Domel has time on his hands. What'll he do? In a glum mood he starts walking through the little town. Looks in the store windows, and they seem unusually colorful and filled with all sorts of things. In front of a clothing store he suddenly imitates the artificial posture of one of the mannikins. People notice him and smile, and he suddenly feels as pleased with himself as a puppy in the springtime, looks at the young girls and the mothers with their baby carriages, in fact, at all the women—which after all is quite normal. You see, otherwise he's always hunched over his steering wheel, and everybody, whether man or woman, is for him just part of the traffic. It's normal, and I'm sure you can understand, even if you aren't a man. Anyway, he doesn't stop. There are lots of girls around, the working day is over, the offices are closed; some are on bicycles, the others are walking in groups to the station, high-school girls are looking at each other to see who's wearing the shortest skirt, mothers are dragging their offspring past the store windows on their way home—all you can say is: there's a lot going on, and Domel's in the middle of it. All at once there's a pedestrian bridge over a street construction site. Domel lets himself go with the crowd, he climbs the steps, climbs and climbs, looks up and sees a pair of women's legs—to another male, I would say: . . . "Hot stuff!" But I can't use such words to describe it to you, so this will be the hardest part of my story. How can I really explain to you as a woman what effect a pair of feminine legs can have on men under certain circumstances? On a man like Domel. Thirty-five. Dependable job. Wife and children. Up to now a model of good sense.

But where is his good sense now? Domel tramps after the woman; with his eyes fixed on her legs, he follows her down the steps and along the street, into stores and out again, around a dozen corners, back over the bridge into the center of town, and there into the bus (where he goes to the rear and has to be satisfied temporarily with the back of her hairdo and forgets to pay) and then, after getting out, follows her on and on, to the edge of town and a housing development and to a block of apartments into which the woman finally disappears. Domel sits down on a pile of cement slabs, he doesn't know that he has long since missed his bus, he doesn't notice that it's getting dark, he stares at the row of apartment units, counts to twenty-three—there the light goes on in a window, and that must be hers. Of course, you know it doesn't make any difference whether it was really hers. For Domel it was hers. He's shaking with a kind of fever now, his knees are beginning to quiver—how lucky that he is sitting down! Otherwise his legs would simply turn him around and propel him across the sand between the trees and on into the pines. And now the moment has come for Domel to ask himself the question you know he will ask. And he takes prompt advantage of the opportunity. But the circumstances dictate that Domel phrase the question somewhat differently: There are so many women, thinks Domel, and there's so much beauty, so much life—but why, Domel, did you get only one portion of each?

And all at once he felt as if he would be missing a very great deal.

So now, of course, he has arrived at the outer limits. And even gone a little beyond. Because a man can have more than one woman. But not more than one life. And he can't have all women either. So why doesn't he just stay with the one, with his, if he loves her? And of course Domel loves his wife—what do you think? He will call her (the last train has also left by now) and tell her she shouldn't worry.

That's almost the end of my story. I would only have to add that Domel looked around when he regained his senses. And saw that he was at the edge of a pine forest that bordered the housing development on one side. You already know: the pines, birches, tall grass, beetles. And more pines, birches, tall grass, beetles. But with the small difference that it now seemed to Domel that he was looking at unexplored territory. He recalled a feeling he'd had in his school days when he first looked at an historical atlas. An ancient map showed the Mediterranean Sea and an approximation of the northern coast of Africa. Where the map should have extended southward into the dark continent there was only an indefinite crosshatching to indicate mountains. And over the whole area these cautious words were printed: Hic sunt leones. Here are lions. Nothing more. And that's just the reason Domel wanted so much to go there . . . .

So now Bruno is really finished with his story about Domel.

He drinks the rest of his coffee and looks quite tired. We can't assume that the story would have turned out differently if he hadn't had to tell it to a woman. But it was probably best this way. Who knows what abysses might have opened up otherwise?

Notes

[1] A popular German card game for 3 to 5 players, only 3 of whom may take an active part in a given hand.

[2] One of the bolder bidding options in the game of Skat.

The Decision

Günter Görlich

That **Wiedenau woman was to blame—she had an insufferable** manner and a voice that was damned penetrating and impossible to ignore.

It's really a contrast—this beautiful woman and her sharp voice.

Yet it is a well-known fact that Wiedenau can handle the worst troublemakers in her 10b class. In her own inconsiderate way, of course; her lack of consideration is what bothered me, and that's why I had lost my temper and pounded on the table.

What's her life like? We don't know much about her. She doesn't have a husband. Or does she? Is that any of my business?

Of course it's my business. Her criticism hurts people's feelings.

And as Party Secretary for the faculty,[1] I'm supposed to be interested in how Comrade Christa Wiedenau lives.

The fact that she dresses well and according to the latest fashion is as obvious as the fact that she prefers toughness and directness in her dealings with colleagues and comrades. But why is she this way?

Then Hoth thought, disconcertedly, to himself: Actually, what do I have against toughness if it's called for?

He was sitting at the table in the teachers' room, at the famous oval table. This shape doesn't allow for any head chair or any spot where one person is automatically singled out as the leader of a meeting or job discussion. Hoth liked this table. An amazing number of people could sit at it, and there was enough room for books, notebooks, briefcases, coffee pots—and sometimes even wine bottles. Everything else had changed in the course of time—bookcases, cabinets, chairs, as the need arose. But the oval table had remained. Through the years various attempts had been made to get rid of it. It took up too much space, didn't fit in with the bright and modern decor of the room; the color was impossible, and on its scratched surface there were unmistakable traces of not exactly serious pedagogical activities.

During the past year Hans Gerber had wanted to get rid of the oval table and install a regular, rectangular conference table. Hoth had defended the old piece of furniture, praised its usefulness; and most of his colleagues had shared his opinion. For Hoth the table was a souvenir of his years at this school; it relaxed the severity, the exaggerated sobriety of the teachers' room. And this was a table top you could feel free to pound with your fist without knocking everything over.

But the question is, Comrade Hoth, whether it is right to pound on a table with your fist at all, however stable it might be? But what the devil!—why shouldn't you pound on the table now and then? It can have a surprisingly healthy effect. And after all, you're only human.

Healthy? That wasn't the way things were at the party meeting this afternoon.

At least that Wiedenau woman hadn't been impressed by what he'd said. She had an answer all ready for him.

But Hoth hadn't let her have the floor a second time. He immediately started to talk and quite loudly too. He could hear himself getting excited and then even more excited. And he didn't want to stop.

Wiedenau's astonished look, which then turned icy and scornful, irritated him.

He made all the general remarks—about past achievements, about the necessity of seeing things in perspective. He asked for a balanced appraisal of the problems and warned against immoderate exaggeration and emotional criticism.

As he spoke he pressed his chest against the edge of the table until it hurt him.

And he looked over at Hans Gerber, who was still the director of the school and also the subject of this last agenda item. It was a question of Gerber's dismissal from the school, and the justification for it.

This justification, one-and-three-quarters typed pages in length, was lying there now on the table in front of Hoth, at this late evening hour.

He had been alone in the room for some time.

In the afternoon he had dictated it to the secretary, and would have liked to hear her opinion on the text; after all she had worked in Gerber's front office for the last two years. Hoth would have liked to have gotten some support from the secretary. She said nothing. But what had he actually said in this drafted statement?

We want to express our gratitude to Comrade Hans Gerber for his successful performance here during these two years, work which he did most willingly, without sparing himself. And our best wishes go with him to his new, responsible position in the school administration, and above all we express the wish that he will soon be restored to good health.

The comrades were supposed to approve the text so that it could be presented to the faculty as a whole.

As Hoth was reading it aloud to them, he glanced at Hans Gerber. His face showed no emotion. He kept loosening and tightening the cap of his fountain pen—something he had done at every discussion and meeting during the two years. At times it seemed as if Gerber were about to smile—that indefinite smile which Hoth in recent months could make nothing of. Gerber was looking toward the window, which framed the gleaming, wet leaves of a chestnut tree. It had been raining all day.

When Hoth had finished reading, no one spoke for a time, until Christa Wiedenau said: "I am not satisfied with the text. Everyone at this table knows that what you say there, Comrade Hoth, is not true. And we of all people must not deceive ourselves and others. Where will we end up otherwise?"

Wiedenau was sitting across from Gerber and she looked right at him, and it was like a challenge to him to say something.

But Gerber was busy with his fountain pen. He held his head down and I could see, under his thin hair, the long scar that came from a sharp edge of a building beam that had almost killed him 25 years ago. It was on a Sunday when they were cleaning up ruins along the Avenue.[2] Hoth had pulled Gerber out from under the beam. At that time Gerber was a hothead, always spouting flame and fire, much too careless, with no experience on construction jobs. Before he went to the university he had been a mechanic. But Hoth had done construction before going on with his studies. Gerber was lucky the way it happened. The falling beam was slowed up by one of the vertical supports. Hoth, who had seen many accidents of this type, was nearby; he tore his shirt in two and bandaged Gerber's head. Gerber was out of school for three months. But he didn't get behind in his studies, the others saw to that. They were a close group, and they wanted to become teachers.

Gerber had his scar, which would always remind him of those hectic days.

Hoth, who saw the scar, could also remember those days.

Perhaps that is why he turned to Wiedenau quite vehemently: "Would you please make yourself clear?"

Christa Wiedenau raised her eyebrows in astonishment. That always happened when she thought everything had been explained and was clear. At such moments her facial expression could seem extremely arrogant.

"The fact is," she said, "that Comrade Gerber is leaving because he wasn't equal to the task. It's certainly not a question of successful performance. And, in the last analysis, all of us, including you, Comrade Hoth, have had a chance to see what the results of ineffective leadership are."

She said that very calmly, with her eyebrows still raised. No consideration or feeling for a colleague in such a situation; only this cold woman, completely convinced of her own value, could do such a thing, Hoth thought, and felt the slight quivering of his hands that was always the sign of an outburst on his part, which he feared because it usually caused trouble.

But it was already too late—because the silence at the table continued, because nobody tried to stop Wiedenau, because he saw Gerber's rigid face and the challenging expression in Wiedenau's face. And he hammered on the table with his fist and spoke loudly and impetuously.

Finally he finished and said in conclusion that, if his comrades had the same opinion of his draft, the whole matter would have to be put on the agenda again.

Then something odd happened.

The people took their briefcases and stood up, apparently considering his words as an adjournment of the meeting.

The room emptied fast; apparently everyone was in a hurry. Some of them, of course, were always in a hurry—children had to

be picked up at the nursery or kindergarten, the stores were closing soon. But there were always a few who stayed behind to talk
about this or that, and often it was a long time before Hoth, as the
last to leave the room, picked up his briefcase and turned out the
light over the oval table.

Today Christa Wiedenau had stayed; she stood behind her
chair and didn't make the slightest attempt to conceal the fact that
she was waiting to talk with Hoth. Hans Gerber was also still in
the room, busying himself with some papers.

Hoth realized that Wiedenau wanted to talk with him. But he
wasn't in the mood at this moment.

What good would it do? She had stirred everything up. She
had provoked his outburst; it was her fault that this meeting had
come to such a sorry end. Hoth felt his excitement changing into
confusion. That was all he needed. To have to sit there before this
self-assured Wiedenau woman like a schoolboy who doesn't know
what to say?

Hoth walked around the oval table to the bookcase, where he
had his shelf, but he didn't take the shortest way because that
wouldn't have led him past Christa Wiedenau.

Then he saw her pick up her briefcase and turn toward the
door. For a fraction of a second he looked into her eyes and was
startled.

No arrogance, no scorn, no smugness.

What *was* in this look that she gave him?

But then Gerber claimed his attention; he had only been waiting for Wiedenau to leave the room. He took Hoth's hand, pressed
it firmly and said: "Thanks, Gerhard, thanks."

Then he left too.

Hoth watched him go and even went to the window. Slowly
and hesitantly, it seemed, Gerber crossed the courtyard of the
school, carefully avoiding the puddles. At the exit gate he opened
his umbrella.

Hoth sat down at his place at the table where the drafted text
about Hans Gerber still lay.

What had happened, Comrade Hoth?

Did you write the evaluation of Hans Gerber this way because
you're thinking of yourself too? You are as old as he is, you belong
to the same generation.

It is not true that Gerber had performed successfully during
the two years. He didn't spare himself, that's true. But he didn't
do his job.

You know that very well, Hoth.

Two years ago Gerber had come to the school; the former director was leaving, to go into retirement. Gerber took over a well-run school; no emergency measures were necessary. You were glad, Hoth, to have your old buddy here, who had the reputation of being a good teacher. And besides Gerber had done some work in theory. So all the requirements for directing a school seemed to be met.

But they weren't. If you're honest, Hoth, you have to admit that you were aware of that after the first six months. Directives accumulated that didn't get beyond the paper they were written on because he hadn't thought them through; there were more and more private conferences between the Director and certain colleagues and comrades, which gradually produced an atmosphere of distrust within the faculty as a whole.

What did you do then, Party Secretary?

Let's not rush things, you thought and often said so too—we have to give him some time. We have to be considerate; after all, he is new here. Quite a few of the colleagues and comrades got used to this way of doing things; it was a comfortable way as long as you did your own work.

And you, Hoth, thought and hoped that with time and with the power of the Party organization that could be changed. A dangerous delusion!

The power of the Party organization is not an abstract quantity, and can't be applied in prescribed doses. It reveals itself—or doesn't—in each comrade.

You waited too long, Hoth, and time was passing. And you also thought of yourself, far too much of your own self. Don't deceive yourself. You were always remembering the difficulties that the Gerbers had had to face in the past two decades. You're one of them. It's been a hard road. Your generation laid many of the foundations that Wiedenau and others build on today and take for granted.

Don't get sentimental, Hoth. A difficult road? It was a new road. And what does it mean to say Wiedenau is building on these foundations. What else should she build on?

Wiedenau doesn't have to keep her eye constantly on you and your difficulties in the past. The sheer contemplation and awe would keep her from her work. She doesn't always have to ask how things were twenty years ago. She was only a child then. Her time is today. And tomorrow much will be expected of her. Once

Gerber said: "You know, Gerhard, our younger comrades seem to lack a certain feeling of respect for the past." Hoth hadn't contradicted him, although he didn't like the words he used. They seemed so vague and pompous.

And then Gerber's health had worsened. So then, Hoth, you saw that the time had come to make an urgently needed change.

To you this seemed the best and fairest way to handle it, and you wouldn't consider any other solution.

But Christa Wiedenau wouldn't let you do it that way.

And that's good, Hoth.

It's not a question of how often a person raises his eyebrows or whether he looks arrogant or not, the question is only: What does the Comrade actually do?

Christa Wiedenau has the right to act this way even if she's only twenty-five years old, because she is a good teacher.

Is she inconsiderate? Yes, when she sees a poor performance, sloppiness, and dishonesty. This is the kind of inconsiderateness we need! It deserves a medal.

You'll have to tell Hans Gerber that there is such a thing as respect for the future—to express it in his terms. We'll have to get used to that, Hans.

So now, Hoth, you're going to tear up this typed sheet, this text that would take us in a different direction. And you know Comrade Wiedenau's address, don't you? She lives on the Akazienweg.

You're going to pay her a visit today.

Notes

[1]Thus he represents the national party (The Socialist Unity Party) and its members within the faculty.

[2]A possible reference to the ruins of Hitler's headquarters on the avenue Unter den Linden.

Eighteen Minutes[1]

Axel Schulze

The train slowly pulled into the covered station, and I saw rivulets of rain running from the roof down over the coaches. Above me a defective neon light buzzed behind its frosted glass, and I was being propelled toward the train, squeezed between travel bags with protruding thermos bottles; I was hemmed in by elbows and suitcases and driven toward the door, whose glass was sprayed by glistening raindrops. In the compartment of the train the heavy dry heat made my throat feel raw. But maybe that was my fever too; the pills weren't working yet. I still had the cold, tarry taste of the mouthwash on my lips and felt a sharp, painful coldness in my stomach.

I took the seat by the window, and the train started, rattling over the first switches on its way out of the station and past the malt-coffee plant, whose smells foretold wind direction and weather for the local people.

Behind me there was a hum of conversation; the clicking of wheels on the rails became regular. I felt the sweat in my armpits and I thought of the talk I'd had with Pokropa in the low barracks that stood within an arm's length of the railroad spur to the refinery, and I heard Pokropa say: You're wrong if you think resignation is a private matter. And: We don't change our work cadres the way a tree does its leaves. He said it and stood at the window looking over at the refinery. The searchlights pierced the evening mists that swirled lazily around them, and in the distance we could see the torch glow of the exhaust stacks. Pokropa had opened the window, and the room was penetrated by the fragrance of a wild jasmine bush that led its straggly existence somewhere on the barrack's wall.

I thought of Pokropa and the jasmine and the refinery, and knew at once that all these things didn't really belong together, that they were assembled from observations and conversations at different times and in different places—assembled and composed into this picture and romantically colored by my damned imagination. But the wild jasmine actually grew everywhere at the refinery. And the elder leaned its lazy, heavy, umbellate blossoms against the walls.

And above all I was thinking of this trip, this eighteen-minute trip that was bringing me inexorably to the refinery. And I began to look around in the compartment, first at the posters in the advertising panels, which showed girls happily waving a welcome to the Black Sea resorts, and then I saw the passengers' faces, with their bristly chin stubble that had resisted their shavers, and their veined eyelids that grew heavy and closed from the regular rocking of the train.

Then the city receded, and more and more gardens were squeezed between the houses, with sheds in them made of boards and tar paper, and there were plots of cabbages and onions, but now they too were gone, and I could finally look out over the meadowlands steaming in the rain, intersected by lazy rivers on which oil spots floated.

Pokropa, I was thinking again and again, Pokropa; I was almost whispering the name like an incantation. The name was close to my tongue, and I swallowed with half-opened mouth because my throat was sore and hot and I knew that the fever was not going away.

You're wrong if you think resignation is a private matter.

We should talk about that, Pokropa, about that very thing, and about my data-gathering at the refinery, because, believe me, it all belongs together. You agreed with me, didn't you, Pokropa? What does "efficient" mean, you said—we have to be more efficient?

My file is right up there on the aluminum luggage rack. There are my figures and my recommendations, Pokropa.

But you aren't at the refinery any more, and I still can hear the politely regretful voice of the secretary on the telephone: Comrade Pokropa has been given a position of greater responsibility in the government. What was that again about not changing our cadres? . . . Help me out, Pokropa, now, while the train is going around this long curve to the right, and the panorama of the city can be sensed through the fog and rain. I know you're living here somewhere in this sea of dark gray tiled roofs, somewhere in one of these buildings that have their stucco crumbling off and a long dark corridor running through them. Once I even wanted to visit you, but your wife opened the door, and you had gone to a conference at Sverdlovsk or Chelyabinsk—I don't remember any more. But you were expected back soon, very soon.

The sun is almost up, and the lights in the compartments are going out. Under a bridge darkened by the soot of many trains, I still can see my pale face with the stringy hair, and for this tiny moment the noises vanish and I am alone with myself, all alone, as I'll probably be the whole day long.

My investigation is over—a good job, everybody says, but the way they say it—I was listening very carefully . . . And now the train shoots out from under the bridge and past the boiler factory, where arcs of light flash behind the windows.

Your illusions won't buy us anything, Pokropa had said as we stood at the window or in the canteen where there were always sausages with lentil soup on Monday. The investigation is over, do you hear, Pokropa? There are no illusions any more. There are only figures, data and diagrams. A year's work is up there in that file case, and then my fever the last two days and the sleepless nights on sheets wet with perspiration.

Rain beats against the panes, and the streaming droplets blur the village clustered around the brick church and the cemetery with lichen-covered gravestones. The train races past the red-framed station and its geraniums planted in woven baskets, and past the red signal tower at the end.

This investigation was very good but too academic. What do you want; after all, the refinery is operating. Did you consider the production rates? And I can give you figures, Pokropa, the figures you wanted, and afterwards, in the evening, we'll say good-bye to each other with a bitter taste in our mouths, too many cigarettes again and a little hoarse again because we got too loud. But we'll have a talk, and when we get tired we'll wonder whether it was enough, whether we've said everything, and we'll take nothing for granted—nothing. The train was slowing down and the network of overhead lines was becoming more closely entwined against the rain-gray sky, and it was time to get my file case down. We rode past slag heaps gouged by erosion, sparsely covered by vegetation, and then came the refinery; the brakes pulled harder and I stood up. At that moment—where was it really, and when? At that moment I wanted to give up everything, and I remember the painful uncertainty of those days, and I remember you, Pokropa, and I see you standing there, looking at the refinery, the living, dirty, breathing refinery that stood there in front of him and in front of me. The door was pushed open, and the air smelled of acid and carbide as always. We walked toward the stained, wooden bridge and the glass-roofed pedestrian bridge that led to the entrance gate, and I saw caps and the backs of heads before me, and the bobbing umbrellas.

Next to the railroad tracks was the racetrack with its dusty, symmetrical columns, and as I climbed up the stairs, jostled and crowded, shivering from cold sweat under my arms, I also saw a jacket and the back of a head, and, when the man turned to go over the pedestrian bridge, I also caught a glimpse of his profile; I pushed forward, squeezed my way through the crowd, was showered with curses and good-natured jibes and then I stood by the man and the sweat ran from my face.

Pokropa, I said, you're here, you're really here.

But it was someone else.

Notes

[1]This is an especially good example of a quite prevalent type of writing in East Germany, which has as its ideal the close linking of literature with everyday work experience.

The Tub

Martin Stephan

Rabinter, a man with an invisible dunce cap on his head, blinked as he looked toward the fence. The sun was high in the sky and the raspberry bushes, where Rabinter was idling away his time, didn't give much shade.

From the neighboring property Rabinter heard the ringing laughter of Widow Rausch, a warm, throaty woman's laughter that took pleasure in its own melody.

Rabinter got up and went to the fence that separated his garden from that of Widow Rausch. In the open door of her garden house stood Widow Rausch, broadly and solidly filling its frame, and laughing. Her whole body shook with pleasure, and her bosom was bouncing so much that Rabinter had to watch it whether he wanted to or not—and he wanted to. Cautiously he glanced around; there was nobody on her property except her, Widow Rausch, and he himself was the only one standing at the fence. Why was the widow laughing that way? Was she crazy or drunk?

Rabinter could feel the hot crumbly summer soil of the garden through the soles of his rubber boots and was about to move back from the fence into the skimpy shade of his raspberry bushes when Widow Rausch called out a robust "Hello!"

"Hello," murmured Rabinter and made a small gesture of acknowledgment.

Widow Rausch burst out in laughter again, and Rabinter found that rather stupid; after all, she wasn't a young girl anymore and her behavior was silly, to say the least. Rabinter figured Widow Rausch weighed a good 200 pounds.

"Would you have a little time for me, Mr. Rabinter?" the widow said with a sweet trill in her voice, and rolled her large brown eyes in a manner that gave Rabinter chills up and down his spine.

Now it was really too late to retreat unnoticed.

"Of course," Rabinter said disconcertedly and started to pull out two boards of the picket fence but then remembered that he didn't know for sure whether the fence belonged to him or to the widow.

Again he felt a chill run down his spine.

And now Widow Rausch launched herself from the door of the garden house and came sailing over to the fence with a suppleness and quick grace which were really remarkable.

Before Rabinter could hide his hands, the widow had seized them and pressed them firmly to her bosom; Rabinter was petrified.

"Help a poor weak woman," she trilled, and smilingly showed her white teeth; they were small and sharp. Rabinter had read of predatory fish that . . .!

"Yes," he whispered and noticed how the widow was examining his shirtfront, unbuttoned at the top, where a tuft of light blond hair peeked through.

He forced a smile: "What can I do for you?"

"Anything!" said the widow jokingly and giggled.

Rabinter wished he'd never come out from behind his berry bushes.

"It's just that I need some water," said Widow Rausch, "and my well is empty."

"I'll be glad to help," sighed Rabinter. He had already given up the battle.

"Wonderful!" cried Widow Rausch and clapped her hands. "You're a man who doesn't desert a poor woman who is alone in her hour of need."

Rabinter laughed nervously.

Widow Rausch leaned forward and seized the crosspiece that held a section of the picket fence together, and, with a quick, powerful movement, tore it out of its moorings: The way was clear.

"I'll be glad to help you," Rabinter repeated softly, turned and went to his garden shed to get his buckets. The widow was suffering another attack of merriment, and this time it didn't sound like laughter intoxicated by its own melody; it was definitely a howl of victory.

Rabinter was sweating and not only from the sun that flickered warmly through the dusty foliage of the fruit trees. She's blowing her trumpet! he thought, and felt a gentle terror come over him. He grabbed the handle of the pump.

The pump squeaked pleasantly and shook off its rust—reddish-brown and powdery. Rabinter was soon sweating, this time from exertion; he felt the salty juices of his flesh run down his forehead and over his broad face. Rabinter groaned and thought: Why does the widow need so much water? It'll be enough to boil a hog in. He was carrying the heavy buckets, filled to overflowing, to the laundry room that was attached to the widow's garden house and emptying them into a wooden tub which stood as tall as a man. Every time he came to the tub—water-carrying is hard work—Widow Rausch, who was now blushingly and unexpectedly referring to herself as "Inge," came and wiped Rabinter's face with the hem of her thin summer dress. She did it matter-of-factly but not without seductive charm—it doubtlessly felt good, and Rabinter was almost sorry when he poured the last bucket into the tub, which was now filled to the brim. Of course he didn't admit to himself that he was sorry. He looked at himself: his hands had brown stains on them; the powdery rust of the pump handle had penetrated his skin like a tattoo. "The tub is full," said Rabinter.

"Yes, I see," cooed Widow Rausch.

"Thirty-two buckets of water!" Rabinter emphasized proudly. "Well water," added the widow appreciatively. Rabinter wiped his forehead; he felt sweat under his arms. Actually he was just now beginning to take a good look at this remarkable woman. She stood tall and stout before him. Her chestnut brown hair, which she had tied loosely behind her neck, was lightly tipped with gray. Her hands were red and strong.

"What do you need all this water for, Mrs. Rausch?"

"You've gotten dirty," the widow answered in a serious tone, "and sweaty and tired from carrying those heavy buckets—you aren't used to that . . . Here you can take a bath and freshen up.

You can splash around as much as you like; it's a laundry room and has a tile floor."

"That's true," Rabinter decided, and closely examined the red, rippled tiles of the little room.

"Towel," whispered the widow and pointed with her finger at the hook where it hung; she smiled mysteriously and left the room.

"Thanks," murmured Rabinter, but she was already gone. It seemed as if he could hear her throaty laughter in the garden; his mind stood still like a clock that had run down.

Slowly Rabinter undressed, laid his clothes carefully on the stool that stood three-leggedly nearby, scratched his chest and tried to summon up the amount of courage that would undoubtedly be demanded of him by this barbaric tub of ice-cold water. Rabinter's unfathomable widow had left the door a hand's breadth open. Rabinter hesitated. But all was quiet. Mild afternoon sunlight slanted into the room; in its flickering path, a fine, otherwise invisible dust was dancing. The room, which was no more than six square meters in size, was pleasantly cool. Rabinter, naked, curled his toes on the welcome, stony coolness of the tiles. With sudden decisiveness he seized the rim of the tub and vaulted into it with a youthful agility which surprised him. For a few seconds he thought he would freeze to death, but soon he could feel his blood excitedly tickling his veins. He dived under, snorted like a sea-monster, then began to splash around in a relaxed way. For a moment he thought he saw a laughing face at the door. But that didn't bother him at all. He thought of those legendary days when the women still washed their men, and scrubbed and rubbed the dusty, bearded warriors with downright worshipful devotion, and afterwards salved and oiled them as if they were valuable instruments. These were very pleasant thoughts that Rabinter surrendered to in the washtub.

When Widow Rausch came in again, no longer so frightening as a short time ago, Rabinter felt ten years younger, no, twenty years. This powerful feeling was so compelling that he couldn't possibly keep it to himself. Three hours later Widow Rausch, who now went by the name of "Inge dear," was busy trimming Rabinter's jagged toenails. At the same time she hummed a soft melody, Mozart, which was just right for that evening—so soft and full of feeling.

How Krabat Lost Smjala[1]

Jurij Brězan

Smjala was the creation of Krabat's first yearnings: Life was only one sunset old and paradise was still in sight. Then paradise sank into the never-has-been and Krabat lost Smjala one autumn. Some say it was long before the invention of the wheel; others think it was at the time of the Great Flood.

In the morning after the fifth night with Smjala, Krabat was fetching water from the Satkula—the well on the little hill was not dug deep enough yet—just as a girl climbed into the brook to bathe. The girl was blond everywhere that Smjala was brown, her breasts shone brighter, the red of their tips was more inflaming. And without taking time to think, Krabat also jumped into the water. The girl swam like a fish, Krabat swam like a fish otter, the otter drew the little fish to the bank, and the little fish was not a fish, the coolness of the brook evaporated, and before the rooster up on the hill had crowed three times, the little fish by the brook had three times found the power of speech and three times lost it. In the night, however, Krabat thought that brown still is warmer than blond, only to think once more, on the following morning, that blond is fresher and brighter in the sun than brown under the stars.

Juri Brĕzan

Lost in such thoughts of color, and because curiosity makes the man, he took longer and longer trips to fetch water and let Smjala thirst.

One morning he avoided the place where the blond girl was bathing and walked upstream to the wooded hills in the south, which from a distance looked like mountains. There, deep in the woods, he came upon a girl gathering berries. A thick black mass of hair tumbled over her shoulders as she bent forward; her hips were round and firm, and her dark eyes became still darker when Krabat reached for her berries. The berries were sweet and rich as Tokay wine, and they made Krabat so giddy and confused that he couldn't find his path and got lost.

When the sun went down he came to a clearing; a hut stood there, surrounded by a jungle of flowers of all kinds, and, before the hut, on a bench of birchwood, a girl sat combing her hair; her hair glowed like the setting sun.

The girl was singing the song of the Lorelei, and, like the boatman in his boat, Krabat steered his course toward her through the sea of flowers; he did not drown in the Rhine like the boatman but in the red flood of her hair and the thousand-flower fragrance of her skin. All night long he counted her freckles and lost count seven times. At sunrise he staggered out of the hut, found the Satkula and followed it home, half like an honest drunkard, half like a dishonest bookkeeper.

When he got home—he had also forgotten his water jug at the Lorelei's hut—the well had been dug deep in the earth and walled with rough stones, the stones in the cool depths were covered with green moss, and the linden tree, grown to a mighty width, had a new trunk growing out of the middle of its hollow body, and out of the hut came a man—Krabat thought he was seeing his own self.

Who are you? Krabat asked this not-other man, who had never seen himself in a mirror and so was not surprised by Krabat's appearance. I am I, answered the man: some call me Serbin.

Krabat asked for a drink of water. The man gave him a cup; the water from the deep well was clear and cold as dewdrops in October.

Krabat sat on the wellstone, saw the blue hills in the distance and the pastures nearby, gently sloping toward the Satkula, and seven villages in the meadowlands.

He sat until the mists rose from the brook, then he went down to the mill. The miller was a cheerful, strange man.

Krabat sat down by the brook, watched the waterbugs run back and forth; it looked as if they were stretching a net to catch the water. But the water flowed along under the net, not to be caught, not to be held.

When the hoot owls hunted and the night owls swept over the fields the water sprite[2] crouched in the trunk of a hollow willow; he broke little pieces out of its bark and dropped them, murmuring, into the brook.

Brother Water Sprite . . . , said Krabat.

Forty-three, forty-four, forty-five, murmured the water sprite more clearly now, and Krabat understood that he did not want to be disturbed.

The last piece of bark fell into the water; one hundred, said the water sprite, one hundred years—he tore a leaf from a twig and let it float away—and one day. No trace in the water, no trace in the wind. Floated away, blown away.

Krabat understood that he had lost Smjala. But the grief was not there yet; it moves more slowly than understanding.

Why did I return, he asked.

The water sprite played with his green beard as if he hadn't heard.

Answer! cried Krabat, suddenly angry; he jumped up and seized him roughly by his beard. Where is Smjala?

The water sprite slipped into the brook, and Krabat held only a clump of rushes in his hand.

A hundred pieces of bark in the brook, a hundred words in the wind, Brother Krabat, said the water sprite. The water stirred and grew cloudy, the darkness vanished and the brook was empty.

A hundred pieces of bark in the brook, a hundred words in the wind, Krabat repeated, and sometime, perhaps in the same night, or in the early morning, or many days later, he started on his journey to look for Smjala where the water flows, where the wind blows.

Sometimes Jakub Kuschk was with him, sometimes Krabat was alone. He found many girls and lay with them in many beds whether of straw or of down, fragrant hay, or young spruce twigs, feathery mattresses of the princess of the peas and the hard clay floor of Cinderella, warm sand on the seashore, perfumed water in tiled baths, and once there was one who stood before him, naked, with her hands under her breasts, her flesh aflame, and she said: What did Smjala have that I do not?

What she had in common with Smjala was that he left her as he had left all and would leave all, and gradually he lost the lost one entirely. He lost even her name and called her The Bright and Dark Dividing of the Ways. Finally he came again to the clearing in the middle of the woods, steered his course again through the colorful sea of flowers, and the deeper he penetrated, the farther all the shores receded from him, and he heard the song of the Lorelei from everywhere, and it was nowhere.

What then became of Krabat no one knows.

Some think he is the old man who sells flowers every Saturday in a pillar recess of the cathedral wall, who comes unseen and goes unseen.

Now and then a buyer of his flowers is said to have found, in the middle of a bouquet of simple asters, a star-shaped blossom of rare beauty not described in any catalog. Others claim that Krabat never found his way out of the sea of flowers and had to stay with the red-haired girl until he could remember Smjala again: what she whispered when she made love to him, and how her tears tasted when she cried. The miller, Jakub Kuschk, claimed his whole life long—however believable the one or the other end of this story might seem to be—that the entire story is nothing but a fairy tale invented by someone who doesn't know that all beauty in life comes from the mystery of the woman and the curiosity of the man. But out of the fairy tale he made a song with which he sang a hundred girls into the bridal bed, where—as he said—the fairy tale has its place, for one night or even three.

Notes

[1]This story is based in part on legends of the Sorbs, a Slavic people living in Saxony and Brandenburg—see remarks on Brězan in the Bibliographical Sketches.

[2]The original German term is "Wasserman," meaning Aquarius or Water Bearer in the Zodiac, as well as water sprite. Here he seems to play the role of a representative of nature who has come to give Krabat a sign or message.

Biographical Sketches

Becher, Ulrich. Born 1910 in Berlin. Studied graphic art under Georg Gross and was a law student at Geneva and Berlin. His writings were banned by the Nazis in 1933. Emigrated to New York via various European countries. Returned to Europe after the war and established residence in Basel, Switzerland. He has written dramas, lyrics, novels and short stories, and many literary critiques. He is known for his ironic humor and preference for whimsical plots.

Bender, Hans. Born in 1919 in Mülhhausen. Studied literature and art history in Erlangen and Heidelberg. Was a soldier in World War II; returned from Russian imprisonment in 1949. Was editor of the feuilleton section of *Deutsche Zeitung* until 1963 and since then has engaged in varied publishing and editorial activity, mostly in Cologne, as editor of *Akzente*, the well-known literary journal. Has been skillful in discovering and furthering youthful literary talent. His short stories are known for their simplicity but also their subtlety, sincerity, and attitude of youthful wonder. Also has written novels, lyrics, critical essays.

Böll, Heinrich. Born 1917 in Cologne. Was apprenticed to a book dealer and briefly studied classical languages and literature. Was drafted into military service and returned in 1945 from an American prisoner-of-war camp. He has become one of the most influential and internationally famous figures of postwar German literature. Has written short stories, novels, radio plays, film scripts, translations, essays. Former president of international PEN society. Won, among other awards, the Büchner Prize in 1967 and the Nobel Prize for Literature in 1972.

Borchert, Wolfgang. Born 1921 in Hamburg, died 1947 in Basel, Switzerland. Was an apprentice in the book trade, and later an actor and cabaret performer. As a soldier on the Russian front he was imprisoned for his opposition to Hitler, and returned home seriously ill in 1945. Wrote his major works in the two-year period before his death, mostly short stories and radio plays. His stylistic innovations, his idealism, and his passionate call for new attitudes and approaches have had a strong impact both in Germany and abroad.

Brězan, Jurij. Born 1916 in Rächelwitz, the son of a Sorbian (a Slavic ethnic group) quarry laborer and farm worker. After secondary school he studied economics, emigrated in 1937 to Czechoslovakia and in 1938 to Poland. He was imprisoned in Dresden because of his participation in a Sorbian resistance group against Hitler. Was forced into Army service between 1939 and 1945. After the war he worked until 1948 as a leader of the Sorbian youth organization. Since 1949 he has been an independent author in Bautzen, East Germany. Brězan has written novels, short stories, children's books, lyrics, TV scripts, and dramas. Has won various literary prizes of the German Democratic Republic. Important themes of his works are the attempt by the individual to find a place in society, the struggle for identity of Brězan's ethnic group, and his own adherence to the socialist principles he sees embodied in the German Democratic Republic.

Claudius, Eduard (Penname for Eduard Schmidt). Born 1911 in Gelsen-Kirchen-Buer, the son of a construction worker. Learned the trade of mason (later becoming a union official) and between 1928 and 1932, he traveled through various European countries. Then became a member of the German Communist Party and was arrested by Hitler's government in 1933, and fled to Switzerland in 1934 after a sympathetic guard let him escape. Was a volunteer from 1936 to 1938 in the International Brigades during the Spanish Civil War. Returned illegally to Switzerland and spent several war years in internment there until he was able to join the Italian partisans in Northern Italy. Worked after the war in the denazification program in Bavaria, then moved to Potsdam in East Germany, 1947. Was named Consul of the German Democratic Republic in Syria in 1956 and was Ambassador to North Vietnam from 1959 to 1961. He has written novels, dramas, journalism, short stories. His works are of a strongly realistic, historical, often adventurous and passionate type that portray what he sees as a new image of humanity—dynamic, moral, conscious of tradition—embodied in proletarian heroes. He has won various East German literary prizes, including the National Prize in 1951.

De Bruyn, Günter. Born 1926 in Berlin. After secondary school, he worked for the German Air Force as a civilian and was then in the work service before entering the army. Was a prisoner of war for a short time in 1945, then a farm worker in West Germany and a teacher in Brandenburg, East Germany. Moved to East Berlin in 1946 and was an apprentice teacher in a nearby village. Attended library school from 1949 to 1953 and worked in libraries in Berlin, then was affiliated as a librarian with the Central Institute for Library Science. Since 1963 he has been an independent author in East Berlin. He has written novels and short stories, radio plays, parodies and essays, and has won, among other prizes, the Heinrich Mann Prize in 1964. He addresses himself in general to the younger generation in East Germany, using subject matter from his own experience and personal as well as general problems of postwar society.

BIOGRAPHICAL SKETCHES

Görlich, Günter. Born in 1928 in Breslau. Was a prisoner-of-war of the Russians. Joined the East German police in 1950. Was a teacher for a time, also an editor and active in a youth organization. Studied from 1958 to 1961 at the Johannes Becher Institute for Literature at Leipzig. He has become a well-known author of books for East German youth. He has received, among other literary prizes, the National Prize in 1971.

Grass, Günter. Born 1927 in Danzig. Soldier and prisoner-of-war in World War II. After the war he took various jobs as a farm laborer, miner, factory worker, and jazz musician. Was also an apprentice stoneworker and stone sculptor. Studied art at Düsseldorf and Berlin. Began writing in 1955 and became an important member of Gruppe 47. Since then has lived mostly in West Berlin, writing lyrics, drama, prose, doing art work, and frequently engaging in political activity for the Social Democratic Party. Grass became internationally famous especially for the novel *The Tin Drum* (1959) and the novella *Cat and Mouse* (1961), in which he satirically lays bare the German past. His most unique feature is his style, which customarily contains grotesquely humorous, often obscene, wordplay and images. The stylistic virtuosity of his writing often seems as important to Grass as the content itself. Besides prose fiction he has also written poetry and drama. He has received, among many other awards, the Prize of Gruppe 47 and the Büchner Prize.

Heym, Stefan (pseudonym for Hellmuth Fliegel). Born 1913 in Chemnitz. Identified himself early with workers' movement. Emigrated in 1933 to Czechoslovakia, worked as journalist. Invited to study at University of Chicago. Had various occupations before becoming editor-in-chief of German language weekly *Deutsches Volksecho* in New York, 1937–1939. Joined U.S. Army 1943, took part in invasion of Normandy and in occupation forces, was officer in division of psychological warfare. In 1945 was cofounder of American "Neue Zeitung" in Munich. Was transferred back to U.S. because of pro-communist activity and discharged. In 1952 left U.S. and settled in East Germany. Lives as independent author in East Berlin. Has written mainly novels, short stories, journalism, essays, frequently concerning historical topics and social criticism. Has won, among other distinctions, the Heinrich Mann Prize (1953) and the National Prize for GDR (1959). Is noted for his passionate battle against fascism and imperialism and for his commitment to individual principles of conduct under any political system.

Kant, Uwe. Born 1936 in Hamburg. The younger brother of the author Hermann Kant. Grew up in Parchim. Studied history and Germanic Language and Literature at the universities of Rostock and Berlin.

BIOGRAPHICAL SKETCHES

Taught from 1961 to 1964 in Lübbenau. Was a professional associate of the German Authors' Organization of East Germany, also became editor of the periodical *Das Magazin*. Lives as an independent author in Berlin. Has written children's books and short stories.

Kaschnitz, Marie Luise (née Holzing-Berstett). Born 1901 in Karlsruhe, died 1974 in Rome. Apprentice in the book trade in Weimar and Munich. Lived from 1924 until 1932 as a book dealer in Rome, married a Viennese archaeologist, Guido Freiherr von Kashnitz-Weinberg, in 1925. Returned to Germany in 1932, settled in Frankfurt am Main after 1941. Won many literary prizes and honors, among them the Büchner Prize in 1955 and the Mackenson Prize for Short Stories in 1964. Made various extended travels and sojourns, notably in Italy and along the Mediterranean coast. Wrote lyrics, prose, essays, radio plays.

Kohlhaase, Wolfgang. Born 1931 in Berlin. Son of a mechanic. Became a journalist in 1947 with a newspaper for young people and collaborated in the publication of the newspaper *Junge Welt*. From 1950 to 1952 was dramaturgist for the German Film Company, DEFA. Since then independent author in East Berlin. Has won, among other distinctions, the National Prize for the GDR (1954, 1968) and the Arts Prize of the East German Youth Federation, 1957. Member of the Academy of Arts of the GDR. Has frequently written about the problems of youth and of the German past and fascism with realistic force and sensitive psychological understanding. Has written short stories, dramas, and scripts for TV, films, and radio.

Körner, Wolfgang. Born 1937 in Breslau. Studied social welfare, later art. Works as business manager in Dortmund, and is a member of the German Writer's Organization. Has written dramas, novels, short stories, essays, film and TV scripts, frequently on themes of social welfare and management under the capitalist system. Was a member of the so-called Dortmunder Gruppe 61, a group of writers, chiefly from the Ruhr industrial area, who had the goal of "coming to terms literarily and artistically with the industrial world of the present and its social problems."

Kusenberg, Kurt. Born 1904 in Göteborg, Sweden. Son of a German engineer. Spent most of his youth in Portugal and Germany. Studied art history in various German universities and received a Ph.D. Worked as art historian in Berlin. From 1935 to 1943 he was acting editor-in-chief of the periodical *Koralle*. Was then a soldier and prisoner-of-war. Settled in Hamburg after the war as writer, art critic, translator, editor. Has written mostly short stories and dramas on fantastic, surrealistic themes.

BIOGRAPHICAL SKETCHES

Lenz, Siegfried. Born 1926 in Lyck (East Prussia). Son of a town official. Was drafted into German Navy shortly before the end of World War II. After 1945 studied German and English language and literature and philosophy at University of Hamburg. Was feuilleton editor of *Die Welt* in 1950 and 1951 and then independent author in Hamburg. Basic elements of his work are the moral commitment of the author, failure of man due to persecution and guilt, and defense of the "little man," frequently expressed in parable form. Has written short stories, novels, radio plays, dramas, and journalism. Has received, among other distinctions, the René-Schickele Prize (1952), the Literary Prize of the City of Bremen (1962), and the Gerhart Hauptmann Prize of the Freie Volksbühne of West Berlin (1961).

Mundstock, Karl. Born 1915 in Berlin. Grew up in Berlin in a class-conscious worker's family, interested at an early age in the cause of the proletariat. As a youth he was imprisoned for political activity for the communists. Later was at various times a packer, teamster, metal worker. Joined the illegal Communist Party under Hitler and took part in the resistance movement. Became a soldier and was imprisoned for two years for political activity within the army. Now lives as an independent author in East Berlin-Pankow. Has written novels, youth and children's books, short stories, TV scripts, poetry, journalism, and has collaborated in various anthologies. Frequent subjects of his realistic writing are the resistance movement and wartime experiences; he likes to lead his heroes into decisive situations which call forth new human qualities in them which resolve things for the better.

Nowotny, Joachim. Born 1933 in Rietschen (Oberlausitz). Studied carpentry and later German philology in Leipzig. Was reader for a publishing house. Has resided in Leipzig since 1962 as freelance writer and teacher of prose composition at the Literary Institute in Leipzig. Writes short stories and novels.

Rinser, Luise. Born 1911 in Pitzling (Upper Bavaria). Daughter of a Volksschule teacher, grew up in village surroundings. Studied at a teacher's institute and at the University of Munich (psychology and education). Was a teacher from 1935 to 1939. After 1939 lived in Braunschweig and Rostock with her musician husband, H. G. Schnell, until his death in the war (1943). In 1940 was forbidden to write and was arrested and imprisoned for high treason in 1944. Was literary critic of the *Neue Zeitung* of Munich, 1945–1955. Was married to composer Carl Orff from 1954 to 1959. Now lives near Rome. Has written novels, short stories, and essays. Her works have a Christian-humanistic character. She has frequently protested against restorative, reactionary, and antidemocratic tendencies in West Germany. Her works often have the aim of improving sociopolitical institutions through the awakening of ethical and religious values in the individual, and are often focused on the particular problems of women and children. Has received, among other distinctions, the René-Schickele Prize (1952) and membership in the German Academy of Arts, West Berlin.

Risse, Heinz. Born 1898 in Düsseldorf. Was a soldier in World War I. Studied economics and philosophy in various universities. After many years as an economist he began writing in 1948. Has produced novels, short stories, and essays. Risse's works are focused on the moral precariousness of modern life. A standard by which his characters are commonly forced to measure themselves is that of a divine justice which is realized in man by the forces of fate and atonement, as in the story presented here, which comes from a collection entitled *Buchhalter Gottes* (Bookkeepers of God).

Schneider, Rolf. Born 1932 in Chemnitz. Studied Germanic and English language and literature from 1951 to 1955 at the University of Halle. Was editor of the cultural and political periodical *Aufbau* in Berlin from 1955 to 1958. Since 1958 he has been an independent author in East Berlin. Has written novels, short stories, poetry, dramas, radio and TV plays. He often presents in a realistic, satirical style the theme of bourgeois intellectuals in moral and political conflict with various forms of fascism and neofascism in the West German postwar scene.

Schnurre, Wolfdietrich. Born 1920 in Frankfurt am Main, spent his youth in Berlin. Was a soldier in World War II. After the war he was a movie and drama critic, first in East Berlin and then West Berlin until 1949, and then became an independent author. Was a cofounder of Gruppe 47 and a leading theorist of the short story. Received the Fontane prize (1958) among others. He is known as a master stylist; his works (novels, short stories, poetry, radio and TV drama) often satirize society and show his efforts to come to terms with Germany's past. He often has used animals in fablelike presentation to illuminate human weaknesses, such as in the story here, which also illustrates the more relaxed, whimsical, and innovative approach he has developed in more recent years.

Schulze, Axel. Born 1943 in Frose bei Aschersleben. Was trained as a lathe operator, worked as a turner and also as a surveyor and laboratory assistant, among other jobs. From 1964 to 1968 he studied at the Johannes Becher Institute for Literature in Leipzig. Lives as an author in East Berlin. Has been a dramaturgist in the State Theater in Halle. Has written short stories, radio plays, lyrics, dramas, journalism, translations of modern Russian poetry. Won a young authors' prize in 1968. He is especially well known as a writer of lyrics which portray socialistic themes.

Seghers, Anna (Pseudonym for Netty Radvanyi, née Reiling). Born 1900 in Mainz, the daughter of an antiques dealer and art expert. Died 1983. Studied philology, history, art history and sinology in Bologna and Heidelberg; obtained a doctor's degree with a dissertation on Rembrandt in 1922; was attracted in the 1920s to the Communist movement and, as she felt, its spirit of genuine humanity and unselfish sense of responsibility. She joined the Party in 1928. Her books were forbidden when Hitler came to power in 1933, and she went into exile in France. She was active in editorial work and as a speaker for German antifascism and the cause of the German writers in exile. In 1940 she fled to Mexico and continued her leadership in political and literary activities. Returned to East Berlin after the war. Was a member of the German Academy of Arts and chairperson of the German Writers' Organization in East Germany. Among other distinctions, she won the Kleist Prize in 1928, Büchner Prize in 1947, GDR National Prize in 1951 and 1959, the Lenin Peace Prize in 1951.

Stephan, Martin. Born 1945 in Köthen. Eleven years of schooling. Has had many different jobs, among them: steelworker, warehouseman, puppeteer, librarian. Has written radio plays and short stories which have been published in periodicals and anthologies.

Wohmann, Gabriele. Born 1932 in Darmstadt. Studied modern languages and music at Frankfurt am Main. Was a schoolteacher for three years in Langood and Darmstadt. Has written novels, short stories, poetry. Her works customarily focus on events of the everyday world and on interhuman relationships described in minute detail and in extraordinarily precise, yet innovative language. Frequent themes are modern man's loneliness, his anxieties, and his failure to communicate. Her excellent short stories, especially, have won her a prominent position among today's German writers.

Wolf, Christa. Born 1929 in Landsberg (Warthe). Moved in 1945 to Gammelin in East Germany and worked as a secretary in the mayor's office. Studied Germanic language and literature in Jena and Leipzig from 1949 to 1953. Employed 1953 to 1959 as technical assistant by a German authors' organization, then became reader and editor for the monthly periodical *Neue Deutsche Literatur*. Worked then for various publishing houses. Since 1962 she has lived in Kleinmachow near Berlin as an independent author. She is one of the foremost writers of the so-called second generation of East German authors who have documented (in her case, with particular courage and honesty) the development and problems of the German Democratic Republic after its first very unsettled years. She received the Heinrich Mann prize in 1963 for her first novel. She has written mostly novels and short stories.